Overboard on the Ocean

A Mollie McGhie
Cozy Sailing Mystery #6

ELLEN JACOBSON

Overboard on the Ocean
Copyright © 2021 by Ellen Jacobson

Digital ISBN: 978-1-951495-17-6
Print ISBN: 978-1-951495-18-3
Large Print ISBN: 978-1-951495-19-0

Editor: Under Wraps Publishing

Cover Design: Mariah Sinclair | www.mariahsinclair.com

First Printing: April 2021

Published by: Ellen Jacobson
www.ellenjacobsonauthor.com

For cats everywhere who wish their humans would stop reading stupid books and pet them instead. Or feed them. Food is always good. Especially the expensive stuff from the cans that we'll throw up later. The litter box probably needs changing too. And those hairballs aren't going to clean themselves up, are they? Put the book down and hop to it, human!

CONTENTS

CHAPTER 1
THE CASE OF THE MISSING NAPKIN

What would you do if your husband decided to hand over your life savings to a con artist? Would you:

(a) Shrug;

(b) Freak out a little;

(c) Hyperventilate; or

(d) Go into full-blown panic mode?

When Scooter first announced his latest hare-brained scheme, I just shrugged. I had recently taken over managing our finances and set up a new password for our online bank account. Scooter didn't have a clue what it was. If he couldn't access the money, he wouldn't be able to give it to that jerk who was trying to con him. So, I was pretty relaxed about the situation.

That feeling of calm lasted exactly two seconds. Then my shrug turned into a weird sort of nervous twitch as I freaked out about the fact that I didn't know what the password was either. Sure, Scooter couldn't access our funds, but neither could I.

Think, Mollie, think, I said to myself as I tried to recollect the new password. I had wanted to use my easy to remember, go-to password—FAROUT—but the system had informed me that it was too weak. It insisted that I come up with a long, overly complicated string of symbols, numbers, and capital letters. Sure, that sort of thing is great for keeping hackers at bay, but mere mortals couldn't possibly remember anything so convoluted. Heck, I struggle to remember to floss my teeth every day. Recalling a complicated password . . . well, that's fairly unlikely.

That's why I had written it down. Except I didn't have a clue where it was now.

I began to hyperventilate. What if someone found the password? What if someone had already emptied our bank account?

I frantically dug through my purse, looking for it. All I found were the usual suspects—my wallet, keys, some glitter pens, a catnip mouse, and a half-eaten Hershey's bar. But no password.

Hoping that it would have a calming effect, I inhaled the chocolate. It didn't help. Instead, things escalated into full-blown panic mode as it dawned on me just where and when I had written the new password down.

Scooter and I had been at Penelope's Sugar Shack for a mid-morning coffee a few days previously. I had scrawled the new password on a napkin, but got distracted when Scooter placed a freshly baked muffin in front of me. The smell of blueberries had been intoxicating, and I devoured it in a few bites. I vaguely remember Scooter shaking his head when he saw the napkin, muttering something about not leaving my password out where everyone could see it. Then he had tucked it in his shirt pocket.

I groaned as I realized what that meant—Scooter had the password. He was about to give our entire life savings away to that scoundrel, Fletcher Tolliver unless . . .

You know what, before we get into all that, maybe I should back up and fill you in on exactly what happened that day. Grab a snack—I recommend the blueberry muffins from the Sugar Shack —and a beverage, and I'll tell you all about it.

* * *

When it all started, I had been standing in the galley of our sailboat trying to remember where I was at in the recipe I was making.

"Hey, M.J., do you know if I added salt to this dough already?"

Not surprisingly, M.J. didn't respond. Honestly, if she had, I would have been startled since M.J. is our sailboat. Boats don't typically talk back. At least ours doesn't.

Actually, she's called *Marjorie Jane* on all the official documentation. Though I wasn't terribly fond of that name, so lately I had taken to calling her M.J. instead.

Truth be told, I hadn't been all that fond of M.J. herself until recently. Scooter had surprised me with her on our tenth wedding anniversary, thinking I would fall in love with the dilapidated sailboat like he had. It was definitely not love at first sight, that's for sure. Still over the past year, Scooter and I had worked hard to tackle an extensive list of boat projects, and I was starting to warm up to her. Which was a good thing, because in a couple of months, we were planning on sailing M.J. from Florida to the Bahamas. I was going to have to trust my life to her on the high seas.

"Salt? Did I add salt already?" I muttered to myself.

"What did you say?" a familiar voice asked.

I turned and saw Scooter climbing down the ladder into the main cabin. "Oh, it's this recipe I'm making. As I was measuring out the flour, Mrs. Moto distracted me."

Scooter laughed when he saw our Japanese bobtail cat perched on the table. "You wouldn't know she was a calico, would you, covered in all that flour."

"She won't let me clean her off," I said. "Maybe you'll have more luck."

As he walked toward Mrs. Moto, she narrowed her emerald green eyes and hissed. He held his hands up and backed away. "I think she needs her space. What are you making?"

"Gnocchi."

Scooter leaned against the counter. "The Italian dumplings made with potatoes, right?"

"Uh-huh."

"Gnocchi. That has a cute ring to it."

"Oh, I know where this is going." I groaned. "This is going to be your latest pet name for me, isn't it?"

He grinned, then kissed me on the cheek. "Sure is, my little gnocchi."

"You seem to be in a good mood," I said.

"I am. Someone made me a very interesting business proposition today. Why don't you come sit with me in the cockpit and I'll tell you about it?"

I stared at the bowl of gnocchi dough, wondering if it had salt in it. "Well, I probably should just chuck this out and start over."

Scooter pulled me out of the galley. "Take a break first."

After we were settled in the cockpit, I turned to Scooter. "Okay, spill."

"Do you remember . . . whoa, look at that." Scooter pointed at a pair of dolphins frolicking in the bay.

I leaned over the side of the boat. "Wow, did you see that leap?"

"Pretty amazing, huh? But it will be ten times better when we're in the Bahamas. Maybe we'll even get to swim with them."

"That would be great, as long as there aren't any sharks. I was talking to a lady in the laundry room yesterday and she told me that her husband was attacked by a shark when they were snorkeling. She said she had never seen so much blood in her life."

Scooter grimaced, and the color drained from his face. I quickly apologized for saying the "B" word. He exhaled sharply three times as he removed his glasses. Closing his eyes, he pressed his index fingers on the bridge of his nose, then tugged on his earlobes while saying something under his breath. After exhaling sharply again, he put his glasses back on and smiled at me.

"It's okay, my little gnocchi. You can say the 'B' word."

My jaw dropped. Scooter had always been squeamish. It was a good thing that he worked in telecommunications. He could have never cut it as a medical professional.

"Go on, you can say it," Scooter urged.

"Blood?"

"Yep, blood," he repeated calmly.

"I'm impressed."

He shrugged. "Well, when we're out

sailing, we'll be on our own. If we have an injury, we're going to have to deal with it ourselves. It's not like there are floating emergency rooms in the middle of the ocean. So, I'm going to have to get over my fear of blood. Besides, there's less chance of having to deal with blood in the Bahamas then there is here in Coconut Cove."

I cocked my head to one side. "Why's that?"

"It seems like every other day you find a dead body," Scooter joked. "This town seems to have become the murder capital of the country ever since we moved here."

"Wait … Did you just say, 'dead body' and 'murder' out loud?"

"Uh-huh. Dead body, murder—they're just words," he said.

Only the confident tone in his voice didn't match the look in his eyes. I squeezed his hand and changed the subject. "Tell me about this business proposition."

"You remember Fletcher Tolliver, don't you?"

"Sure. The scumbag who embezzled money from his business, right?"

"That was just a rumor," Scooter said.

"Where there's smoke, there's fire."

"I did a couple of deals with him back when we lived in Cleveland."

I shook my head. "You lost your shirt on one of them too."

"That wasn't Fletcher's fault." Scooter folded his arms across his chest. "There was a supply chain problem. That won't be an issue this time around."

"This time around?"

"Fletcher has a sure-fire investment opportunity, and he's offered to let me get in on the ground floor." Scooter looked at me intently. "Do you have any idea what this would mean for us? We would be set for life. We'd never have to work again. Imagine sailing around the world and never having to worry about money again."

I ticked items off on my fingers. "First, I never said I wanted to sail around the world. Let's just focus on getting to the Bahamas in one piece. Second, I don't want to quit my job. I know I don't make a lot of money, but I love what I do. And third, when someone describes something as 'sure-fire,' I'm suspicious."

Scooter furrowed his brow. "Don't you trust me? I know a good deal when I see it."

"I trust you," I said. "It's Fletcher I don't trust."

"I'm not asking you to trust Fletcher. I'm asking you to trust me."

"Exactly how much money are we talking about?" When Scooter hesitated, I felt my stomach twist into knots. "It's a lot, isn't it?"

"You have to spend money to make money," he said.

This is when I realized Scooter didn't know the password to our online account, so I shrugged. Fletcher Tolliver wasn't going to be able to get a hold of our life savings without me, and I certainly wasn't going to hand it over to him.

"What's wrong with your shoulders?" Scooter asked. "They seem to be spasming."

As my shrug turned into a nervous twitch, I frantically tried to remember what the password was. I darted out of the cockpit in search of my purse. I searched everywhere, eventually finding it on our bed.

"I wonder why my purse is covered in white paw prints," I said pointedly to the cat lying on Scooter's pillow. Mrs. Moto ignored me and continued her bath, licking the last of the flour off her tail.

After I dumped the contents out of my purse, the calico helped me search for the piece of paper with the password on it. Her idea of "help" consisted of batting various items onto the floor, then meowing plaintively for me to pick them up so that she could knock them down again.

"What's going on?" Scooter said behind me.

I crumpled up the Hershey bar wrapper and tucked it in the pocket of my shorts before turning around. "Nothing."

He arched an eyebrow. "You have chocolate on the side of your face. What are you hiding? A cookie from the Sugar Shack?"

My eyes widened. The Sugar Shack, that's it. I wrote the password down on a napkin at the Sugar Shack. But what had happened to it?

"Hey, are you okay?" Scooter asked, sitting next to me on the bed. "You look like you're going to have a heart attack."

"The nap ... the nap ... the napkin," I spluttered. "What did you do with the napkin?"

"What napkin?"

I tried to calm my breathing, then said, "The other day at the Sugar Shack—"

"Wait a minute, are you talking about the one you wrote on? This is why I didn't want you to manage our finances. You can't go around writing passwords down."

I pursed my lips. "What did you do with it?"

"I destroyed it."

I felt the tension in my shoulders dissipate. "So, you can't access our bank account."

"Don't worry." He tapped the side of his head. "I memorized it."

My breathing became shallow, and my shoulders started twitching again. I clutched Scooter's hand. "You can't give our money to that man."

"Listen, you may not be fond of Fletcher, but once you see the investor presentation, you'll be completely on board. You don't always have to like the people you do business with."

"But you do have to trust them," I said firmly.

He pulled his hand away. "I do trust him. And you will too after the cruise this weekend."

"Cruise … This weekend?"

"Didn't I mention it?" When I shook my head, he said, "Oh, I probably should have led with that. Fletcher has invited us to join him with other potential investors on a cruise to the Bahamas. We leave from Miami on Friday afternoon. The boat sails overnight and we'll wake up in the islands the next morning. We'll spend a couple of days there, then head back on Monday."

"So, let me see if I've got this right . . . we're going to spend a fortune on a cruise so that Fletcher can con us out of our life savings."

Scooter narrowed his eyes. "Fletcher is paying for our trip. He wouldn't do that if he was a con artist, right?"

"It's called a convincer," I said. "It's

what all good con artists do. They put up their own money at first to suck you in. Then they—"

"Enough, Mollie," Scooter said coldly. "I get it. You don't trust Fletcher. Fine. Just come on the cruise and listen to the presentation. If you don't think it's a good deal after that, then we won't invest in it. Simple as that."

As if sensing the tension, Mrs. Moto crawled into my lap and purred loudly. I chewed on my bottom lip as I stroked her. Scooter and I had been married for almost eleven years, and I could count the number of fights we'd had on one hand. I couldn't figure out what had gotten into him. Usually, my husband was good-natured and easygoing. I had never seen this side of him before, and I didn't like it.

"Well?" Scooter asked.

"I can't go," I said. "I told Anabel that I'd look at wedding venues with her this weekend."

"I'm sure she'll understand if you postpone."

"I don't want to postpone. She's my best friend. I promised I'd help her."

"I thought I was your best friend," Scooter said quietly as he got to his feet.

"Where are you going?" I asked as he started to walk out of the cabin.

"I need some time to think," he said back over his shoulder.

I lay on the bed, tears welling up in my eyes. Mrs. Moto snuggled against my face. "Fletcher Tolliver," I muttered to her. "Something needs to be done about that man."

CHAPTER 2
CHOCOLATE NEVER ASKS ANY QUESTIONS

Feeling M.J. rocking back and forth in her berth, I peeked out the porthole. Sure enough, Scooter had leaped off the boat onto the dock. As he walked away, my heart sank. He hadn't even bothered to tell me that he was leaving.

Sinking back onto the bed, I ran several scenarios involving Fletcher Tolliver's disappearance from our lives past Mrs. Moto. She was disinterested until I used her catnip mouse and a pillow to demonstrate how an avalanche could eliminate the man who was coming between my husband and me.

While the calico snaked her paw under the pillow to retrieve her toy, I chastised myself for having such horrible thoughts. Surely, there had to be a way to get rid of Fletcher that didn't involve foul play. Besides, an avalanche was impractical. It's not like snow was something you could count on in southern Florida.

"We need a change of scenery," I said to Mrs. Moto. "What do you say we go to the library?"

She dropped her mouse on my chest and then meowed enthusiastically. The library had become one of her favorite haunts as of late, primarily because of its new resident feline, Dr. McCoy.

After I pulled into the library parking lot, I scooped Mrs. Moto into my arms. "You're going to behave today, right? No more sitting on the checkout desk and begging the librarian for treats, okay?"

Of course, the first thing Mrs. Moto did once we entered the library was to squirm out of my arms, leap onto the checkout desk, and headbutt Hudson, the librarian on duty.

The librarian set aside the book he was scanning into the system. After scratching the cat's head, he opened a drawer and pulled out a foil pouch. Mrs. Moto went crazy, pacing back and forth until he placed a fish-shaped treat in front of her. After she gobbled it up, Hudson pointed at the periodical section. "Dr. McCoy is over there, if you want to go say hi."

Hudson grinned at me while Mrs. Moto scurried off to find her feline friend. "Sorry, I don't have any human treats for you, Mollie, unless you want to buy one of these." He pointed at a box of chocolate bars sitting next to the computer monitor. "It's a fundraiser for the Coconut Cove Historical Museum. If you buy one, you also get a sticker."

"One of your stickers?" I asked.

After Hudson showed me the sticker he had designed with the museum's logo, he held up a chocolate bar. "So, what do you say?"

Despite having eaten a Hershey bar less than an hour ago, I nodded. The fight with Scooter had rattled me and I needed something to console me. Chocolate is a good listener. It never asks questions and never judges you. Chocolate just listens quietly, then whispers comforting things as you savor each morsel, making your problems easier to deal with. My problem with Scooter was a real doozy. I was going to need all the chocolate I could get.

"How much for the whole box?" I asked.

Hudson cocked his head to one side. "You want all of them?"

"Yep." I ripped one of the bars open

and popped a piece in my mouth while he calculated how much I owed.

After I paid him, Hudson gave me a wistful smile. "My wife would have been really impressed with the fact that I sold all this chocolate so quickly. She used to be on the Board of Trustees for the museum. She oversaw all the fundraising activities, but the annual chocolate drive was her favorite."

"She sounds like my kind of girl," I said.

"She was a great girl," Hudson said in a strained voice. Then he cleared his throat and motioned to the man standing behind me. "I need to help this gentleman. Thanks again for your contribution, Mollie."

I slung my purse over my shoulder, grabbed my box of chocolate, and headed over to the periodical section. Mrs. Moto and Dr. McCoy were having a grooming session together in an armchair next to the large bay window. I settled into the chair next to them and grabbed a stack of bridal magazines, looking for ideas for Anabel's bachelorette party. As her matron of honor, I was in charge of organizing the event. Since Anabel and her ex-husband were remarrying, she wanted something low-key and casual.

My original plan had been a champagne brunch at a popular local eatery, the Tipsy Pirate. However, out of the blue, the owner had closed the restaurant indefinitely, citing personal reasons. The Coconut Cove grapevine had gone into overdrive with rumors about what exactly those personal reasons were too. I personally thought the theory that he had moved to Antarctica to become a camel trainer was the most plausible.

Though, to be honest, figuring out why the Tipsy Pirate had closed was the least of my concerns. What I really needed to focus on was finding another place to hold Anabel's bachelorette party. No mean feat at this time of the year when Coconut Cove was overrun with tourists and snowbirds. Plus, Anabel wanted my help to find a wedding venue.

I ran my fingers through my hair, attempting to smooth down the frizzy sections, and sighed. Mrs. Moto looked over at me. She did that slow blinking thing that cats do to tell you they love you. I blinked back at her, then returned to perusing the magazines. The wedding dresses were stunning, the bouquets were gorgeous, and the cocktail recipes were enticing, but it all seemed so generic. Anabel was as far from generic as you could get. If you pictured an eccentric, bohemian artist in your mind, you'd probably come up with someone like Anabel. Her quirky imagination lent itself to the whimsical paintings she created. Paintings that featured fanciful creatures such as fairies, unicorns, and dragons, along with more common animals such as hamsters, yellow-bellied marmots, and kittens. She was quickly developing a national reputation for her work, with people clamoring to own one of her paintings.

It still amazed me that she was remarrying her ex-husband. The only thing whimsical about him was his name —Tiny Dalton. There wasn't anything tiny about him though. As the chief of police of Coconut Cove, his burly stature came in handy when facing off against bad guys or intimidating seagulls. Of course, no one but Anabel dared to call him Tiny to his face. To the rest of us, he was simply Chief Dalton.

I chewed on my lip as I thought about Anabel's bubbly personality. Maybe it was a good thing that the Tipsy Pirate had shut down. Obviously, not for the owner of the Tipsy Pirate, unless he really had always dreamed of becoming a camel trainer. A champagne brunch would have been too ordinary of a bachelorette party for Anabel. I needed to come up with something creative and unique, and needed to do it fast. The party was taking place in a little over a week's time.

"Darn it," I muttered to myself as I accidentally tore one of the pages in the magazine. It happened to be a recipe for a chocolate wedding cake. Perhaps my subconscious at work? One of the things I had always regretted about my own wedding was that my mother had talked me into a boring vanilla cake. It was horrible, had took bland to a whole new level.

My phone beeped. I glanced at the screen and saw that it was a text from Scooter. Did he know I had just been thinking about our wedding? Was he texting to apologize?

I shook my head. I wasn't ready to deal with Scooter yet and shoved my phone into my purse. I went to the front desk to own up to what I had done. When I showed the torn magazine to Hudson, he waved his hand. "Don't worry about it. That magazine is really old. It's due to come out of circulation, anyway."

"Old? Well, that explains the article about recording your wedding with a VHS camcorder."

Hudson furrowed his brow. "VHS? Oh, yeah, those old-fashioned tapes. My Uncle Ned has a bunch of them with old movies on them. My Aunt Nancy is always complaining about how much room they take up."

"Nancy? Complaining? Imagine that," I muttered sarcastically.

"What was that?" Hudson asked, as he scanned the magazine.

"Oh, I was just wondering if you knew that it was Ned who gave Mrs. Moto her name. It's from one of those old movies he loves to watch."

Hudson snapped his fingers. "The Mr. Moto movies, right?"

"Uh-huh. They're about a Japanese secret agent who wears thick, black-rimmed glasses. Since Mrs. Moto is a Japanese bobtail cat who has black markings around her eyes that resemble glasses. Ned thought it was a perfect name for her."

"It's a cute name." He handed the magazine back to me. "There, I've removed it from the system. It's all yours."

"I'm not sure I need a bridal magazine."

"No problem. Do you mind sticking it in the free box by the entrance for me? Someone else will grab it."

As I turned around, a petite blonde woman holding a large flat package wrapped in brown paper squealed. "Mollie McGhie, is that you?"

After setting the package down next to a new release display table, she rushed toward me. I was in shock as she hugged me. Questions rushed through my head—like "What is she chewing on?" "How can someone so tiny have such freakishly powerful arms?" "I can't breathe, is this hug ever going to stop?" "I can't free myself, is this how Mrs. Moto feels when I'm holding her and she wants to jump out of my arms?" "What in the world is Fletcher Tolliver's wife doing in Coconut Cove?"

When she finally released me, I quickly filled my lungs with air. Breathing never felt so good. "Sylvia Tolliver," I gasped.

She beamed at me. "Surprise!"

"It certainly is," I said. "What are you doing here?"

"When Fletcher first called Scooter a couple of weeks ago—"

"A couple of weeks ago? I had thought the two of them spoke for the first time today?"

Sylvia smacked on her gum for a

moment. "No, they've been talking for a while. Scooter raved about what a charming town Coconut Cove is, and we thought we'd come check it out for ourselves. Honestly, I don't think I can handle one more gloomy winter in Cleveland. I've been telling Fletcher for years that we should get a place in Florida. He's always resisted the idea. But now he's seriously considering a move down south, and it's all thanks to Scooter."

My head was reeling. I don't know what was worse—Scooter lying to me about when he first talked with Fletcher or the thought of the Tollivers moving to Coconut Cove. I shook my head. I'd deal with my husband later. First things first, I needed to convince Sylvia that living here was a bad idea. A really bad idea.

"You know, it's actually overcast in Coconut Cove ninety-eight percent of the time. If you're looking for sunshine, you've come to the wrong place."

Sylvia looked out the window, perplexed. "But the sun is out now. This is Florida, the Sunshine State."

"Ah . . . Yes, most of Florida is sunny, but there's some sort of weird weather vortex over Coconut Cove. Always cloudy. You lucked out and got here on the only sunny day we've had all year."

"Well, at least you don't have snow. I hate driving on icy roads, and I'm worried Fletcher is going to have a heart attack one of these days shoveling the driveway."

Hmm . . . why didn't I think of that earlier? A fatal heart attack wouldn't be the worst thing to happen to Fletcher, I thought. Then I mentally slapped my hand. Fletcher might be a horrible person, but even he didn't deserve to die.

"We actually had a really horrible snowstorm last month," I said. "There was hail the size of gerbils, and power was cut off for days. It was so cold that people were having to knit sweaters out of plastic shopping bags. The National Guard even had to airdrop an emergency supply of mittens."

"A snowstorm in November? Here in Coconut Cove? Really?" Sylvia turned to Hudson for confirmation.

Hudson cleared his throat, then glanced at me. "Um . . . I don't remember that."

"You were probably too busy reading. Books can be really distracting," I said to him. Pulling Sylvia away, I lowered my voice. "That's not the worst of it. Right after the snow melted, we had a swarm of locusts come through town. They ate the leaves off everything."

Sylvia pointed at the palm trees lining the walkway to the library. "They have leaves."

"Oh, those are fake," I said. "The town council attached plastic leaves to the trees. They look pretty realistic from a distance, but when you get up close, you can tell that they're not real."

Someone chuckled behind me. "I think Mollie is pulling your leg."

I spun around and saw Hudson rearranging books on the new release display table next to us. He grinned at me, then turned to Sylvia. "Coconut Cove is a great little seaside town. Lots of nice restaurants and shops, the fishing is great, and the annual boating festival is a blast. It's a wonderful place to retire to."

"Sounds like it would be a great place for young families as well," Sylvia said.

"It is," Hudson said quietly as he toyed with his wedding band.

"But your children are grown," I said to Sylvia. "The two of you should retire someplace quieter. The kids around here are so noisy. You wouldn't get a moment of peace."

"Our oldest daughter just got married," Sylvia said. "We're hoping there will be grandchildren on the way soon. Coconut Cove would be a wonderful place for them to come visit us, especially if there are built-in playmates."

I was running out of ideas for how to discourage Sylvia from moving here, so out of desperation I turned to Hudson. "Surely, there's something you don't like about this town?"

He pondered this for a moment, then shook his head. "No. I was born and raised here. It's a wonderful place. But . . ."

"But what?" I prompted.

"I am thinking of moving."

I clapped my hands together. "Aha. See, Sylvia, even Hudson doesn't want to live here."

"Oh, no, that's not what I meant." Hudson ran his fingers through his hair, making his unruly dark curls even more erratic. "I just need a change of scenery. Too many memories here. But I'd still recommend Coconut Cove as a great place to live."

Sylvia looped her arm through mine. "That's settled, then. What do you say to showing me around town?"

I looked at the bridal magazine I was holding. "Um, I wish I could, but I have to—"

Before I could explain about Anabel's bachelorette party, the door to the library swung open. I groaned when I saw my arch-nemesis, Fletcher Tolliver, standing in the entryway. He looked the same as when I had last seen him— short, overweight, and balding.

"I've been looking everywhere for you," he said icily to Sylvia. "I had told you to wait in the car."

Sylvia stage whispered to me. "He hasn't had lunch yet. His blood sugar levels are low. It makes him cranky."

"You know I can hear you, right?" Fletcher said.

She patted his arm, then pointed at me. "Look who I ran into it. What's wrong with you? Don't you recognize Mollie McGhie?"

The expression on Fletcher's face flickered from annoyance at his wife to surprise at seeing me. Then it changed to something that reminded me of how grizzly bears size you up before they eat you. He gave me an oily smile, kissed my cheek, then looked me up and down. "Mollie, it's wonderful to see you again."

I nodded, not trusting myself to respond politely.

Fletcher slung his arm around Sylvia's shoulders. "Did you know that Scooter has agreed to invest in the company?"

"That's wonderful, dear," she said. "When did that happen?"

"A few minutes ago. I just got off the phone with him."

"He said he was going to invest?" I said, my voice cracking. When Fletcher nodded, I blurted out, "The only way that's going to happen is over my dead body . . . or yours."

* * *

After my announcement, there was dead silence. It was eerily quiet, even for a library.

Okay, I realize that "dead silence" probably isn't the best choice of words, especially considering I had just mentioned dead bodies. However, if you had found as many dead bodies as I have since moving to Coconut Cove, you'd find yourself unconsciously uttering words like 'dead,' 'murder,' 'corpse,' and 'homicide' way more often than you'd like.

I glanced at the others. Hudson and Sylvia looked uncomfortable. I was definitely uncomfortable. The only person who didn't seem fazed was Fletcher. Instead, he seemed to regard me with a sort of grudging respect. Probably because there had been whispers that he had once threatened a business competitor with bodily harm.

After a beat, Sylvia laughed nervously. "Oh, Mollie, you're such a card! Isn't she a card, dear?"

Fletcher ran his hand down Sylvia's back while he stared at me. "She sure is."

Hudson muttered something about checking on the cats.

"Hang on, I'll come with you," I said to Hudson as he retreated to the periodical section. Turning back to the Tollivers, I explained, "My cat probably needs a snack or something."

Fletcher gave me a dismissive nod and Sylvia smiled weakly at me. Then they proceeded to bicker loudly about the fact that Sylvia hadn't waited in the car for Fletcher.

Walking behind the open shelving unit that divided the periodical section from the lobby, I spied Hudson perched on the edge of an armchair with both cats vying for his attention. I watched for a few moments as he took turns petting them. Mrs. Moto certainly was more demanding, but Dr. McCoy held his own, getting his fair share of scratches under his chin.

"How are they doing?" I asked.

"The cats or your friends?"

"They're not really my friends," I said. "Scooter did some work with Fletcher back when we lived in Cleveland, and I would just see Sylvia occasionally at dinners and cocktail parties."

Hudson cocked his head toward the lobby. "They seem to have forgotten that this is a library."

"They are pretty loud. I wonder what they're arguing about?"

"Whatever it is, they should do it in private." He looked down at the cats sprawled on his lap. "I really should go over and tell them to keep it down."

I walked over to the shelving unit and peered through a gap. Sylvia had placed her package on the new release display table and unwrapped it. Fletcher was pointing at it, a sour expression on his face.

"That is the ugliest painting I've ever seen," he said.

"It's not ugly." Sylvia placed her hands on her hips. "I think it's charming. The colors are so bright and cheerful. It will go great with our living room furniture."

Fletcher bent down to inspect it. "Are those unicorns?"

"Actually, the artist told me they're quadricorns. See how they have four horns? And those are pixies braiding their manes."

I smiled at Sylvia's description, realizing that it must be one of Anabel's paintings. My smile quickly faded when Fletcher clenched his fists, took a step toward Sylvia, and glared at her.

"Quadricorns? Pixies? How could you waste money on something so ridiculous?"

To her credit, Sylvia didn't back down. "Me waste money? Are you kidding? You're the one who drops thousands and thousands of dollars at poker games every weekend. Thank goodness for my inheritance. If it wasn't for that, we'd be flat broke."

"You're exaggerating as usual," Fletcher said. "I work hard all week. So what if I play poker with the guys to relax?"

"Well, I work hard too."

Fletcher scoffed. "You mean with that silly little business of yours? I'd hardly call that work."

Sylvia jabbed Fletcher in the chest. "All I did was buy one little painting. Living with you, I need something to cheer me up."

A commotion prevented me from hearing Fletcher's response. I turned and saw Mrs. Moto yowling as Hudson tried to extricate her from his lap. He finally managed to stand, placing her back on the chair next to Dr. McCoy.

"I need to put a stop to this," Hudson said as he walked toward me.

I grabbed his arm. "Hang on a sec. They've lowered they're voices. I can't hear what they're saying, which means they're not causing a disturbance anymore, right?"

"Are you eavesdropping?" Hudson whispered.

I put my fingers to my lips, then leaned around the corner of the shelving unit.

Fletcher had picked up the painting and was studying it dispassionately. "It's hideous."

"I like it, and I'm keeping it." Sylvia folded her arms. "I can enjoy it long after you're gone."

"Gone? I'm not going anywhere, sweetheart. The doctor gave me a clean bill of health."

Sylvia chewed her gum while she gave her husband an appraising look. "Really? Even your liver?"

Fletcher ignored her question, then hurled the painting on the ground. He forcefully pulled the door to the library open before he stormed out.

"Hey, where are you going?" Sylvia yelled before rushing after him.

Hudson looked at me. "Maybe it would be better if they didn't move to Coconut Cove."

* * *

Hudson picked the painting up and inspected it.

"Any damage?" I asked.

"I don't think so," he said. "Looks like Anabel's work. I have one of her paintings hanging in my bedroom. When I wake up in the morning, it always makes me smile."

"I wonder if they're going to come back for it?"

Hudson rolled his eyes. "I hope not. They've already made enough of a commotion in here for one day. Do you think you could return it to them?"

"Hmm, I'm not really sure where they're staying. But I suppose—" I chewed my lip. Scooter would know how to track them down, but I wasn't ready to talk with him yet.

Hudson thrust the painting into my hands. "Thanks, I appreciate it. You can leave Mrs. Moto here if you want while you drop this off."

Realizing that there wasn't an easy way to get out of this task, I hauled the painting to my car. After stowing it in the back seat, I considered the accommodations in town. Fletcher had always flaunted his wealth, so my guess was that they had a suite at the Golden Astrolabe Hotel. As I pointed the car in that direction, I hesitated. Sylvia had given Fletcher a hard time for gambling his money away. Sure, she had mentioned her inheritance, but were we talking millions or thousands? Could they afford to stay at a luxury boutique hotel? Perhaps they were staying at the Honeysuckle Cottages, a reasonably priced bed-and-breakfast that was popular with tourists?

When I got to the intersection at Main Street, my intuition told me to turn left toward the Honeysuckle Cottages. I was trying to pay more attention to my intuition lately. It seemed to know when there was a sale at my favorite bookstore, when Mrs. Moto was about to hack up a hairball on my pillow, and even when a killer might be after me. It didn't fail me this time. I spotted a flashy car with Ohio license plates as I pulled through the gate to the bed-and-breakfast.

"Thanks, intuition. You were right again. They're here." I grabbed my purse, but before I could open the car door, I felt a tingling sensation in my left hand. I knew it was a message from my intuition again, but it wasn't a very specific one. As I stared at my hand, my wedding band glimmered in the sunlight.

"Darn it, intuition. Are you saying that I should read Scooter's text?"

The tingling stopped immediately. Sighing, I pulled my phone out of my purse. Scooter hadn't just sent one text; he had sent several.

The first one was pretty straightforward, asking me to call him so we could talk. The next couple were variations on that theme, but the fourth one was different. Based on the number of meows in the message and the cat emojis, it almost appeared to have been sent by Mrs. Moto.

Meow, meow, meow. Call Scooter meow.

I have to confess; it did make me smile. Only I was pretty sure that Mrs. Moto hadn't sent it. While she was a whiz at typing on my computer, pressing her paws on the keyboard and coming up with highly creative sentences like,

"Pfzg urrrr oooosff," she hadn't mastered texting yet. Scooter was trying his best to tug at my heartstrings by pretending to be our cat.

I replied with a GIF of a scary-looking Chihuahua

He responded right away with a GIF of his own—a kitten wiping away tears from its enormous eyes. The words written underneath said, "I'm sorry."

My heart melted a little bit. Kittens will do that to you.

"Stupid kittens," I muttered as I called Scooter.

He answered the phone right away. Scooter apologized for his reaction and storming off the boat. When I asked him about why he had behaved so uncharacteristically, he was at a loss.

"I don't know why I did that, Mollie. Maybe it's the stress of getting ready to go to the Bahamas. Maybe it's because I worry about our finances ... maybe it's because ..." his voice trailed off.

"Why don't we talk more about it tonight?" I suggested.

He agreed, then added that he understood my concerns about Fletcher. "I promise we won't invest anything unless both of us agree that it's the right thing to do."

"Then why did you tell Fletcher this morning that you were in?" I asked.

"I never said that."

"Well, he's got a different story."

"When did you talk to—"

I spotted Fletcher coming out of his cottage. "I have to go," I said, abruptly ending the conversation.

Fletcher looked surprised to see me step out of my car. I gave him a wave, then retrieved the painting from the back seat. His eyes narrowed as I walked up the pathway.

"You left this at the library," I said.

"Consider it a donation."

I set the painting on the porch swing. "I don't think Sylvia would like that."

"She bought this on a whim. When she comes to her senses, she'll realize how ridiculous this is. I mean, look at it. Unicorns and pixies, are you kidding? This isn't art."

"I think there are many people who would beg to differ. Anabel got a commission from a very famous movie actor just last week."

"Anabel?"

"Anabel Dalton. The woman who painted this. She's a local artist."

"Hmm . . . a commission from a movie star, huh?" I nodded. "So, this could really be worth something. Maybe we will keep it after all."

The door to the cottage opened and Sylvia peeked her head out. "Fletcher, your phone is ringing."

"Why don't you answer it?"

"I tried, but all I ended up doing was making it ring louder."

"Well, don't just stand there, hand it to me," he demanded. Then he muttered,

"That incompetent woman doesn't have a clue how to work a toaster, let alone a cell phone."

After a moment, she came back out with his phone. "Looks like Scooter tried to call you. Oh, hey, Mollie, I didn't see you standing there."

"I just came to return your painting," I said.

While she took it into the cottage, I listened to Fletcher's side of the conversation with my husband.

"No, no, there's been a misunderstanding. I never told her that . . ." Fletcher rocked back and forth on his heels while he listened to what Scooter was saying. "Uh-huh . . . I see . . . . well, are you sure I can't change your mind? Herbert will be really disappointed. Maybe you want to talk with Mollie first before you decide? Let me pass you to her."

As Fletcher thrust his phone into my hand, I said, "Did I just hear you mention Herbert? Herbert Miller?"

"Yeah. What about it?"

"Are you still partners with him?"

"Sure. We started the business together."

"And he's going on the cruise?"

"Of course—" Fletcher scowled, then stuck his head through the cottage door. "Stop yelling, Sylvia. I'll be right there."

I waved Fletcher away, then pressed the phone to my ear.

"What are you doing at the Honeysuckle Cottages, my little gnocchi?" Scooter asked.

"I came to return something. It's a long story. I'll explain later."

"Sounds like we have a lot to talk about tonight," Scooter said. "Maybe I should get a bottle of wine to go with dinner. I finished making the gnocchi and I have some sauce simmering on the stove."

"I forgot about the gnocchi," I said. "I hope you threw out that dough and started from scratch. It either has too much salt in it, or not enough."

"Sure did," he said brightly. I laughed, knowing from the tone in his voice that he hadn't thrown the dough out and started over. "Listen, before you go, you should know that I told Fletcher that we wouldn't be going on the cruise to the Bahamas."

"Actually, you know I've been mulling it over and I think we should go. I'll reschedule looking at wedding venues with Anabel."

"You think we should go?" Scooter sounded stunned.

"Yes, I for one would be very interested in hearing more about Fletcher's investment opportunity."

"Really," Scooter said dryly. "Why do I have a feeling that you're up to something?"

"Me? Never," I said, crossing my fingers. A little white lie never hurt anyone, did it? And, besides, hadn't

Scooter just fibbed to me about the gnocchi dough?

CHAPTER 3
TELECOMMUNICATIONS GEEKS

A couple of days later, Scooter and I were standing in line, waiting to check in for the cruise. I grabbed his hand and gave it a squeeze. He glanced at me, and I smiled. "I'm so glad we kissed and made-up. I hate the fact that we fought."

"That's ancient history," Scooter said, squeezing my hand back. As the group in front of us shuffled forward, he added, "I still can't believe the only reason you agreed to come is because of Herbert Miller."

I shrugged. "Well, Fletcher did say that Herbert would be disappointed not to see you. I didn't want to let him down."

Scooter chuckled. "We both know that's not why you agreed. You can't rest until you know why Herbert and Fletcher are still business partners."

"Aren't you curious too? Fletcher embezzled money from their business —"

"Allegedly."

"Fine. Fletcher *allegedly* embezzled money, and Herbert is still working with him. Don't you want to know why?"

"Look, for the record, I don't think Fletcher is an embezzler. Herbert and Fletcher's partnership works well. They've made a lot of money together over the years. What I don't get is why you're so interested. Usually, someone has to be murdered . . ."

Scooter paused to do that weird ritual of his—exhaling three times, pressing his fingers on the bridge of his nose, tugging his earlobes while muttering something, then exhaling again. After he was finished, he just carried on talking about dead bodies like it was no big deal.

"When someone gets killed in Coconut Cove, you dive straight into investigating who did it. But no one has died. Why are you getting involved?"

"Just listening to my intuition," I said. "And, as it turns out, Anabel and the chief are thinking about having their wedding on a cruise ship. I told them I'd check this one out as an option."

"Getting married aboard a boat," Scooter mused. "That's not a bad idea. Although wouldn't they rather do it on a sailboat than on a big ship like this?"

"I'll suggest it to her."

"You should, my little jellybean."

"Jellybean. Hmm . . . I guess that's better than calling me your little gnocchi. Wait, is that because I was eating jellybeans in the car?"

Scooter frowned. "I know, it's not very original. I'm off my game."

"Maybe it's time to retire the pet names," I suggested.

"What? Never." He tucked a lock of my hair behind my ear. "Besides, I thought you liked them."

I smiled. "I do, just don't tell my husband."

"Your husband? Does he know you're going on a cruise with your handsome boyfriend?" Scooter quipped.

"No, he has no idea." Scooter ran his finger down my cheek. "He's a lucky guy, that's for sure."

"And I'm a lucky girl."

Scooter looked intently into my eyes. "You know, with all this wedding talk, I was thinking maybe we should—"

"Next, please." The agent at the check-in desk waved us forward.

As the agent scanned our passports and boarding passes, I heard a loud voice bellowing.

"There you are." Fletcher clapped Scooter on the back. "Boy, do you drive fast. We couldn't keep up."

"Mollie was driving, not me."

"Well, I do like fast women," Fletcher said, putting his hand on my shoulder and squeezing it.

As I squirmed out of his grasp, Sylvia walked toward us, dragging a suitcase behind her. It was one of those roller bags, but one of the wheels was broken. It was apparent that Sylvia was struggling to carry it.

"Fletcher, where did you go? I could have used some help," she said.

"Just checking us in, sweetheart."

"But we can't check in without Anthony and Madison."

Fletcher let out an exasperated sigh. "Where are they?"

"Madison needed to stop at the ladies' room."

"How many times does that girl need to touch up her lipstick?"

Sylvia glared at Fletcher, then looked at Scooter and me. "Madison is Anthony's girlfriend. Anthony met her when she was competing in a beauty pageant sponsored by the company. I think Herbert was one of the judges that year. Anyway, now she works for the business as a secretary. I don't think you've met her before, but I'm sure you remember my nephew, Anthony, don't you?"

"Sure," Scooter said. "We met him at your Christmas open house. I think he had just gotten his MBA."

"That's right. He's such a smart boy." She beamed at a man in his early thirties who was walking toward us. He was accompanied by a stunning woman. She was tall and slender, with one of those figures that would make even a potato sack dress look glamorous on the catwalk. "There they are now."

Fletcher drummed his fingers on the

check-in desk while he waited for the couple to join us.

The agent looked at Fletcher, then asked Scooter, "Excuse me, sir. Is this gentleman with you?"

"Of course, I am. You see me standing here, don't you?" Fletcher said curtly.

The couple standing behind us started murmuring, then the man tapped Fletcher on his shoulder. "Hey, buddy, wait your turn."

"It is my turn."

"No, it isn't. You cut in line."

Fletcher squared his shoulders. "Mind your own business, fellow."

Actually, he didn't say "fellow." He used another word, but it's not one that I want to repeat here.

The other man lunged at Fletcher, but Anthony intervened. He nudged Fletcher toward the check-in desk, then tried to pass Fletcher's bad behavior off as a medical condition. "Sorry about what he said. It's his medication. Makes him say things he doesn't mean to."

The man's wife whispered something to her husband, likely trying to avoid the conflict from escalating any further. He relented, allowing Fletcher to check in.

"Medical condition?" I mouthed to Scooter.

"First I've heard of it," he whispered.

I was pretty sure that the only medical condition Fletcher had was being a jerk. This wasn't the first time I had seen him cut in front of other people. It was always him first. Standing in line was for others, not for someone like Fletcher Tolliver.

While the agent completed the check-in process, Sylvia patted Anthony on his arm. "Do you remember Scooter and Mollie McGhie? You met them at our Christmas open house."

Anthony shook Scooter's hand and nodded at me. "It's nice to see the two of you again."

"Anthony is working for the business

now. When Fletcher retires, Anthony is going to take over."

"Now, Aunt Sylvia, I think you're getting ahead of yourself. I'm not sure Herbert would see it that way. And Uncle Fletcher isn't going to retire for years yet. In any case, that's not how their partnership agreement is structured. Their shares are split fifty-fifty. But you know that if either of them retires, the other one gets controlling interest of the company." Anthony turned to us and smiled. "The idea of me taking over the company is just my aunt's wishful thinking."

Sylvia lowered her voice. "There's no way that Herbert could run the business. He can barely cut it as the company's CFO. He'd never cope taking on the CEO role. Ever since his wife died, he's lost his focus. We all know that he's why so many deals have gone bad."

"You've had deals go bad?" I asked. "Is there a problem with the business?"

Sylvia waved her hands in the air. "No, I'm exaggerating. What I'm really trying to say is that Fletcher keeps Herbert around out of a sense of loyalty. He feels sorry for him. But he has every intention of handing over the reins of the business to Anthony."

"But if Fletcher and Herbert are partners, how could he do that?" I asked.

"Oh, I don't really understand all that legal stuff," Sylvia said breezily before changing the subject. "Fletcher, dear, isn't that one of your potential investors there?"

Fletcher yelled out, "Hey, Dominic, over here."

The man standing behind us in line scowled. "Seriously? You're going to let someone else cut in front of us?" Then he turned and saw the person Fletcher was waving over. The guy looked like he could bench press an elephant without breaking a sweat. His black t-shirt was several sizes too small and was struggling to contain his bulging biceps and broad shoulders. Protein drinks, weightlifting, and possibly even steroids looked like they had factored into his physique.

When the large man reached us, he grunted some sort of greeting.

Scooter made the mistake of shaking Dominic's hand. When he retracted his hand, Scooter's pinkie looked a bit mangled. Fortunately, pinkie fingers aren't completely necessary for everyday activities.

"So, how long have you been in telecommunications?" Scooter asked as he gingerly massaged his hand.

"Telecommunications?" Dominic had a blank look on his face as he struggled to pronounce the word.

I held up my cell phone. "You know, telecommunications."

Dominic reached into the back pocket of his jeans and pulled out his phone.

He showed it to me, then shoved it back in his pocket.

While Fletcher handed everyone their boarding passes, Scooter and I exchanged glances.

"Do you think that guy is really in the telecommunications business?" I whispered.

"Doubtful," Scooter said.

"Does he seem like a potential investor to you?"

"Not really."

"Then what is he doing here?" I asked.

"No idea. You going to add it to your list of things to investigate?" Scooter asked.

"Definitely."

* * *

After the cruise ship departed, Scooter and I made our way to the Reef Beach Bar to join the others for drinks before dinner.

"Yoo-hoo, over here," Sylvia said, waving her arms over her head.

Anthony was seated next to his aunt, swirling ice cubes around in his glass. When Madison pulled a pack of cigarettes out of her evening bag, he shook his head. "Put those away."

As she shoved the pack into her purse, one of the cigarettes fell out and rolled toward me. When I handed it to her, I said, "I haven't seen pink cigarettes before. If my friend, Penny, smoked, she would love those. Pink is her favorite color. In fact, I don't think she even knows that any other colors exist."

Madison smiled at me. "I can relate." As she tucked the cigarette back in the pack, she snagged one of her fingernails, smudging the nail polish. She turned to Anthony. "See what you made me do?"

Anthony rolled his eyes and took a sip of his drink.

Sliding into a chair next to Sylvia, I asked where Fletcher was.

Before Sylvia could respond, Madison pointed at the bar and said, "He's over there, schmoozing."

Anthony frowned. "He's building relationships with the new investors, not schmoozing."

"Building relationships, right," Madison scoffed. "That's just a classier way of saying 'schmoozing.'"

"Maybe if you quit smoking, you'd have some more class," Anthony said to Madison.

Sylvia shot them a look, then plastered a smile on her face. "Aren't the two of them just adorable with the way they tease each other?"

"How many investors are there?" I asked, trying to change the subject.

"Four, not including Scooter," Sylvia said.

Scooter cleared his throat. "I've still not decided. I told Fletcher that I'd ..."

He looked at me, then continued. "I told him that *we* would make a decision after we saw the investor presentation. Hopefully, that's not a problem."

Sylvia toyed with her necklace. "But I thought—"

Anthony put his hand on Sylvia's arm, then looked at Scooter. "That's absolutely fine," he said smoothly. "But I'm sure once you see the presentation, you'll be the first in line to sign up. I promise you won't want to miss the boat on this opportunity."

I felt someone put their hands on my shoulders and squeeze them. When I turned and saw that it was Fletcher, I shuddered.

"How come Mollie and Scooter don't have drinks?" Fletcher snapped his fingers and summoned a waitress to our table.

"Yes, sir?" she asked.

The young woman had an accent that reminded me of our friend Melvin, the owner of Coconut Cove's marine supply store. "Are you from the Bahamas?" I asked.

She beamed. "Yes, ma'am. Will this be your first time visiting the Bahamas?"

Before I could answer, Fletcher interrupted. "You're not paid to make chit-chat," he said. "Don't you see all these empty glasses here? We need refills."

Her smile faded. "Certainly, sir."

"Mollie, Scooter, what do you want? Gin and tonic still your tipple of choice?"

We nodded, and the poor woman hurried off to get our drinks.

"You didn't have to be so rude," Sylvia said.

Fletcher rolled his eyes. "She's a waitress, not our friend."

I gave Scooter a meaningful look. No matter how fantastic the investor presentation was, I couldn't imagine wanting to do business with someone who was such a jerk.

After the waitress returned with our drinks, Fletcher asked Anthony and Scooter if they were interested in a poker game after dinner. "The other investors are here without their wives," he explained. "It's a good opportunity to play cards without the little women complaining."

"You're not going to go on cruises without me once we're married, are you?" Madison asked Anthony.

"Oh, are you engaged?" I asked.

Madison looked pointedly at her ring finger. "Not yet."

Anthony tugged at his collar. "Poker sounds good. You in, Scooter?"

"Um, I'm not sure," Scooter said. "I'm not a big poker player."

"No problem, we can hit the craps table instead."

"Why don't you skip the casino tonight?" Sylvia suggested.

Fletcher ignored his wife and slapped Scooter on the back. "You and me, buddy. We're going to make a night of it."

Sylvia pressed her lips together. "While the guys are losing all their money . . ." she stared at her husband for a moment, then smiled brightly at Madison and me. "The girls can go to the magic show."

"Magic? I love magic," Scooter whispered to me. "Can't I be one of the girls?"

"Sorry, mister," I whispered back. "Someone has to keep Fletcher company, and it looks like you've been nominated."

* * *

Fletcher completely monopolized the conversation over drinks. He bragged about his golf handicap, raved about his new convertible, and even talked up his latest business venture. The only person who was able to get a word in edgewise was Sylvia. Unfortunately, her topic of conversation involved way too many details about her recent colonoscopy.

I was relieved when it was time to head to dinner. Sylvia said that she needed to pop back to her cabin to get something, and would meet us there. Scooter and Anthony led the way, chatting about the latest trends in telecommunications. Fletcher, Madison, and I trailed behind them. When Fletcher started telling us about the industry awards that he had received over the years, I veered off to the ladies' room. Even though I didn't need to go to the bathroom, it was a good excuse to get away from 'Mr. Aren't I The Most Wonderful Thing Since Sliced Bread.'

After splashing cool water on my face, I applied some lip gloss and futilely attempted to smooth down my frizzy hair. When I came out of the ladies' room, I had to do a double take.

Fletcher and Madison were standing across the hallway in a small alcove. Why weren't they in the dining room? The last thing I wanted was for them to see me, and have Fletcher subject me to more of his self-aggrandizing stories.

I darted back into the ladies' room, leaving the door slightly ajar so that I could see when they left.

They had their eyes locked on each other, neither of them saying a word. I gasped as Fletcher grabbed Madison and pulled her toward him forcefully.

"Let go of me," Madison said sharply

When he didn't release her, she reached over with her free hand and dug her long fingernails into his arm. Fletcher cursed, then released her.

I glanced at my short, ragged and unvarnished fingernails. I usually resisted having my nails done, but seeing how Madison had used her talons for self-defensive purposes was making me reconsider my nail grooming routine. When I got back to Coconut Cove, I was going to head straight to my friend Alejandra's nail salon and get a manicure.

"Just admit it," Fletcher said. "You don't give two figs about Anthony. You only care about what he can do for you."

Madison put her hands on her hips. "That's not true. I love Anthony."

Fletcher shook his head. "You love his money . . . or rather the money that he'll have one day when he takes over the business."

"You're wrong. I'd be with Anthony no matter how much he made."

"You know, there's a reason why he hasn't asked you to marry him yet."

Madison's eyes widened. "You haven't told him—"

Fletcher held up his hand. "Don't worry. Your secret is safe with me. As long as you do your part, that is. You have until the end of the cruise to take care of things."

"Don't worry. It will get done. Herbert is a problem for all of us."

"Good. Because if it doesn't get done, well, you know what will happen." Fletcher held out his arm. "Now, can I escort you to dinner?"

Madison raised her hand as if to slap Fletcher.

"Don't even think about it, sweetheart." He sneered when she dropped her hand. "Smart girl."

"I can find my own way to the restaurant," she snapped.

He chuckled quietly as he watched her sashay down the hall.

When Fletcher finally made his own way toward the restaurant, I emerged from the ladies' room. My mind was whirring. I had originally come on this cruise, because I wanted to know more about Fletcher and Herbert's partnership, especially after the rumors that Fletcher had embezzled money from their company. Only now I had other things to occupy myself with. What was Madison's secret? Why was Herbert a problem? And what was Madison supposed to do to 'take care' of Herbert? I have to admit, it was refreshing to have an investigation that didn't involve murder.

* * *

When I got to the restaurant, everything seemed normal. Or at least as normal as things can be when you're seated with a dysfunctional family and a bunch of telecommunications geeks.

Fletcher was at one end of the long table, chatting with potential investors about the latest advancements in 5G networks. At least I think that's what they were talking about. I tend to struggle when sentences contain too many references to data transmission, software algorithms, and antennas.

Madison was feeding Anthony an hors

d'oeuvre. She giggled when a drop of sauce landed on the tablecloth. I saw a flicker of annoyance in Anthony's eyes, but when she stroked his cheek, he smiled.

Sylvia was telling Scooter how fabulous her new ear wax removal specialist was. Apparently, the man could work miracles with ear swabs and organic peanut butter. Sylvia's ears hadn't felt better in years. Scooter gave me a pleading look as I sat next to him. To put him out of his misery I changed the subject.

"Do you think Mrs. Moto is doing all right?" I asked. "We're out of cell phone range, so Ben won't have a way of texting us if anything goes wrong."

"Don't worry," Scooter said. "Ben is more than capable of taking care of our cat."

"Who's Ben?" Sylvia asked. "Your housekeeper?"

I snorted. "A housekeeper? You do

realize that we live on a sailboat, don't you? We're not exactly the type of people to have a housekeeper."

"Ben lives aboard his sailboat at the Palm Tree Marina. He also works there," Scooter explained. "He's crazy about Mrs. Moto. When we decided to come on this cruise, he offered to watch her."

"Ben could use a housekeeper for his boat," I said. "The place is a pigsty. I'm surprised Nancy doesn't read him the riot act."

"Nancy and her husband Ned own the marina," Scooter told Sylvia.

"I can't wait to see it," she said. "Fletcher and I are getting excited about our move."

My shoulders slumped. "So, you've definitely decided to relocate to Coconut Cove?"

"Absolutely," Sylvia said. "Now, tell me, who is the best acupuncturist in the area?"

"Acupuncture?" Scooter's face grew pale as Sylvia described the sensation of needles being stuck into your body. Although he quickly recovered after exhaling sharply, pressing the bridge of his nose, and tugging on his earlobes.

I pointed across the room. "Hey, isn't that Ned and Nancy over there?"

Grateful for the interruption, Scooter said, "What are the chances that they'd be on the same cruise as us, especially since we were just talking about them?"

"Let's go over and say hi," I said.

Scooter almost knocked over his chair in his eagerness to leave the table and escape Sylvia for a few moments.

When we approached their table, Nancy scowled. "What are you doing here?"

In contrast to his wife's grumpy greeting, Ned beamed at us. "What a pleasant surprise. Are you having a romantic getaway?"

"We're here on business," Scooter

said.

After he explained Fletcher's investment opportunity, Ned said, "If you're looking for something to invest in, you could always buy the marina."

"You're selling the marina?" I asked.

Nancy interjected. "We're considering it."

"It's a lot of work," Ned said. "I'd like to enjoy retirement and have more time with our grandkids. But Nancy isn't convinced. She likes to stay busy, you know."

Staying busy for Nancy involved bossing people around, telling everyone what they're doing wrong, and enforcing ridiculous rules and regulations. Ned should be careful what he wished for. If they sold the marina, Nancy would focus all of her energy on him. I could imagine a future for him that involved lessons on how to tear paper towels off the roll correctly, detailed manuals on how to clean the kitchen appliances, and being chastised for wasting time watching old movies.

"Our kids surprised us with this trip," Ned said. "We had no idea it was happening until our daughter picked us up and drove us to the cruise ship terminal. She had already gotten our passports and even packed our bags."

"What a lovely surprise," I said.

Ned nodded, then added ruefully. "To tell you the truth, I'd much rather be heading to the Bahamas on a sailboat. Don't get me wrong, the cruise ship is nice. But it's not the same as feeling the wind in your face as you trim the sails. I'd love to get another boat."

Nancy's expression softened as she patted Ned's hand. "I think those days are over. You don't want to have to get your knees replaced again, do you? And your arthritis keeps acting up."

"I suppose you're right." Ned sighed, then looked at us. "Are the two of you still planning on heading to the

Bahamas after Christmas?"

"Yep, with the first decent weather window, we're gone," Scooter said.

Nancy pursed her lips. "Are you sure that boat of yours will make it in one piece?"

A year ago, if someone had asked me that, I would have hesitated before answering. Only now, I jumped to M.J.'s defense. "Of course, she'll make it. We've put a lot of time, money, and sweat into her. You won't find a finer sailboat anywhere."

Nancy looked at me doubtfully, then she tapped Ned's arm. "There's that nice fellow we were chatting with earlier."

As Ned waved the man over, I realized they were talking about Fletcher's business partner.

"How do you know Herbert Miller?" I asked.

"He was standing next to us on deck when the ship left port," Nancy said.

"We got to talking about the times Ned and I sailed to the Bahamas back when we had a boat."

"Funny how sailors gravitate toward each other," Ned said. "It's almost like we have a sixth sense that another like-minded person is nearby."

"Super nice guy," Nancy said. "He even gave us a free phone charger. Says that his company got a box of them to test. He complained about their secretary. Apparently, she was supposed to order five, but she ordered five dozen instead. Now, they have so many they don't know what to do with them."

Herbert greeted Ned and Nancy, then shook Scooter's hand. "It's been a long time, hasn't it?"

"Sure has," Scooter said. "You remember Mollie, don't you?"

"Of course," Herbert said. "The roller derby girl."

"It's been ages since I've skated," I

said.

"They don't have a roller derby rink in Coconut Cove?" Herbert asked.

"No. But I'm not sure I'd have time for skating these days. Our sailboat keeps us pretty busy."

Herbert slapped Scooter on the shoulder. "So you finally did it, huh? You bought a sailboat."

"I used to go sailing with Herbert on Lake Erie," Scooter explained to Ned and Nancy.

"We were telling Herbert about what a great boating town Coconut Cove is," Ned said. "He's thinking of bringing his boat down to Florida."

"Ideally, I'd have a boat in the south to sail on during the winters and one up north for the summers. When I eventually decide to stop working, which is a long way off, maybe I could retire down here."

"We convinced Herbert to spend some time in Coconut Cove after the cruise and check it out," Ned said. "The timing is perfect. We have the fundraiser at the yacht club next weekend. It will be a great opportunity for Herbert to meet some local sailors."

"What are you raising money for?" Herbert asked.

"It's for a new maritime exhibit at the historical museum," Nancy said.

"Sounds good," Herbert said.

"They're selling chocolate at the library to raise funds for it too," I said.

"I'm not sure they have any left," Nancy said dryly. "Hudson told me that you cleared out their inventory."

"Just doing my part for a good cause." I turned to Herbert. "Did you know that Fletcher and Sylvia are considering moving to Coconut Cove too?"

"No, I didn't," Herbert said slowly. "That's interesting."

I cocked my head to one side. "I was surprised to find out that you and Fletcher were still business partners after all these years."

"Well, it isn't easy to end a relationship with Fletcher. Just ask Sylvia." When I raised my eyebrow, he added, "I'm kidding, of course. Fletcher and I have been together since the beginning. It's kind of like a marriage in a way. I can't imagine us ever splitting up."

The smile on Herbert's face didn't quite reach his eyes. Did he know Fletcher had it out for him? Did he realize that Madison had plans to 'take care of him'?

CHAPTER 4
LADY LUCK

"Ragno, the Master of Illusions," Madison said, reading the sign outside of the theater. "Sounds pretty corny. Maybe we should have joined the guys in the casino. I don't think I can take three hours of hokey magic tricks."

Sylvia did a double take. "Did you say Ragno? It can't be." Stepping forward, she peered at the picture of the magician who would be performing shortly. "Goodness, it is him. I saw Ragno in Vegas a few years ago. You girls are in for a real treat. He was absolutely amazing."

"If he's so amazing, why is he on the cruise ship circuit?" Madison asked. "This is where acts go to die."

"Maybe he just wanted a change of pace." Sylvia said snippily, then turned to me. "Did you know I used to be a magician's assistant?"

I cocked my head to one side. "Really?"

"It was before Fletcher and I were married. I worked with all the top magicians in Cleveland. You should have seen the outfits I wore—mini-skirts and fishnet stockings."

I tried to reconcile the older, slightly dowdy woman in front of me with an image of a young, sexy magician's assistant. "Did they saw you in half?"

"Yes, but they always put me back together at the end," she said with a smile.

"How do they do that?"

"Sorry, can't say. Code of silence." Sylvia twisted an imaginary key over her lips.

Madison shrugged. "I'm sure there's a video on YouTube that shows how it's done."

"That's horrible," Sylvia said. "Anyone who would break the sacred magic code of silence should be ashamed of themselves."

"What would happen if someone breaks the code? Get sawed in half?" I asked.

Sylvia smiled, then got a faraway look in her eyes. "One of the magicians I worked for made it big. He asked me to go on tour with him, but I had just met Fletcher. I was madly in love. Now I wonder what my life would have been like if I had made a different decision."

"I guess you think about things like that when you get older," she mused as she fiddled with her necklace. "The road you didn't take."

"But you're happy with Fletcher, aren't you?" Madison asked.

"Oh, sure." The tone in Sylvia's voice wasn't very convincing. "If I hadn't chosen Fletcher, I wouldn't have my kids."

"You have two daughters, right?" I asked.

"Yes. They're both living on the west coast now. They don't visit us as much as I'd like, but once we move to Florida, I bet we won't be able to keep them away." Sylvia pulled out her phone and showed us photos. "My oldest became a doctor and my youngest is an entertainment lawyer."

"Neither of them wanted to take over the family business?" I asked.

"No. And we didn't pressure them either. That's why I'm glad Anthony was interested. It will be nice to keep it in the family." When Madison bit her lip, Sylvia said, "Don't worry dear, you'll be an official part of the family before you know it."

Madison clasped her hands together, as though she wanted to hide the lack of an engagement ring. "I don't know. I keep thinking he's going to pop the question, but then he never does."

"I bet it will happen at Christmas. You wait and see. Sometimes men need a bit longer to realize what's missing from their lives." She grabbed Madison's hand and nodded at me. "Come on, girls, let's go find our seats."

"How long have you and Fletcher been married?" I asked Sylvia as we walked into the theater.

"We celebrated our fortieth this year."

"Wow, that's impressive," I said.

"Marriage is a commitment. When things aren't going great, you can't just walk away."

As we sat down, I asked Sylvia if everything was okay between her and Fletcher.

She smoothed down her dark slacks.

"He's been a little stressed lately."

"Stressed? Is that what you call it?" Madison quirked an eyebrow. "He's been hitting the bottle pretty hard."

"You think I don't know that?" Sylvia pulled a tissue out of her purse and dabbed her eyes. "He promised that he'd quit again when we're back home. I don't know why he had to drag all the investors on this cruise. He could have done the presentation back in Cleveland. There are too many temptations here—booze, gambling . . ."

As her voice trailed off, I wondered if she also worried about women tempting Fletcher. There were rumors that he had strayed more than once.

"Don't worry," Madison said. "Anthony is going to keep an eye on him tonight. He'll make sure that he doesn't gamble or drink too much."

"That's a tall order," Sylvia said ruefully. "If you tell Fletcher not to do something, then he does it."

The loudspeakers crackled. "Welcome, ladies and gentlemen," an announcer said. "Please take your seats. The show is about to start."

Sylvia squealed. "This is so exciting. I get to see Ragno again. Wait until you see the illusion he does with tarantulas."

"Tarantulas?" I asked, my voice cracking. "As in big, hairy spiders?"

Sylvia's eyes gleamed with excitement. "It's almost as good as the trick he does with snakes."

My eyes grew wide. Our seats were awfully close to the stage. "Um, you know what, I feel a headache coming on. I'm going to go back to my cabin and lie down."

"No, you can't go now," Sylvia said. "I think I have some over the counter pain relievers in my purse."

I rubbed my fingers on my temples. "I think I might need something stronger."

As the lights dimmed, I hightailed it out of the theater. Dead bodies, blood, murderers—I'd rather deal with all of that any day over a big, hairy tarantula.

* * *

Okay, I'll be honest. I didn't really have a headache. Though if I had stayed for the magic show, something worse would have happened. When the tarantulas appeared on stage, I would have screamed—loudly, really, really loudly. I can deal with a lot of things, but creatures with eight legs, well, that's just wrong. Four legs are the most that anything should have or six at a stretch. But eight? That's downright terrifying. And you want to know what else really creeps me out about spiders? They have *eight* eyes. More eyes to see you with in the dark right before they pounce on you.

Anyone who doubts the existence of extraterrestrial life should examine spiders carefully. From a safe distance, of course. Preferably behind a sturdy, impenetrable plexiglass barrier. Once you get a close look, you'll realize that spiders clearly originated on a planet where eight legs are the norm. Aliens must have dumped them here on Earth as some sort of practical joke. Don't even get me started on centipedes . . .

Anywho … where was I? Oh, yeah. I had rushed out of the theater, closing the door firmly behind me to prevent any spiders from following. I decided to head to the casino to see what the fellows were up to. Fletcher had always been one of those guys who drank too much at parties and then blamed his bad behavior on the booze. Except from what Sylvia had said, it sounded like his drinking problem had gotten worse. Scooter might need my help to run interference.

I haven't visited many casinos, but the one on the cruise ship seemed to fit the general pattern—plush carpeting, dim lighting, people in zombie-like trances mindlessly feeding coins into slot machines, and the occasional cheer when someone hit a jackpot. The only difference was that this casino had a view of the ocean. Moonlight reflected off the water, and I swear I could see a sailboat off in the distance.

Craps, roulette wheels, and blackjack tables were in the center of the room. To the right of the entrance was a bar and to the left was the VIP Room. A red velvet rope was barricading it from the rest of the casino. Inside, the potential investors were playing high-stakes poker.

As I looked around for Scooter, someone tapped me on the shoulder. I turned and saw Dominic. He was dressed in a similar fashion to when I had met him earlier in the day—a black t-shirt two sizes too small for him paired with jeans. The only difference was that he had a large diamond stud in one of his ears. Maybe that was his way of dressing up for the evening.

Dominic smiled at me. It was an odd smile. His mouth looked so tiny in comparison to his bulky build. His teeth appeared to be the size of baby teeth. I wondered if this was a side effect of doing too many steroids. When your muscles grow bigger, do your teeth shrink?

He pointed at the roulette wheel. "Play?"

"Uh, no thanks," I said. "I'm looking for my husband. Have you seen him?"

Dominic shook his head. "Play?"

"No, I can't," I repeated.

"Okay, I play." Dominic pointed at himself, then at me. "You, good luck."

Grabbing my elbow, he steered me toward the roulette wheel. When we reached it, he asked, "Favorite number?"

"Six million, four hundred and thirty-two."

Dominic's brow furrowed, and I wondered if English was his first language. He pointed at the numbers running around the outer edge of the roulette wheel. "Pick again."

"But I don't have a second favorite number," I said. "That's the only one."

He nodded slowly. "One. Good. Good number. Favorite color?"

"Oh, this question is harder," I said. "I can tell you what my least favorite color is—pink. But as for my favorite, well, I'm torn between blue and green. Orange is nice too."

Dominic cracked his knuckles and stared at me. The noise was so loud that it could be heard over the robotic chirping and beeping noises from the nearby slot machines. "Red or black? Pick."

"To be honest, I don't really like either color. Unless you're talking about licorice, in which case, red, for sure."

"Red. Good. Good color." Dominic

placed a stack of chips on top of the number one, then another stack on top of a red diamond. Never having played roulette before, I wasn't sure if this was a good betting strategy. However, given the number of chips he was gambling, I hoped so.

The dealer spun the wheel. Dominic watched intently as the white ball whizzed around. When it landed on the number one, Dominic clapped his hands together. After the dealer pushed a pile of chips toward him, Dominic patted me on the shoulder.

"Good. Good job. Pick again."

I stared at the numbers on the roulette wheel—zero through thirty-eight. None of them spoke to me. Then an image of a giant tarantula popped into my head. Dominic was a scary-looking guy. Tarantulas were scary too. Maybe the universe was trying to tell me something. "Eight," I suggested.

Turns out eight is a lucky number

when it comes to roulette. Dominic was on fire. He spent the next twenty minutes asking me to pick numbers. Somehow, each one I chose was a winner.

As I was trying to decide between twelve and twenty-two, I heard a commotion on the other side of the room. "That sounds like Fletcher. A very drunk Fletcher."

Dominic and I wound our way around the gaming tables and through the rows of slot machines. Fletcher was standing outside the VIP Room, gesturing at Scooter and sloshing the contents of his drink on the ground. "That dealer is crooked. That's why I lost."

Scooter tried to steady Fletcher. "I think you're just having a run of back luck."

Fletcher handed the glass to Scooter and pulled his wallet out of his pocket. He frowned as he rifled through it. "Sylvia will kill me if she finds out I'm out of cash."

"Why don't we go to the lounge and get some coffee?" Scooter suggested.

"I don't want coffee. I want another drink." Fletcher looked blearily in our direction. "Dominic, there you are. Do me a favor. Lend me some money."

Dominic stared impassively at Fletcher, not saying a word.

Fletcher spied the bucket of chips that Dominic was holding. "Lady Luck has been treating you right, hasn't she?"

Dominic pointed at me. "Lady Luck."

Fletcher grabbed Dominic's arm and whispered something in his ear. Dominic shook his head. Fletcher narrowed his eyes, then whispered something else to him.

Dominic stared at the ground, considering what Fletcher had said. After a beat, he said, "Watch."

Fletcher took a deep breath, then removed a heavy gold watch from his wrist and handed it to the other man.

Dominic examined it closely before handing Fletcher the bucket of chips.

"Thanks," Fletcher said, slurring his words. "I can feel my luck changing already."

As we watched Fletcher weave and totter his way toward the craps table, I said, "Anthony should be here. Madison said that he was going to keep an eye on Fletcher."

"He's with the other guys at the poker game," Scooter said. "That kid is sharp. He knows the telecommunications industry inside and out. From the sounds of it, he's the one that put this deal together, not Fletcher. Maybe it's not such a bad investment opportunity after all."

I turned to look at Scooter and noticed a red stain on his shirt. "What happened?"

"Fletcher spilled his daiquiri on me. I should probably go change, but . . ." his voice trailed off as Fletcher bellowed for a drink.

"Go ahead. I can keep an eye on him."

Scooter cocked his head to one side. "Hey, aren't you supposed to be at the magic show?"

"Tarantulas," I said.

"Ah . . . I see."

After Scooter left, I walked over to the craps table. A waiter was handing Fletcher another drink when Herbert elbowed his way through the other gamblers and snatched it away.

"Don't do this," Herbert said. "Fletcher, you're better than this."

"Stop being such a stick in the mud," Fletcher said, trying to grab the drink.

Herbert spotted me. "Here, take this," he said in an undertone.

While I took a sip of the daiquiri, Fletcher leaned over the large oval table and dumped some chips out of his bucket. "Give me the dice."

After the other players placed their bets, Fletcher blew on the dice before throwing them down the table. A silver-haired lady squealed and high-fived her friend. Fletcher frowned as the dealer scooped up his losing chips. Then he demanded a rum and coke from a passing waitress.

I groaned when I realized the waitress was the same woman who Fletcher had been rude to earlier in the evening. Though if she resented having to put up with his bad behavior again, she didn't show it.

Herbert pulled the waitress aside, and I heard him suggest that she bring Fletcher a non-alcoholic drink.

After losing some more of his chips, Fletcher slammed his fist onto the craps table. Herbert clasped him on the shoulder. "Why don't we call it a night?"

Fletcher let out a loud belch, then jabbed his finger in Herbert's chest. "We're here to have fun, for goodness sake."

"You're drunk," Herbert said flatly.

Fletcher waved his hands around. "We're on a boat. It's not like I'm going to get in a car and drive drunk." He nodded toward the VIP Room. "Why don't you go play poker?"

"You know I don't gamble."

"You don't gamble, you don't drink, you don't do anything except cost the company millions." Fletcher lurched toward Herbert. "You haven't been pulling your weight for a long time. If we don't get these guys to invest and close this deal, something is going to have to change."

"Oh, don't worry, Fletcher. Something is going to change," Herbert said darkly.

"Good, we're in agreement for once."

Herbert took a deep breath. "Fine, I give up. We'll talk more tomorrow when you're sober."

The waitress bustled over and handed Fletcher his drink. He downed it, then glared at her. "This doesn't taste right. Bring me another one." She simply nodded, then scurried off.

Herbert narrowed his eyes as he watched the exchange. Leaning forward, he said quietly, "Listen, buddy, this time, I won't be so understanding. Make sure that the money you lose tonight is yours, and only yours."

* * *

I watched as Fletcher continued to place chips on the table and stare in disappointment when he didn't win. I wasn't the only one keeping an eye on things. Dominic was perched on a stool, carefully observing the action at the craps table. When Fletcher reached into the bucket and realized it was empty, he made eye contact with Dominic. Some sort of unspoken agreement seemed to have been reached. Fletcher shuffled over to Dominic and handed him his car keys. In exchange, Dominic handed him a wad of bills, which Fletcher promptly exchanged for chips.

Realizing that almost a half hour had passed, and Scooter still hadn't returned, I decided to leave Fletcher to his own devices. Watching him wasn't going to make a difference. The man was bound and determined to gamble, drink, and insult everyone that crossed his path. More power to the jerk, I thought as I left the casino.

Scooter wasn't in our cabin, although I did find his stained shirt crumpled up in the bathroom sink. Next, I peeked into the theater. Maybe Scooter had thought that I had braved the magic show again. The lighting was dim, so I couldn't see who was in the audience. I glanced at the stage and saw a magician wearing a red cape with black spots. He waved a wand in circles while he recited some sort of incantation. I gasped when I saw the black spots on his cape move. Realizing that the spots were in fact tarantulas, I fled.

Wishing our cell phones had coverage while at sea so I could text Scooter, I made my way back toward the casino. He was probably there looking for me while I was looking for him everywhere else. As I walked through the lounge, I spotted Ned and Nancy having a nightcap.

"Have you seen Scooter?" I asked.

"No," Ned said. "Where did you last see him?"

After I explained how Scooter had gone back to our cabin to change his shirt, Nancy pursed her lips. "I thought you were the klutzy one."

"Scooter didn't spill the drink. It was Herbert's business partner, Fletcher. He's drunk as a skunk."

"Some people go overboard when they're on vacation," Ned said.

"It's not really a vacation," I reminded them. "Fletcher and Herbert are here to drum up business. I thought I had Scooter convinced that investing was a bad idea, but he seems to be wavering again."

"There's always the marina," Ned joked.

"Don't be silly. They're not going to buy the marina." Nancy looked at me. "Are you sure it was Fletcher you saw drinking?"

"It's not like it's the first time I've met him."

"I thought Herbert told us that his business partner didn't drink," Nancy said to Ned.

Ned shrugged. "Maybe they have another partner?"

"Or, more likely, this Fletcher fellow is an alcoholic and fell off the wagon," she said. "That sounds like a certain someone who works at the library."

"Do you mean Hudson?" I asked.

Nancy's eyes widened. "What? No, our nephew isn't an alcoholic. Although, I'd understand if he had turned to the bottle after what he's been through."

I frowned. "What happened to him?"

Ned and Nancy exchanged glances.

"I guess it was before you moved to Coconut Cove," Ned said after a pause. He reached over and squeezed Nancy's hand before continuing. "Hudson's wife died in childbirth."

"And the baby?" I asked tentatively.

"It was a boy," Nancy said, her voice cracking. "He didn't make it either."

I put my hand over my mouth. That poor man. To lose your wife and child— was there anything more heartbreaking?

"It was hard on the entire family. My sister was over the moon that her first grandchild was on the way, then . . ." Nancy stared at her brandy as her voice trailed off.

Ned attempted to change the subject. "The person at the library who has an addiction issue is the custodian. He was in a terrible car accident and got hooked on painkillers. He's been through rehab and is clean now. Knock on wood it stays that way."

"Makes me glad the only thing I'm addicted to is chocolate," I said.

"Sugar can cause serious health problems," Ned said. "Maybe you should think about cutting back." He smiled when he saw the expression on my face. "Just a little."

"Maybe, but not until after the Daltons' wedding," I said. "I can't very well skip sampling their wedding cake, especially if Penelope is making it."

"Have they set a date yet?" Ned asked.

"No, they're still trying to decide on a venue. I told Anabel I'd check out this cruise ship as an option. I sent her some pictures before we left port, but I don't really think it's for her."

"Isn't her bachelorette party this weekend?" Nancy asked. "Why would she schedule it now before they pick a date for the wedding?"

"With the holidays coming up, she

thought it made more sense to have it now." I ran my fingers through my hair. "I don't know what I'm going to do about the party though. The Tipsy Pirate shut down and I need to find another venue. That's why I didn't want to go on this cruise. I have too much to do."

"Maybe Nancy could help you," Ned said. "She's great at organizing things."

Both Nancy and I blanched. I think the last thing either of us wanted was to work together planning a party. Fortunately, I was spared from having to come up with a polite way to say no.

"Gotta scram," I said as I spotted Scooter on the opposite side of the lounge.

* * *

Scooter marched through the lounge and out on to the deck before I could catch up with him. He was walking down the stairs to the deck below and I followed in close pursuit.

When I got to the bottom step, the only people I saw were a young couple locked in a passionate embrace. I paused for a moment, breathing in the salt air. As the cruise ship slipped through the water, I pictured what it might be like when Scooter and I sailed for the first time to the Bahamas.

Not sure which direction my husband had gone in, I left the decision up to my intuition. It told me to take a left turn toward the stern. Rounding the corner, I saw Scooter leaning against the rail, staring glumly at the water.

"What are you doing out here all by yourself?" I asked gently. "I was getting worried."

"Hey, Mollie," he said without glancing at me.

"Mollie, huh? Should I be concerned that you're using my proper name? What happened to all your pet names for me? What was the one you called me last week? My little agave?"

He gave me a faint smile. "That was only because we were drinking margaritas made with agave syrup."

"Do you want to go to the bar and get one?"

He shook his head. "I'd rather stay here."

"What's going on?" I placed my hand on his. "There's obviously something bothering you."

Scooter sighed. "I feel like a fool."

"A fool? What are you talking about? You're the smartest guy I know."

"Yeah, right. So smart that I almost invested our life savings in Fletcher's business venture."

"But you didn't, and that's the important thing."

He pushed himself off the railing and paced back and forth. "Don't you see? After talking with Anthony this evening, I was convinced that it was a good investment. I almost got suckered in again."

"Something must have happened between now and then," I said.

"When I went to our cabin, I found an envelope which had been slipped under our door. I opened it, thinking it was for us, but it was really for Fletcher."

"How did it end up in our cabin?"

"Fletcher made the booking. Maybe there was a mix-up and his name is in the system instead of ours. Anyway, that's not the important thing. What's important now is that I know this so-called investment opportunity is a scam. We would have lost everything."

"Is it some sort of Ponzi scheme?"

"No, nothing like that. Look, it's too complicated to explain right now—"

I grabbed Scooter's arm to stop his pacing. Standing on my tiptoes, I put my hands on either side of his face, forcing him to look in my eyes. "Ah, it's complicated. See, you are a smart guy. You understand complicated things."

Scooter pulled away, then shook his head. "No, if I was smart, I would have figured it out from the start. I was so excited about the possibility of doubling, even tripling our money, that I was easily duped. I was blinded by the fact that I want us to have a considerable nest egg. If we do want to sail around the world, then we wouldn't have to worry about going back to work. We could just do it."

"Look, I know I'm not pulling my weight financially, but—"

"No, it's not that at all. You're passionate about what you do. It doesn't matter how much you make. And that's the point. It shouldn't be about money. It should be about enjoying what we do. I just got taken in by Fletcher's smooth talk and sales pitch. I got greedy and lost sight of the fact that we're so much better off than most people in the world."

"That's for sure," I agreed. "There are so many homeless people. We're fortunate to have a roof over our head."

Scooter smiled. "One that floats in the water and can go in any direction we want to point her to."

"And plenty of food to eat." I patted my belly. "Do you think I need to lose weight? Should I cut back on my chocolate intake?"

Scooter laughed. "There's no way you're going to get me to respond to that question. No married man with any sense would ever answer that."

"See, not only are you smart, but you're also sensible."

"You know you're my best girl, don't you?" Scooter pulled me into his arms. As he lowered his head to kiss me, a loud voice on the deck above us spoiled the romantic moment.

"Maybe we should go someplace quieter," Scooter suggested.

"Shush," I whispered. "Doesn't that sound like Fletcher?"

"You're never going to get what you

want," the man said, slurring his words. "Never."

"Yep, that's Fletcher," Scooter said.

Someone responded to Fletcher, but their voice was muffled.

Fletcher's response came in loud and clear, though. "What are you doing?" he shrieked.

I leaned back against the railing and peered upward, trying to see what was happening on the deck above us. A man was silhouetted in the moonlight, holding his arms up in what looked like a defensive posture.

I pulled Scooter back so that we wouldn't be seen. Then I heard a grating noise, like metal rubbing against something. That was followed by a piercing scream. When I saw a body hurl past us into the ocean, I gasped. "I think Fletcher has gone overboard."

CHAPTER 5
MAN OVERBOARD!

By the time one of the ship's officers had finished questioning us about Fletcher's death, the moon had set. Not that anyone officially confirmed that Fletcher had died mind you, but I had overheard one of the crew members saying that the chance of surviving something like that was extremely low.

While I went back to our cabin to try to get some shut eye before the sun came up, Scooter headed to the restaurant in search of coffee. He didn't seem upset from having seen someone plummet past us to their probable death. I think I was more in shock than he was, and a large part of my shock was that he wasn't more upset than me. That strange calming ritual of his appeared to really do the trick. He even refused the chocolate I offered him, telling me that I probably needed it more than him.

I was so frazzled after what had happened, that I wondered if tugging on my earlobes, pressing my fingers on the sides of my nose, and doing breathing exercises might help me as well. Once I crawled into bed, I tried it. The only effect it had was to cause me to cry out in pain when I almost yanked one of my earrings out of my ear.

After tossing and turning for what seemed like ages, I gave up and went in search of Scooter. As I was walking through the lounge, I saw Anthony and Madison. He was leaning against a wall, his arms folded across his chest.

Madison was curled in a ball on a nearby couch, clutching a box of tissues in her hands.

"How's Sylvia?" I asked.

Madison looked up at me, her large eyes still stunning despite the mascara smudged underneath them. "They've locked her up and won't let us talk to her."

"Locked her up?" I asked.

"Madison is exaggerating," Anthony said. "My aunt is with the captain."

"I'm not exaggerating," Madison huffed. "She's been in his office for hours. Those two goons guarding the door won't let us in."

"You're overstating things as usual. It hasn't been hours." Anthony looked at his watch. "Uncle Fletcher fell overboard before midnight. It's . . . oh, I guess she has been in there for hours."

Madison wailed, yanking several tissues out of the box. For someone who seemed to have had a bitter relationship with Fletcher, she was awfully devastated by his demise.

I picked up a tissue which had fallen on the floor, then looked at Anthony. "You're her nephew. Shouldn't you be allowed to be with her?"

"That's what I said." Madison dabbed her eyes. "Sylvia shouldn't be alone at a time like this. She needs her family with her."

Anthony clenched his fists. "Don't you think I know that? I tried."

"Well, try harder." Madison had a hard edge to her voice.

"Why don't I see what I can do?" I suggested, eager to get away from the tension that was bubbling up between the two of them. "If you see Scooter, can you tell him where I've gone?"

When I reached the captain's office, I gulped. The two crewmen standing in front of the door looked like they could give Dominic a run for his money in the weightlifting department. The one to my right had a rigid stance and buzz cut. Perhaps he was ex-military. The other man had a more relaxed posture and sported a goatee.

The man with the buzz cut stepped forward. "Can I help you, ma'am?"

"Yes, you can open the door, please."

"I'm sorry, ma'am, but I can't do that."

"Of course, you can," I said. "Look at those muscular arms of yours. How much can you bench press?"

He puffed up his chest. "Three hundred pounds."

"So, pushing that door open would be like child's play to you."

The man with the goatee snickered. "Three hundred pounds? Give me a break. You'd be lucky to manage one-fifty."

Buzz cut guy glared at him. "Watch it, buddy."

"Hey, easy there, fellows. There's a simple way to settle this." I pointed at a marble statue of Poseidon standing across from the entrance to the captain's office. "How much do you think that weighs?"

The two of them sized it up. "I dunno," buzz cut guy said. "A lot."

"Could you lift it over your head?"

"Piece of cake." He removed his jacket, rolled up his sleeves, and cracked his neck.

As he walked toward the statue, I turned to goatee guy. "Shouldn't you spot him?" The question seemed to stump him. "Safety first, right?"

That spurred him into action. While the two hulking men tried to figure out the best way to grip Poseidon—his trident kept getting in the way—I started to pull the door to the captain's office open. The squeaking noise of the hinges alerted the guys.

Goatee guy rushed over, pushing the door closed. "What are you doing? You can't go in there."

I wracked my brain for another ruse.

These two were marginally smarter than I had assumed. Whipping my FAROUT badge out of my purse, I said, "I'm here on official business related to the death of Fletcher Tolliver."

"What kind of badge is that?" he asked.

Before he could grab it in his beefy hands, I snapped the badge holder shut. If he saw the spaceship logo and I admitted that my credentials consisted of being an investigative reporter for the Federation of Alien Research, Outreach, and UFO Tracking, he might ask questions.

"The kind that can get you into big trouble if you're not careful. Now are you going to open the door for me, or should I contact my superior officer?"

He took a step back, clearly intimidated by my authoritative demeanor. Then he sheepishly opened the door for me. A win for this FAROUT reporter.

I pointed at crew cut guy who was struggling to yank Poseidon off his stand. "I think your buddy needs help." Giving him a dismissive nod, I strode into the captain's office, closed the door firmly, and bolted the latch.

Sylvia and the captain were sitting on a couch. The captain looked puzzled by my presence. He started to rise, but I flashed my badge and motioned for him to sit back down. To my surprise, he complied. I made a mental note to try using my FAROUT badge the next time I got stopped for speeding. Maybe the officer would be so impressed by my credentials that he would let me go without even so much as a warning.

"Mollie, what are you doing here?" Sylvia asked.

"Anthony and Madison are worried sick about you." I turned to the captain. "Those buffoons guarding your office wouldn't let them in. You should be ashamed of yourself, separating a distraught widow from her family."

The captain glanced at the door to his office. "But I didn't—"

"Save it. I don't want to hear another word out of you," I motioned to the captain to move over on the couch, then squeezed in between him and Sylvia. "How are you doing?" I asked her.

"As well as can be expected, I guess," she said. "I think I'm still in shock. Do you know that I haven't cried once?"

"Grief hits us in the strangest ways," I said.

The captain cleared his throat. "I'm sorry, who exactly are you?"

"Mollie McGhie," I said, turning to fix my gaze on him. "Don't make me show you my badge again."

Sylvia furrowed her brow. "Badge?"

"That's not important. What's important is if they're treating you okay. Have they given you anything to eat or drink?"

She pointed at her teacup. "Earl

Grey."

"What about a lawyer?"

"Why would I need a lawyer?"

"Because they're interrogating you. They're trampling all over your rights."

"This isn't an interrogation," the captain said. "I simply asked Mrs. Tolliver a few questions about her husband. Then she started telling me stories about her time as a magician's assistant."

"I've probably bored him silly. But it's been such a lovely distraction. I haven't had to think about what happened until now." As Sylvia took a sip of her tea, a lone tear fell down her cheek. "Where did you say Anthony was?"

"He's in the lounge with Madison."

Sylvia set her cup on the table and stood. "I think I'll go find him. I'll need his help making arrangements."

"Here, let me go with you," I offered.

"No, I'd rather go by myself." Sylvia kissed the captain on the cheek and thanked him for his hospitality.

After she left, I grilled the captain. "I assume you've recovered Fletcher's body, correct?"

"I can't comment on that," he said.

"What about the murder investigation? I assume you've examined the scene of the crime. What clues have you found?"

"Ma'am, it was most likely an accident," he said crisply. "Not murder."

"But my husband and I heard him arguing with someone. Fletcher was pushed overboard."

"According to his wife, he was drinking heavily. It wouldn't be the first time someone who was drunk fell to their death on a cruise ship." The captain looked at me thoughtfully. "Or it could have been suicide. Do you know of any reason why Mr. Tolliver would have killed himself?"

"Fletcher was too full of himself to even consider taking his life. But I think there's at least one person who would have wished him dead."

* * *

"Who exactly did you say you are?" The captain asked.

"I'm a friend of Sylvia's."

"If you really are her friend, then I'd advise you to keep this idea that her husband was murdered to yourself. She's dealing with enough. The last thing she needs is for someone to suggest there was foul play. It would traumatize her unnecessarily."

"But don't you think it's possible that someone killed Fletcher?"

"Murder on a cruise ship? The idea is preposterous." The captain narrowed his eyes. "And if I hear you've been spreading rumors to that effect . . ." his voice trailed off, leaving the rest of his threat unsaid.

"Oh, I see what's going on," I said. "This isn't about Sylvia. This is about protecting the cruise line's reputation. You don't want to lose future bookings when word gets out that someone was killed on your watch."

The captain stood. "I think it's time you left."

As he escorted me to the door, I asked why he had guards outside his office. "What are you afraid of?"

"Guards? What guards?" When he saw crew cut guy and goatee guy struggling to put the statue back on its pedestal, the captain sighed. "Oh, those two. They aren't guards. I told them to wait outside my office so that I could speak with them about an operational issue."

"Then why did they try to keep people out of your office?"

"Because they're idiots."

He had a point. The two self-appointed guards had managed to place the statue back in place. Only now they were trying to decide if they could use duct tape to reattach an arm that had broken off.

While the captain dealt with his two crewmen, I headed to the restaurant in search of some caffeine.

Scooter was sitting at a table with Ned and Nancy. He waved at me, then held up his coffee cup, indicating that it was empty. Ned and Nancy spotted me, but shook their heads when I mimed getting them coffee as well.

I grabbed two cups from the beverage station and filled them up, adding double the usual amount of sugar to them. It had been a long night, and my body was crying out for an energy boost. Then I spotted a tray of brownies on the buffet. Chocolate and sugar together in one delectable morsel? Yes, please. This is what makes cruises so enjoyable—delicious snacks twenty-four hours a day.

I placed two brownies on a plate, then added a couple of slices of pie and a few donuts for good measure. A waitress came to my rescue when she saw me struggling to balance my tray and walk at the same time.

"Here, let me help you with that, ma'am." She expertly placed the tray on her shoulder.

Her soft Bahamian accent and intricately braided hair were familiar. "Weren't you working at the casino earlier tonight? Or was that last night? What time is it, anyway?"

"It's four-thirty, ma'am."

"In the morning?" She nodded. "So, it's tomorrow. Or rather today." I rubbed my eyes. "It's like I have jet lag. I can't stay up all night like I could when I was younger."

As we walked toward the table, I asked her what she knew about Fletcher's death.

"Such a tragedy." Her face clouded. "We're not supposed to talk about it. Captain's orders."

"I was with the captain discussing what happened just moments ago. I'm sure he would be fine if we discussed it."

She shifted the tray she was carrying. "Really?"

"Of course. You were serving Fletcher at the casino last night. You're a key witness to what transpired."

"I am?"

"Definitely. How did Fletcher seem to you? Did you notice anything unusual?"

"The gentleman seemed to be enjoying himself," she said diplomatically.

"That's one way of putting it," I said wryly.

"I already told my manager everything I know." The waitress set the tray on the table. "I'm sorry, but I really need to help set up the breakfast buffet before it gets busy."

As she bustled off, I handed Scooter his coffee. Noting the dark circles under his eyes, I asked how he was doing. "Maybe you should try to get some sleep."

"At this point, I might as well stay up," he said. "What about you? You didn't take a very long nap."

"No, I couldn't sleep."

"I have a meditation app you could try," Scooter suggested.

"I use one of those occasionally when I'm having insomnia," Ned said.

Nancy peered at Ned over her reading glasses. "Only weak-willed people need help falling asleep. I simply tell myself that it's time to go to bed, and I'm instantly asleep. I've told you a million times, it's a matter of self-discipline."

"Not everyone is as regimented as you are, Nancy," I said. "And it's no surprise that I couldn't sleep. We witnessed someone plummeting to their . . ." I glanced at Scooter who was calmly sipping his coffee.

"It's okay," he said. "You can say it out

loud."

I pushed a brownie toward him. "Are you sure?"

"Fletcher fell to his death," Scooter said, ignoring the brownie. "It was an accident."

"Accident? No way. I can understand the captain trying to convince himself that it was an accident or suicide, but you were there. You and I both heard Fletcher arguing with someone. It was definitely murder."

"You didn't tell us you were there when he died," Ned said.

"You didn't mention that?" I asked Scooter. "What in the world have you guys been talking about?"

"We've been discussing the fundraiser at the Yacht Club," Scooter said. "Nancy is in charge of the event. She's been showing us her project plan."

Nancy held up her tablet, showing me the colorful spreadsheet that she had created.

"I told you she was organized," Ned said to me. "You should let her help with the bachelorette party."

"Oh, I don't think that's necessary. I'll figure something out."

"Do you even have a project plan?" Nancy asked.

I pulled a notebook out of my purse. "It's all in here."

Nancy scoffed. "There's a spaceship, unicorns, and gnomes on the cover. You can't plan a party properly in something like that."

"You can if you have these." I showed her my collection of glitter pens, washi tape, and cat stickers, which I had used to jazz up the pages.

Ned seemed interested in the pens, but Nancy told him they would create a mess. "Stick with normal ballpoint pens, dear."

"What are the two of you doing up so early, anyway?" I asked.

"I couldn't sleep," Nancy said.

"Which means no one could sleep," Ned muttered under his breath.

I grinned mischievously. "Didn't you just finish telling us how it was a matter of self-discipline."

She scowled. "The sheets are a very poor quality. They're scratchy and hadn't been ironed. No one could sleep in those sheets. Wait until I see the captain and tell him about it."

"I think the captain will be busy today. I could loan you one of my pens so you could fill out a comment card instead," I suggested.

"Speaking of the captain, you mentioned something about him saying that Fletcher's death was accidental," Scooter said. "When did you see him?"

"I just came from there. Anthony and Madison were worried sick about Sylvia. She had been in the captain's office ever since she found out about her husband's death. I told them that that I'd check on her."

"She was with the captain this whole time?" Ned cocked his head to one side. "If he was questioning her for that long, maybe there was foul play."

I leaned forward, glad that someone believed murder was a plausible explanation. "Fletcher's death happened when we were in international waters, right? What does that mean for jurisdiction? Who's responsible for investigating?"

"Those are all very good questions." Ned grabbed his wife's tablet. "Let's see what we can find out."

"We don't have cell phone coverage." Nancy plucked her tablet out of his grasp. "And we're not paying the exorbitant rates the cruise ship charges to connect to their WiFi."

"I suppose you're right," Ned conceded.

Nancy looked at Scooter. "You're in telecommunications. How come it costs so much to use WiFi at sea?"

He held up his hands. "Not really my department."

"Did anyone notice that the ship isn't moving?" I asked. "When did that happen? How come I didn't notice that before?"

"They would have stopped the boat to search for Fletcher once the crew was alerted," Ned said. "I wonder if we'll continue to the Bahamas or return to the States."

I looked at the clock on the wall. "It's already after five. Other passengers are going to wake up soon and wonder what's going on."

"I'm sure they'll make an announcement in due course," Nancy said.

The four of us sat quietly for a while. Nancy worked on her project plan, Scooter and Ned polished off the pie, and I ate all the brownies while I stared out the window. When I glanced back at the clock to see what time it was, I noticed framed pictures of islands in the Bahamas on the wall.

"I think I have an idea for Anabel's bachelorette party," I said.

"What's that, my little . . ." Scooter shrugged. "Sorry, I can't think of a new pet name."

"I have some ideas," Nancy said.

Ned, wisely sensing that perhaps Nancy's pet names for me wouldn't be very flattering, chimed in. "What's your idea, Mollie?"

"We could sail to Destiny Key and have the party there. The island isn't that far from Coconut Cove."

"That's a great idea," Scooter said. "We haven't taken *Marjorie Jane* out of the marina in a while. I'd love to get back out on the water."

"Sorry, it's girls only."

"You can't fit everyone on your boat," Nancy said. "If you had a project plan, you'd know that."

"Well, I was thinking Penny could take

her boat as well. Between the two of us, we can ferry everyone to the island."

"There's another flaw in your plan." Nancy looked almost gleeful. "You need to set up for the party in advance. How are you going to do that if you're sailing half the guests over on your boat?"

"There's an easy solution to that," Scooter said. "Why don't the guys go over earlier on Ben's boat and get everything ready. Then we'll make ourselves scarce once you ladies get there."

Ned's eyes lit up at the prospect. "Count me in."

"See, Nancy," I said. "Everything is figured out for the party and I didn't need a project plan."

A frail voice behind me said, "How can you think about a party at a time like this?"

Turning, I saw Madison clutching her box of tissues in her hands. Her eyes were bloodshot and swollen. Anthony was standing behind her, a worried look on his face.

I started to apologize, but Madison cut me off. "Someone murdered Fletcher and you want to celebrate?"

Scooter cleared his throat. "I thought it was an accident."

"We just came from the captain's office," Anthony said. "It was definitely murder."

CHAPTER 6
MY LITTLE SEXADECIMAL

I took a deep breath, then exhaled slowly. "Oh, my gosh. I was right. It *was* murder."

"That isn't the type of thing you want to be right about," Scooter said quietly to me. Then he turned to Madison and Anthony. "Grab a seat. I'll get you some coffee."

"Herbal tea for me, please," Madison said. "My nerves can't take the caffeine."

"What about you?" Scooter asked Anthony.

Anthony pulled a chair out for his girlfriend. "Strong and black, please."

While Scooter went to grab their drinks, I introduced everyone.

"Ah, yes, Herbert told me about the two of you," Anthony said to Ned and Nancy. "You own the marina in Coconut Cove."

"Are the two of you sailors?" Ned asked.

"Heavens, no," Madison said. "I'm scared to death of the water. Besides, I get terrible seasickness."

"Fortunately, cruise ships are so big and have stabilizing systems that seasickness isn't typically a problem," Ned said. "I guess that's one advantage of them over smaller boats."

"It's always cracked me up that you'd have to wear bathing suits in beauty pageants, but you've never actually been swimming," Anthony said.

"I don't think they have the girls in beauty pageants wear bikinis, because they expect them to swim," Nancy said dryly. "I think it's more for the judges. The male judges, that is."

"Oh, no, we didn't wear bikinis," Madison said. "Only one-pieces. It was all very modest."

Nancy shook her head. "I bet you wore high heels with your modest swimsuits too."

"Of course," Madison said. "Heels are great for posture. You carry yourself better when you wear them."

While Nancy muttered something about sensible shoes and her bunions, Scooter set steaming mugs in front of Anthony and Madison. "I brought some Danish pastries too. They'll start serving a full breakfast soon, but I thought you might be hungry now."

"Thank you. That was very sweet of you." Madison batted her long eyelashes at Scooter. I'm not sure it had the effect she was going for with all the mascara and eyeliner smeared under her eyes. "But I'll pass. We girls have to watch our figures."

I looked down at my belly, shrugged, then grabbed Madison's pastry.

Scooter sat next to me, then asked Anthony and Madison how they knew that Fletcher had been murdered.

"They recovered his body," Anthony said matter-of-factly.

"They could tell from the body that it was homicide?" I asked.

Anthony looked blankly at me for a moment, and Madison jumped in. "Yes, of course. It was obvious."

I furrowed my brow. "Did you see his body?"

Madison and Anthony exchanged glances. Madison started to say something, but Anthony put his hand on hers. "No, we didn't. We overheard one of the stewards say something to the captain about it."

Madison nodded. "Yes, that's what happened."

"The news was too much for my aunt to bear," Anthony said.

"Should she be by herself at a time like this?" Ned asked.

"She asked that we give her some space," Anthony said. "The ship's doctor gave her a sedative. She's resting comfortably in her cabin."

After wiping icing off my fingers with a napkin, I asked Anthony and Madison if they had any theories as to who killed Fletcher.

"You don't need to answer," Nancy said. "Mollie is just being nosy. She's been involved in so many murder investigations in Coconut Cove that she thinks she's some sort of private investigator."

"I *am* an investigator," I said.

"You investigate UFO sightings," Nancy said. "This sort of thing is a matter for the police, not someone who believes in the Force."

"I'm kind of impressed that you know

what the Force is," I said.

"Ned and I have watched *Star Wars* with the grandkids. Believe me, it wasn't my choice."

Scooter put his arm around me. "Actually, I think Mollie is an excellent investigator. I'm sure Chief Dalton would agree."

I snorted. "You think the chief would agree? The man can't stand it when I get involved in investigations. He only tolerates me, because Anabel and I are friends."

"That's not true," Scooter said. "He's a stoic sort of fellow. Keeps his cards close to his chest. But I can still tell what he's thinking."

"Really? Have you suddenly developed ESP? Ooh, did you learn how to do that from one of the apps on your phone?"

"Yep, there's an app for everything." Scooter smiled. "There's probably even one to keep track of my pet names for you."

"What kind of pet names do you call Madison?" I asked Anthony.

"Pet names?" Anthony scratched his head. "Nothing too original, I guess."

"Scooter can probably give you some pointers."

"We should focus on the murder, my little sexadecimal," Scooter said.

My eyes widened. "Sexadecimal? That sounds pretty racy."

"Racy? It refers to numbers that relate to sixteen or sixteenths. It has to do with computation of . . . hang on a minute, you almost got me off track." He tapped my notebook. "We should make notes while our memories are still fresh."

"Notes about what?" Madison asked before taking a sip of her tea.

"About the murder," Scooter said. "Possible suspects, motives, and alibis."

"What happened to my husband?" I asked. "This is the type of thing you tell me to stay out of."

"Not this time. This time, I'm going to help you." Scooter pushed the notebook toward me, then removed his glasses and polished them.

Anthony shifted in his chair. "Maybe it would be better if we left this to the professionals."

"But what professionals?" I asked. "We don't know how jurisdiction works for this kind of thing. We don't even know if we're heading back to the States or continuing on to the Bahamas."

As if on cue, a voice came on over the loudspeaker. "Ladies and gentlemen, this is your captain speaking. I'm sorry to inform you that due to circumstances beyond our control, we are going to have to return to Florida. At present, we do not have an estimated time of arrival. I apologize for the inconvenience. We will update you as soon as we know more."

"Circumstances beyond their control," I said. "That's a new spin on describing murder."

Scooter dug through my purse. After pulling out one of the glitter pens, he said, "Okay, who do we think did it?"

Madison sipped nonchalantly on her tea while Anthony toyed with a spoon. Ned and Nancy looked perplexed. And I was utterly dumbfounded. Who was this man sitting next to me? He could talk about death, blood, and other gory subjects with ease. Surprisingly, now he wanted to be involved in a murder investigation.

"Suspects?" Scooter prompted.

Before anyone could answer, one of the crew came up to our group and addressed Anthony. "Excuse me, Mr. Wright. Your aunt fainted on deck. The ship's doctor is with her, but there's a concern about her condition. The captain requests your presence."

As Anthony and Madison rushed off, I pointed at the notebook. "That's something you should write down. They told us that Sylvia had taken a sedative and was lying down in her cabin. That doesn't seem to have been the case, does it?"

"Good point," Scooter said. "What was she doing walking around on the deck?"

* * *

Nancy and Ned excused themselves, saying that the breakfast buffet was calling them.

"I know you're hungry," Scooter said to me. "But I think we should check the crime scene first."

"The crime scene," I spluttered.

"We should have checked it earlier," he said. "Hopefully, it hasn't been tampered with."

"Let me get this straight. You actually want to see the place where Fletcher was pushed to his death?"

He furrowed his brow. "Isn't that how you properly conduct an investigation?

You're always telling me about the clues you and Mrs. Moto find at the crime scene."

"Well, yes, that's true. It's surprising how many things get overlooked."

"Okay, then. Let's get going. No time to waste."

As we walked past the buffet, I looked longingly at the omelet bar. "They make them to order," I said. "Are you sure we don't have time for a quick bite to eat?"

Scooter smiled as he ushered me away from temptation. We walked out of the restaurant, through the lounge, past the casino, and down a maze of hallways. The only way to access the crime scene was via the stairs located at the rear of the ship on the port side. As Scooter opened the door to the stairwell, I noted that this part of the ship was rather quiet. Unless your cabin was in this section of the ship, you weren't likely to come back this way.

"Chop, chop," Scooter said while I

followed him up the stairs. "Time is of the essence. Now, what cover story should we use if someone tries to keep us from examining the scene?"

"Earlier, I flashed my FAROUT badge and threatened to call my superior officer."

"Hmm, your superior officer. Is that me?"

"You're a smart guy, what do you think?"

He glanced over his shoulder and grinned. "Don't worry, I know my place in the pecking order. You're the boss."

"Actually, I was going to say that Mrs. Moto is the boss. She's our superior officer and we're just her humble human servants."

He chuckled, then asked if the same ruse would work again.

"I'm not sure. The guys I used it on weren't the brightest."

"Maybe I should get one of those badges too."

"Are you saying you believe in aliens now?"

He stopped on the landing and gazed at me with those dark brown puppy-dog eyes of his, which always make me feel gooey inside. "I want to take more of an interest in what's important to you. You enjoy investigating things—both real and . . ."

"You were going to say make believe, weren't you?" I teased.

"I'm trying to keep an open mind. We're partners, right? I was the one who was passionate about sailing. Heck, I even bought you a sailboat as an anniversary present. You've been fantastic at supporting my dream. You help with fixing up the boat, you've learned how to sail, you—"

I stopped him mid-sentence with a kiss. When we came up for air, I said, "I really like sailing now."

"What about *Marjorie Jane*?"

"I've become rather fond of M.J. She's

as much a part of our family as Mrs. Moto is."

"That's what I'm saying. You embraced my dream. I need to be more open to what's important to you." He tugged on my hand. "Come on, let's go. I got distracted with all this sailing talk. The crime scene awaits."

As we exited the stairwell, I paused and peered over the side of the boat. "It's a long way down. Fletcher must have been terrified."

"Try not to think about that," Scooter said.

The frothy, churning water that the cruise ship was plowing through on her way back to Florida was mesmerizing. Despite that I managed to tear myself away. Then I stopped in my tracks. Yellow barricades had been erected in front of the area of the deck where Fletcher and his assailant would have been standing. Pointing at the two muscular men standing guard, I said, "I had to talk my way past those guys to get into the captain's office."

"Those are the ones you showed your FAROUT badge to?

"Yeah, but I'm not sure the same trick is going to work twice."

"Leave it to me," Scooter said. "I have an idea."

Scooter strode up to the two men. After exchanging a few words, he reached into his pocket and pulled out his wallet. Crew cut guy saw me and frowned. Scooter offered something to him—I couldn't see what as his back was turned to me—but crew cut guy refused. Goatee guy nudged his partner and said something which must have made him change his mind. They both held out their hands and took what had been offered.

The two men nodded as they walked past me, then Scooter waved me over. "Okay, we're good to go."

"What did you do?" I asked. "Show

them your business card?"

"Something like that," he said.

"You bribed them, didn't you?"

"A bribe? Me?" Scooter feigned shock. "I prefer to think of it as a contribution."

"Contribution to what?"

"They mentioned something about needing to get a statue repaired. Now, let's hustle before anyone comes by."

As he moved one of the plastic barricades aside, I told him to hang on for a minute. I pulled my phone out of my purse and took photos of the area. When murders happened in Coconut Cove, I had been able to revisit the crime scene. Granted sneakily at times, but it had been feasible. Though with this particular situation, once we disembarked the cruise ship, I doubted even I would be able to sweet talk my way back on board.

When I was done, I nodded at Scooter. "Okay, let's check things out more closely."

The crime scene was located on the uppermost deck that was open to the public. While some of the other decks below wrapped around the entire ship, this deck only extended across the stern of the ship. And, unlike some of the other decks which had open railings, this one was enclosed.

Being careful not to touch anything, Scooter leaned over and pointed at the deck below us. "That's where we were standing."

"Fletcher would have been somewhere around here," I said, positioning myself with my back facing the water. "We could only see the upper portion of his body from where we were standing."

Scooter planted himself in front of me. "His attacker could have been standing here."

"He or she might have been standing further back," I said. "Remember, we couldn't hear that person clearly."

"She," Scooter mused. "Do you think it was a woman?"

"I don't see why not. In my experience, women are as likely to kill as men."

"But it would have taken a certain amount of strength to push Fletcher backward over the railing." Scooter placed his hands on my shoulders, trying to figure out how the killer might have done it. "Fletcher was quite a bit shorter than me, maybe five foot five, five foot six?"

I nodded. "He was short, but squat."

"Yeah, he was certainly packing the pounds," Scooter agreed. "It would have taken some considerable force to lift him off his feet and push him over the railing."

I paced back and forth for a few moments, then said, "Aha!"

"Did you find a clue?"

"Not exactly. There doesn't seem to be anything out of the ordinary around here."

"Then what was the 'aha' for?"

"It falls more into the 'means' category." I pointed at a gate situated in the middle of the enclosed railing. "I heard a grating, metallic noise that night. What if the killer opened this gate and then pushed Fletcher overboard? That would have made it easier."

Scooter gave me an appreciative look. "Smart thinking."

"But wouldn't Fletcher have sounded the alarm when the killer opened the gate," I mused. "That should have seemed strange to him, even considering how inebriated he was."

"He was pretty drunk when I left the casino," Scooter said. "I can only imagine how much more he drank between then and when he was killed."

"Herbert did intervene at one point and whispered to the waitress to bring Fletcher a non-alcoholic drink. But Fletcher could tell right away that something was off about it. I'm sure that he made sure all the rest of his drinks that evening were full of booze."

Scooter pursed his lips. "Or his killer made sure they were full of booze."

"Do you have a napkin or something on you?" I asked.

"Will this work?" Scooter handed me a cloth that he used to clean his glasses with.

"Perfect." Using the cloth, I tried to open the latch on the gate. "This isn't easy to budge."

"Here, let me try," Scooter said. He had an easier time of it, but not by much. After the bolt was retracted, he swung the gate inward. "There's that noise we heard."

I stepped forward and peered through the opening at the water below. "Why didn't we notice that the gate had been opened? Wouldn't we have seen it from where we were standing?"

"We only looked up at this deck for a short period. Then you pulled me back so that Fletcher and his killer wouldn't see us," Scooter reminded me.

"Yeah, first rule of eavesdropping. Make sure you aren't seen."

"Come back from there," Scooter said. "I don't want anyone else to go overboard, especially you."

"That makes two of us," I said as Scooter shut the gate.

"Hey, buddy, time for you and the missus to go." Crew cut guy waved us toward the stairwell. "The captain is headed this way. Hurry."

As we dashed toward the stairs, I saw a flash of hot pink out of the corner of my eye. Bending down, I gasped when I saw what was wedged behind a lifebuoy.

"Come on, lady," crew cut guy said.

"Just a sec . . . got it." I darted down the stairs, then followed Scooter through the maze of halls. When we reached the lounge, I showed him what I had found.

"Is that what I think it is?" he asked.

"Uh-huh. A cigarette butt. A hot pink cigarette butt."

Scooter's eyes widened, then we both said at the same time, "Madison."

* * *

"That was a close call," Scooter said as we stood in line at the omelet station. "The captain almost caught us."

"Usually, it's Chief Dalton I'm trying to avoid at crime scenes," I said, eyeing all the potential omelet fillings. Deciding to go for a healthier option, I opted for mushrooms and bell peppers. "Actually, can you add some cheese too?" I asked the chef. "Maybe some of that bacon and ham as well?"

Scooter requested his usual—a Denver omelet. While we waited for our eggs to be prepared, I poured some orange juice and Scooter grabbed some toast.

As we looked for an empty table, I

heard people sharing theories about why we were returning to Florida.

"I heard someone had a heart attack," one woman said.

"No, it was an aneurysm," her companion said. "The ship's doctor had to do emergency brain surgery, but there were complications."

At another table, people were convinced that a celebrity was on board. When the diva's cell phone died and she wasn't able to update her social media sites, she demanded that the captain turn the boat around.

A couple walking in front of us were certain that it was a government conspiracy. What exactly the government was hiding wasn't clear, but it had something to do with coconuts and dolphins.

"This looks good," Scooter said, setting his tray on a table in the far corner of the room. It was positioned behind a column, offering a bit of privacy.

After devouring our food—investigating murder makes you hungry —Scooter was eager to get down to business. On our way to the restaurant, we decided that although we had found a cigarette butt at the crime scene that could have belonged to Madison, we needed to keep an open mind. I had been fooled by red herrings before.

"What should we start with? Motive, means, or opportunity?" Scooter asked.

"Motive," I said. "Figuring out why someone would take a life is always fascinating."

"I can see how the whole psychology of it would be interesting. Usually people commit murder, because they're jealous, greedy, or want revenge, right?"

"Those are some of the main motives, but don't forget that murder is often a way to hide something, either another crime or a secret." I looked up at the ceiling, trying to recollect the conversation I had overheard between Fletcher and Madison. Even though it had only happened the previous night, it seemed like ages ago.

"Earth to Mollie," Scooter said. "What are you thinking about?"

"I don't think I had a chance to tell you about the conversation I overheard between Madison and Fletcher. Given the cigarette butt, it's taken on more significance."

"Overheard or eavesdropped on?"

"Does it really matter?" I asked, cocking my head to one side.

"I guess you're right," Scooter conceded. "When people don't think anyone can hear them, they say things that are meant to be a secret."

"Exactly. And Madison has a secret. Fletcher knew what it was and threatened to reveal it to Anthony if Madison didn't do what he wanted."

"What did he want her to do?" Scooter asked.

"For Herbert to be taken care of."

Scooter frowned. "That sounds ominous."

"Fletcher is the one who was killed, not Herbert," I pointed out.

"Okay, so Madison could have killed Fletcher to keep her secret safe." Scooter pointed at my purse. "Shouldn't we be writing this down?"

I handed him the notebook and a pen. After he jotted down a few notes, I said, "The next person on the list is Herbert."

"Herbert? But I thought you just said that Madison was supposed to take care of him."

"Ah . . . but that's what makes investigations so tricky. Sometimes, you're not sure who are the good guys and who are the bad guys. Herbert and Fletcher definitely had some issues. Maybe Herbert snapped and wanted to get rid of Fletcher."

"Is this about the alleged embezzlement? That was years ago. If it had really happened, and if Herbert was really upset about it, he would have offed Fletcher a long time ago."

I held my hands up. "All I know is the exchange I heard between the two of them after you left the casino."

"Go on." Scooter had his pen poised over the paper.

"Well, Fletcher told Herbert that he was costing the company millions. Fletcher sounded like he was going to take some sort of action if they didn't close this deal with their potential investors."

Scooter considered this. "After that letter I saw last night, I certainly wasn't planning on investing. And I heard some of the other guys say that they were iffy about the whole thing too. I think they only came along for a free cruise."

"So Herbert knew that the deal was likely to fall through. Maybe he decided to get rid of Fletcher before Fletcher got rid of him."

"This pen is out of ink," Scooter said. After I handed him another one, he scrawled down what I had said. "We've got Madison and Herbert on our list. Who else had a motive?"

"What about Anthony?" I suggested. "Sylvia was hoping that he would take over the company when Fletcher retired. Anthony might have decided to push Fletcher's retirement date up to a more permanent basis."

"I'll mark that motive down as greed. We'll have to look into how the partnership agreement was structured. Who would Fletcher's shares in the company have gone to in the case of his death?" He tapped the pen on the table. "Okay, who else would have wanted Fletcher dead? I'm drawing a blank."

"There's one obvious person you've missed."

"Who's that?"

"Sylvia."

Scooter leaned back in his chair. "But

she's his wife."

"Yeah, so?"

"How could anyone kill their husband?"

I laughed. "It happens all the time."

"You're not still upset about the fight we had, are you?" Scooter asked warily.

"Don't worry," I said. "I'm not going to kill you. But Mrs. Moto, on the other hand, might want to seek revenge."

"Revenge for what?"

"Remember how you tried to give her a bath right before we left for the cruise?"

Scooter examined his forearm. "The scratches seem to have healed up. I don't get it though. She loves swimming. Why was she upset about a bath? She really needed one after knocking over that can of engine oil."

"She loves swimming when it's *her* idea."

"Great, now I have to worry about my cat wanting to 'take care of me' in my sleep," Scooter said, making air quotes. "But getting back to Sylvia, why would she have wanted to kill her husband?"

"You saw the two of them together. They were constantly bickering. The fact that he was always drinking, gambling, and possibly even chasing after other women, wouldn't have helped either."

"Alright, I'll write her name down."

As he started to close the notebook, I said, "Hang on, we're not done yet."

"There's someone else?"

"Dominic, maybe?"

After I explained how Dominic gave Fletcher money at the casino the previous night in exchange for his watch and car keys, Scooter shrugged. "I don't buy it. Dominic would have wanted him alive. You can't collect from a dead man."

"Yeah, you're probably right. Okay, that leaves us with four suspects that we know of—Madison, Anthony, Herbert, and Sylvia."

"Aren't we doing this backward?" Scooter scrubbed his jaw. "They may all have had reason to want Fletcher dead, but who had an alibi?"

"That's our next step, finding out where everyone was when Fletcher was killed."

The loudspeaker crackled. "Would Dominic Kalchik please come to guest services? You have an urgent message. I repeat, would Dominic Kalchik please come to guest services?"

"Well, that's interesting," I said. "I wonder what's so urgent that requires Dominic's attention?"

Scooter flipped the notebook open, wrote Dominic's name down and put a large question mark next to it. Then he rose to his feet. "Race you to guest services?"

* * *

Trying to keep up with Scooter was

impossible. His nickname was apt. It had been a long time since his college basketball days, but the man certainly could still 'scoot.' By the time I reached the lobby, I was gasping.

I found Scooter crouched behind a potted palm tree. If he was trying to hide, it wasn't very effective. When I put my hand on his shoulder, he startled, nearly knocking the plant over.

"Where's Dominic?" I asked, bending down next to him.

Scooter put his finger to his lips to shush me, then pointed toward a seating area opposite the guest services desk. Dominic was sitting next to a frail-looking elderly couple, his bulky frame taking up the majority of the couch. He was staring at a piece of paper with a perplexed look on his face. After a moment, he said something to the couple. The man put on a pair of reading glasses and examined the paper. After a brief exchange, Dominic looked satisfied. Then he proceeded to tear the paper up before shoving the pieces into his mouth.

"Is he eating it?" Scooter whispered.

"I think he's seen too many spy movies," I said.

After Dominic finished chewing and swallowing, he nodded at the elderly couple. When he got on the elevator, we rose to our feet.

"Excuse me, sir," I said to the elderly man. "Can I ask what you and that man were talking about?"

"The big fellow? He wanted to know what 'extortion' meant." Scooter and I exchanged glances. "He didn't seem like the sharpest knife in the knife drawer."

"What did the rest of the note say?" I asked.

The elderly man looked suspicious. "Why do you want to know?"

"Like you said, he isn't the sharpest knife. We're kind of keeping an eye out for him. Want to make sure he doesn't get into any trouble, if you know what I mean."

The man relaxed. "Oh, I see. My wife had a cousin like that."

"So, what did the note say?" Scooter prompted.

The man scratched his head. "Something about financial records. Sorry, that's all I remember."

We thanked the couple for their time, then Scooter told me to get the notebook out.

"It's not in here," I said, digging through my purse.

"I gave it back to you at the restaurant," Scooter said.

"No, you didn't. If you did, it would be in here."

"That means it's on the—" Scooter stopped mid-sentence, then sprinted down the hall.

I almost collapsed when I reached the restaurant. I nearly made a vow to start exercising and swear off sugar, but then

I saw a tray of freshly baked chocolate chip cookies. Grabbing a couple, I slowly walked toward the rear of the room. Scooter was leaning against the table we had been sitting at, looking through the notebook.

"Another close call." I handed him one of the cookies. He munched on it while I jotted down what we had learned about Dominic.

"I see Madison and Anthony sitting by the window," Scooter said. "Want to go check their alibis out?"

"Okay." I made a show of closing the notebook and placing it in my purse, then wiped some crumbs off Scooter's shirt. "Do you want to take the lead in questioning them?"

"Sure." He grinned. "This is kind of fun."

"Well, except for the fact that someone died."

Scooter's smile faded. He quickly pressed his fingers to the side of his nose and tugged his earlobes, then strode toward Anthony and Madison's table.

"How's Sylvia doing?" I asked.

Scooter nudged me, reminding me that he was on point. "Is she feeling better?" he asked.

"She's resting," Anthony said, motioning for the two of us to join them. "The doctor says she'll be fine."

"That's good," Scooter said. "And how are the two of you doing?"

Anthony squeezed Madison's hand. "We're coping. It's been tough, but—"

"Tough, I can imagine," Scooter said, cutting Anthony off. Clearly that had been enough chit-chat and now Scooter wanted to get down to business. "Any news on who killed Fletcher? Have they arrested anyone? Do you know who the murderer is? Why was he killed?"

I kicked my husband under the table. The man didn't seem to realize that he shouldn't bombard them with questions, subtlety goes a long way.

Scooter pulled his leg away, then apologized. "Sorry, lack of sleep."

"Understandable," Anthony said graciously.

That was all he said. No answers to any of Scooter's questions. Just silence.

The silence was broken when a cheery voice greeted us. "Good morning, folks. We're handing out complimentary jars of Bahamian mango jelly." The woman set down two small jars on the table. "They're handcrafted on Cat Island. It's our way of saying thank you for being so understanding about the change in itinerary."

As she bustled off, I heard people complaining at nearby tables.

"Do they really think a jar of jelly is going to make up for canceling our cruise?" one woman asked.

A man examined one of the jars. "Do you think this is what caused that man to have a heart attack?"

"It wasn't a heart attack," his wife said. "The ship's doctor removed his appendix."

A group of women who looked like they played bingo professionally chatted about one of the latest government conspiracies.

"You shouldn't eat mangoes. They add chemicals to them to make you crave chocolate," one woman said.

"Why would the government care if you ate chocolate?" another woman asked.

A third woman tapped the side of her nose. "Exactly," she said in a conspiratorial tone. The other ladies nodded their heads sagely, probably not sure what they were agreeing with, but also not wanting to seem like they were the only ones who didn't get it.

Anthony grabbed one of the jars. "Maybe I'll try some on my toast." He tried to open it, but was unsuccessful. "They must have used superglue to seal it."

Madison picked the jar up and twisted the lid off effortlessly. She smiled at her boyfriend. "Easy-peasy."

"That's only because I loosened it for you," Anthony joked as he smeared some jelly on his toast.

Scooter leaned forward. "So, where were you two when Fletcher was killed?"

Anthony choked on a piece of his toast. When Madison slapped him on his back, he scowled at her. He took a sip of water, then said, "I was in the VIP Room."

"People were pretty intent on their poker games," I said. "Does anyone remember seeing you?"

"Sure, I have someone who can back up my alibi." Anthony leaned back in his chair. "That's what you're getting at, isn't it? Whether we have alibis or not?"

"What about you, Madison?" Scooter asked, taking back the reins of the conversation.

While she put the cap back on the jelly jar, she said, "I was at the magic show with Sylvia."

Scooter looked deflated at the fact that three suspects had alibis. He folded his hands on the table, and said in a quiet voice, "That means Herbert—"

"Don't mention that man's name." Madison stabbed her eggs with her fork.

"Why not?" Scooter asked.

Anthony leaned forward. "Well, isn't it obvious? Herbert killed my uncle."

CHAPTER 7
BREAKFAST SALAD

The rest of the day aboard the cruise ship was excruciating. After Anthony announced that Herbert had murdered his uncle, both he and Madison clammed up saying they shouldn't say any more about the subject until they spoke with the appropriate officials. Madison was confident that Herbert was going to be taken into custody the minute the ship docked in the States. In her opinion, the authorities would lock Herbert up, throw away the key, and no one would ever hear from him again.

When some of the potential investors stopped by the table to inquire about the impact of Fletcher's death on the business, Anthony told them he intended to take over leadership of the company effective immediately. When one of the investors said that they had assumed that Herbert would be in charge going forward, Anthony made some snide comments about Herbert's financial mismanagement. He told them that Herbert planned to retire in any event. Then he made assurances that their investment would be safe in his hands, even promising to triple their money.

Dominic and Herbert were nowhere to be found. If they were inside their cabins, they never answered when we knocked. Scooter and I complied with the do-not-disturb sign hanging on Sylvia's door. With nothing else to do, we whiled away the hours playing backgammon in the lounge. I even suggested having a nap, but Scooter was adamant that we needed to stay sharp in case there were any breaks in the case.

Sylvia stayed in her cabin until we arrived at the cruise ship terminal. We watched as the captain ushered her off the ship before the rest of the passengers were allowed to disembark. The large sunglasses and broad-brimmed hat she wore obscured her eyes, and her up-turned coat collar shielded the rest of her face from view. Anthony and Madison trailed behind, stony-faced.

We didn't see any police come on board to take Herbert away. Despite persistent questioning of the crew, we hadn't been able to determine if he had in fact been arrested.

After a prolonged wait, we finally cleared immigration and customs, and made the long drive back to Coconut

Cove. Mrs. Moto was overjoyed to see us, seemingly to have forgotten that Scooter had given her an unwelcome bath the day prior.

When I woke the next morning, I found a cup of coffee on the nightstand along with a note telling me that Scooter had gone to help some friends remove the mast from their boat. I checked my phone while I sipped my coffee and saw a text from Anabel asking if I wanted to meet her for breakfast at the Sailor's Corner Cafe.

That was a no-brainer. The only food we had on board was a shriveled up lemon, granola, and a lone can of cream of celery soup. The can of soup had been on board when we first got the boat. We were never going to cook anything with it, and should have thrown it out ages ago. Despite that, for some reason, I had started to consider it as a good-luck charm and couldn't bear to get rid of it.

When I walked into the cafe, the owner called out to the cook, "Mollie's here. Better save that last cinnamon roll for her."

"Thanks, Jim. I can always count on you to look out for me," I said.

Jim smoothed down his trademark Hawaiian shirt. "We take care of our regulars. Besides, you're always telling tourists about this place and sending them our way."

"That's probably not the smartest move on my part," I said. "Sometimes, the line stretches down the block and it takes me forever to get a table."

"Well, I'm not complaining. Business has been great. I had to hire another cook. And look at all those bare spots on the walls. I barely get a piece of artwork hung up before someone buys it."

As Jim smiled, his rosy cheeks and white beard reminded me that the holidays weren't too far away. "Are you playing Santa Claus in the Christmas parade again this year?"

"Absolutely." He let out a cheery ho-ho-ho, then said, "Hey, a friend of yours was in here last week. Mentioned that she and her husband are moving to Coconut Cove. She's one of the reasons I have gaps on the walls. When she saw Anabel's painting, she snapped it up."

"Oh, you must mean Sylvia. She's not really a friend, more of a . . ." My voice trailed off as I tried to figure out what Sylvia was to me. What was the difference between a friend and someone you saw occasionally? I might not have liked Fletcher, but Sylvia needed friends at a time like this, not acquaintances.

"I'm not sure if my friend will still be moving here," I said. "She just lost her husband."

"Oh, no, that's a shame," Jim said. "She seemed like a nice lady. What was it? A heart attack?"

I grimaced. "No, he was actually murdered."

"You're kidding." Jim put a hand to his chest. "We've had another murder in Coconut Cove? Ever since you and Scooter moved here, the homicide rate has skyrocketed."

"You can rest easy," I said. "Her husband died on a cruise ship, not here in town."

"Phew. That's a relief." Jim pointed over at my favorite booth by the window. "Better grab it while it's open."

Anabel came in a few minutes later. "I ran into Nancy on my way here," she said as she sat down. "She told me that someone had died on the cruise ship. Though I think she was more miffed that I had heard about it on the news this morning."

I laughed. "She's probably telling everyone she meets. I was surprised that Jim didn't know about it already."

After we placed our order—in addition to the cinnamon roll, I asked the waitress to bring me some pancakes— Anabel leaned forward. "On the news, they only mentioned that a man had fallen overboard. But Nancy said that you thought it might be murder. Why does it not surprise me that you're involved?"

I raised an eyebrow. "Involved in killing a man?"

She chuckled. "No, you know what I meant."

"Unfortunately, I was involved in a very up close and personal way. Scooter and I saw the whole thing. We were on the deck below when Fletcher plummeted into the water."

"Oh, my gosh, how awful. Usually, you just find dead bodies, but this is the first time you've seen someone die, right?"

"Actually, it's not." I felt my appetite dissipate as I recalled seeing someone die from poisoning by a fishing pier.

Then the more recent memories of Fletcher's screams as he plunged to his death filled my mind.

"Hey, let's talk about something else," Anabel suggested.

I gave her a faint smile. "Sure. I had an idea for your bachelorette party."

"What is it?"

"I thought we could sail to Destiny Key and have a picnic there."

"That sounds fantastic."

I cocked my head to one side. "Are you sure? Especially after what happened there—"

Anabel held up her hand. "I'm a firm believer in facing your demons head on. In fact, Tiny and I took the ferry to Destiny Key last weekend. We had a long walk on the beach with the dogs. I brought some rocks that I had painted and left them scattered about for other people to find too."

"Those will be collector items," I said. "You're a world-renowned artist now."

"Hardly. Selling a painting to someone in Mongolia doesn't make you world-renown. Now tell me what you had in mind for the party."

While we chatted about plans for Anabel's bachelorette party, my appetite returned and I cleared my plate in record time. As I crumpled up my napkin, I saw Sylvia walking into the cafe. She pushed her sunglasses onto the top of her head and waved at me.

When I introduced Anabel to her, Sylvia squealed. "Can I shake your hand?"

"Sure, why not." Anabel winced as Sylvia took hold of her hand. When Sylvia finally ended the handshake, Anabel rubbed her fingers. "That's a powerful grip you have there."

"It's a special exercise regime designed to strengthen your hands and forearms. I play badminton. You know, it would probably be great for you too, holding brushes in your hands all day."

Sylvia beamed at Anabel and squealed again. "Pinch me. I can't believe I'm meeting a famous artist in person."

Anabel looked like she wanted to crawl under the table. "Um, I'm not really famous."

"Nonsense," Sylvia said, scooting into the booth next to Anabel. "When I enter 'Anabel Dalton unicorn fairy elf Florida painter' on my computer, your name comes right up."

"Imagine that," Anabel said.

"I'm surprised to see you here," I said to Sylvia. "I would have thought you would have gone back home to Cleveland."

"This is my home now. I have an appointment with a real estate agent lined up." Sylvia beamed at Anabel. "I told him that I want a place with a large fireplace so that I can display your painting above it."

The waitress handed Sylvia a menu. After a quick glance at it, she ordered a cup of black coffee and a side salad.

"Salad for breakfast?" I asked.

"Fletcher never liked salad," Sylvia said. "Now that he's gone, I'm going to eat salad morning, noon, and night."

Personally, I thought that salad seemed like an odd way to grieve someone. But to each his own.

"So, what are you gals up to?" Sylvia asked.

"We're talking about Anabel's bachelorette party," I said.

Sylvia clapped her hands together. "A wedding, how exciting. Just the thing I need to take my mind off what's happened. Now, tell me all about it. What's your theme?"

Anabel furrowed her brow. "Theme?"

"You know, the overall look and feel that you want your big day to have. Art Deco is really popular. A black and gold color scheme, glass and mirror details, geometric shapes—it's all very luxurious."

Anabel looked at the peasant blouse and patchwork vest she was wearing. "I'm not sure Art Deco luxury is really my thing."

"Don't worry, there are lots of other themes to choose from. When's the wedding taking place?"

"We haven't set a date yet," Anabel said. "Maybe early next year."

"Did you say 'maybe'?" Sylvia pursed her lips. "You have to be decisive when it comes to planning a wedding."

Anabel's brow creased. "I do?"

"Absolutely. There are lots of decisions to make, not to mention all the logistics that need to be dealt with. It's a good thing I ran into you. I'm a professional. I can help you organize everything."

"I'm sorry, you're a professional what?" Anabel asked.

"Didn't I say? I'm a wedding planner."

"I thought you worked at a gift shop?" I asked.

"Not anymore," Sylvia said. "Now I help brides make their dreams come true."

While Sylvia picked at her salad, she peppered Anabel with a million questions. By the end of the discussion, Anabel wasn't any closer to figuring out what her wedding theme was.

"Okay, girls, I've gotta run." Sylvia pushed her half-eaten salad to the side. "Now, think about what I said, Anabel. We'll catch up tomorrow, same time, same place, and go through options for your wedding dress."

After she darted out of the cafe, Anabel looked at me with a dazed expression on her face. "What just happened?"

"I think you just hired yourself a wedding planner."

* * *

As we walked out of the cafe, I told

Anabel that she shouldn't hire a wedding planner if she didn't want one.

"But Sylvia seems so passionate about it." Anabel's frowned. "And when she told me how planning my wedding would help keep her mind off her husband's death, my heart broke for her. I feel like I should let the poor woman help."

"You're too nice for your own good," I said. "Considering you're the wife . . . I mean ex-wife . . . wait, no, I mean wife-to-be-again of a chief of police—"

Anabel smiled. "It's confusing, isn't it?"

"It's sweet, is what it is. After some time apart, the two of you realized that you really do belong together. Anyway, what I was trying to say before I got tongue-tied is that because you know about police work, you'll be a good sounding board for Sylvia. She's going to have to deal with a lot while they look into Fletcher's death.

"It's hard for the families," Anabel

agreed. "There's the investigation, then the trial and sentencing. On top of all that, people treat you differently. And media coverage, don't even get me started on that circus."

"I'm still not sure how the investigation is going to work. Fletcher was killed when the cruise ship was in international waters. But Sylvia's nephew, Anthony, and his girlfriend were convinced that the murder would be subject to American law."

"Tiny might know. He has some buddies in the Coast Guard."

While she sent her soon-to-be-again husband a text, I checked my own phone. "Listen, I've gotta go. Scooter is at Melvin's. If I don't hurry, he might max out our credit card again buying stuff for the boat."

Anabel chuckled. "Okay, see you here tomorrow for round two of wedding planning with Sylvia."

When I arrived at the marine supply

store, Melvin jerked a finger to his right. "Scooter is back there checking out grills." Then he pointed toward an inflatable dinghy on display by the front windows. "And Mrs. Moto is having a nap in there."

I found the calico nestled underneath an oar. She protested when I scooped her out, but once I pulled a cat treat out of my purse, she seemed happy enough to see me.

When I carried her to the checkout counter, Mrs. Moto squirmed out of my arms. She yowled, then walked across the price scanner toward Melvin. When the machine beeped, Melvin laughed and scratched the cat's head.

"It sounds like you and Scooter are almost ready to head to the Bahamas," he said. "If you make it to Mangrove Cay, you'll need to say hi to my family."

"Shush, don't jinx it," I replied. "It seems like every time we cross one thing off our project list, another two appear."

"You know that you'll never get everything done on that list, right? That's what keeps sailors in port. Perfectionists never leave. Perfect is the enemy of done. All you need to do is make sure *Marjorie Jane* is safe and seaworthy. Get out there and enjoy life."

"You're right." I crossed my heart. "I promise we'll be gone after Christmas."

"I hear you almost made it to the Bahamas this weekend," Melvin said. "Terrible thing, that man going overboard."

"Let me guess, Nancy stopped by and told you."

Melvin moved a display of floating key chains out of Mrs. Moto's reach. "No, I actually heard about it last night. One of my nieces works on the cruise ship. She's staying with me for a while. I have some pictures on my fridge from that party at the yacht club. You and Scooter were in one of them, and she recognized the two of you."

"Wow, small world. What does she look like? Do you have a picture of her?"

"I can do better than that," Melvin said. "You can see her in real life."

As a young woman with intricately braided hair walked through the door, I said, "I know her. She's the poor waitress who had to deal with Fletcher. He treated her terribly."

"Velma, come say hi to Mollie." Melvin waved his niece over, then turned to me. "She was named after my wife, you know. God rest her soul."

Velma greeted me shyly. As she stroked Mrs. Moto, Melvin said, "Mollie told me someone treated you badly on the cruise? What happened?"

"I was telling your uncle about Fletcher," I said.

"That's the poor man who died," Velma said quietly. "He was a friend of yours, wasn't he, ma'am?"

"He was a business acquaintance. We

were on the cruise for my husband's work," I said, wanting to distance myself from Fletcher's rude and drunken behavior. "Do you know if they arrested Herbert when the ship docked?"

"Herbert? Sorry, I don't typically remember passenger names."

"Here, I'll show you a picture of him." I scrolled through my photos until I reached a group one which I had taken at dinner. Anthony's arm was slung around Madison's shoulders. He had a gloomy expression on his face. She was a natural in front of the camera, angling her body so that her curves were displayed to maximum advantage. Fletcher was standing next to Madison. His smile reminded me of a used car salesman, ready to pounce and sell you an over-priced lemon. Sylvia was gripping her husband's arm tightly. Herbert was at the far edge of the group. He had a faraway look in his eyes, as though he was contemplating something serious.

As I pointed Herbert out to Velma, I wondered what he had been thinking about when the photo was taken. Had he been plotting Fletcher's murder?

"Take your time." I enlarged the photo so that she could see Herbert's face more closely. "Do you know if he was taken into custody?"

"I'm sorry, I told my manager everything I know." Velma handed me back my phone, then turned to her uncle. "You're out of eggs. I'm going to the grocery store. Is there anything else you need?"

"Hang on a minute, child. You haven't answered Mollie's question yet."

"But—"

"No 'buts,'" Melvin said. "Mollie has been involved in many investigations here in Coconut Cove. If she's asking you questions, it's for a good reason. If anyone can get to the bottom of what happened, she can."

As Velma's eyes widened, I reassured her. "It's okay. All you'll be doing is repeating what you told your manager."

She nodded, then asked to see the photo again. Pointing at Herbert, she said, "This man came into the VIP Room with the man who died."

"This man, right?" I indicated Fletcher.

"Yes ma'am. The two of them exchanged words. It got a little heated, and Herbert suggested that they finish their discussion somewhere else. I saw the two of them leave together."

"Do you happen to remember what time that was at?" I asked.

She shook her head. "No, but it was after you were in the casino with them."

"And did you see either of them after that?"

"No, ma'am. Not during the rest of my shift."

I rubbed my temples. While Velma hadn't seen Herbert kill Fletcher, her eyewitness account of them fighting and then leaving together was pretty compelling.

"This man was in the VIP Room all night," Velma said. "I told my supervisor that."

Glancing at the phone, I saw that she was pointing at Anthony. "Makes sense," I said. "He would have been keeping an eye on the guys playing poker and using every opportunity to try to get them to invest in his business deal. Thanks, Velma. You've been a really big help."

Melvin put his hand on his niece's shoulder. "See, that wasn't so hard. Now, about that grocery list."

While the two of them discussed how many eggs they needed, I went in search of Scooter. I found him trying to decide between two different grills.

"This one costs more, but it's larger," he said. "I anticipate catching a lot of fish when we get to the Bahamas, so maybe that's the way to go."

"Speaking of the Bahamas, guess who I just met? One of Melvin's nieces."

"He has a lot of nephews and nieces," Scooter said.

"Yeah, but this one was the waitress on board the cruise ship. You know the one that Fletcher was such a jerk to."

"We should go talk to her." Scooter's eyes lit up. "I bet she has the inside scoop on Fletcher's murder. Maybe she knows if Herbert was arrested."

"Sorry, Velma and I already chatted."

Scooter's shoulders slumped. "You mean you questioned her without me?"

"Sometimes, you have to take advantage of opportunities as they present themselves. She was there, her uncle encouraged her to talk to me, and she told me what she knows."

"Which is?"

"It sounds more and more likely that Herbert killed Fletcher."

Scooter chewed on his lip. "Does that mean our investigation is over?"

"Nope, not by a long shot. There are still a lot of loose threads to pick up. So, pick a grill and let's get going."

CHAPTER 8
SARDINE AND JELLYBEAN
RASHES

After setting Mrs. Moto on the backseat,
I popped the trunk of the car so Scooter
could put our new grill inside. He
caressed the box, his eyes gleaming
with excitement about his new gadget.

"Can we consider that your Christmas
present?" I asked.

Scooter gave the grill one last look,
then snapped the trunk shut. "Wouldn't
it be more like *our* Christmas present?
You'll enjoy the meals we make on this

as much as I will."

"I was hoping for something a little less metallic."

He ran his fingers down the necklace I was wearing, stopping when he reached the lighthouse pendant. "I seem to remember you liking it when I got you this. It's made of gold. That's a metal."

I smiled at him. "I should clarify. Metal is good when it's decorative. Even better if there's a diamond or two involved."

"Duly noted." He leaned back against the car and rubbed his hands together. "Time to strategize. What are our next steps in the investigation?"

"Velma's account of what happened that evening in the VIP Room seems to point the finger at Herbert. I think talking to him is our number one priority."

"You're assuming he hasn't been arrested."

"If he had been, I think it would have made the news. If he did kill Fletcher, he should be behind bars."

Scooter rubbed his jaw. "You don't suppose he's dangerous, do you?"

"I don't think he's a mass murderer or anything. If we tread lightly and don't tip our hand, I think it would be okay to ask him some questions and find out more about what happened that night."

"Agreed. But first we need to find him. Everyone else seems to have shown up in Coconut Cove. Maybe Herbert is here too."

I knocked on the car window and wagged a finger at Mrs. Moto. "No scratching the upholstery." Then I looked at Scooter. "Herbert was real buddy-buddy with Ned and Nancy."

"That's right. They invited him to go to the yacht club." He pulled his phone out of his pocket and called Ned. After telling him about the new grill, Scooter asked him if he had seen or heard from Herbert. "Bingo," he said after hanging up. "Herbert is in town and Ned is meeting him at the yacht club in an hour."

"Let's go." Before I could open the passenger door, my phone buzzed. "Hang on, it's a text from Sylvia."

"What's it say?"

"She's at the library and asked me to come meet her. Apparently, she has important information to share with me."

"Okay, let's split up. I'll go to the yacht club and you go to the library."

"Makes sense," I said. "Who is going to take Mrs. Moto with them?"

"That's easy," Scooter said. "Do you think she'd rather spend the afternoon at the yacht club or at the library with her buddy, Dr. McCoy?"

At the mention of the library's resident cat, Mrs. Moto made her opinion known by standing up on her hind legs and yowling through the gap in the cracked car window.

"Library it is," I said.

* * *

When I walked into the library, Hudson held up a chocolate bar. "Back in stock."

"Okay." I pulled out my wallet. "It's for a good cause."

"Do you want the whole box again?"

"I think one bar is probably enough today." Torn between a milk chocolate bar and one with caramel filling, I closed my eyes. "Surprise me."

"I hope you like cereal," he said.

When I saw what he had placed in my hand, I breathed a sigh of relief. "Phew. I was worried when you mentioned cereal, I thought you were going to give me a bowl of oatmeal. Corn flakes are so much better."

"Especially when they're covered in dark chocolate. I think you're going to enjoy it." As I popped a morsel in my mouth, Hudson smiled at me mischievously. "If I was a betting man, I'd say that you won't be able to stop with just one."

"Oh, go on then. Give me another

one," I said. "It is pretty delicious."

"That was too easy. I didn't even have to do my hardcore sales pitch."

"You must have hypnotic powers."

"Hypnotizing people isn't as easy as you think. The hypnotist I go to has had years of training."

"Why do you get hypnosis therapy?" When Hudson's eyes grew cloudy, I instantly regretted my question. What if it had to do with the death of his wife and son?

"I'm scared of spiders," he said after a beat.

I suspected that wasn't the real reason, but I went along with it. "Me too. Especially tarantulas."

"They're the worst. Someone was just telling me about a magician who features tarantulas in his act. I think you know her. The lady who was in here last week arguing with her husband."

"Sylvia." I cocked my head to one side. "Did Nancy tell you what happened on the cruise?"

"No, I haven't spoken with my aunt for a few days. Although, I am going over to her place for dinner tonight."

"Well, Sylvia's husband was murdered. Someone pushed him overboard."

"Oh, wow, that's awful." He took a deep breath. "She's here right now, you know. Over in the periodicals section. Dr. McCoy must have sensed what she's going through. He's been sitting quietly in her lap for the past twenty minutes."

"It will be interesting to see if Mrs. Moto realizes Sylvia needs consoling too." I looked around the lobby. "Where did that cat go?"

"When you walked in, she made a beeline in that direction." Hudson pointed toward the staff room. "Probably getting herself a snack."

"I'm sorry that she keeps eating Dr. McCoy's food."

Hudson waved a hand in the air. "That's what it's there for."

"For all the cats who wander into the library? How many come in here?"

"True. Only Mrs. Moto is a regular. But Anabel Dalton brings her Yorkies in here sometimes. They've been known to sample the cat food."

I chuckled. "Frick and Frack spend so much time with Mrs. Moto that sometimes I think they've forgotten that they're dogs."

"Anabel told me that she wants to figure out a way to include Frick and Frack in the wedding, but she's not sure how."

"Maybe her wedding planner can help with that," I said.

"Wedding planner?"

"Sylvia offered her services."

"That's right. She showed me some pictures from weddings she's worked on." Hudson furrowed his brow. "But they seemed pretty elaborate, not to mention expensive. I never figured Anabel to be the type to have a wedding planner. She always seems so . . . ."

"Bohemian?" I suggested.

"Yes, that's it. I picture her getting married on the beach barefoot with flowers in her hair, not having a fancy wedding and reception."

"I need to find a way to get Sylvia to tone down her ideas for Anabel's wedding. It's not going to be easy though." I looked toward the periodicals section, steeling myself for my conversation with Sylvia. "You know what, I'm going to need even more of that chocolate."

As Hudson handed me a few more bars, he said, "Do you want the name of my hypnotist? He can help you with your sugar addiction."

* * *

I found Sylvia nodding off in one of the

comfy armchairs by the window. Dr. McCoy was curled up on her lap. When he saw me, he lifted his head and meowed softly.

"You're a sweet kitty," I told him.

As if sensing that I was complimenting another cat, Mrs. Moto raced out of the staff room. She leaped onto the coffee table and yowled. Everyone looked over at the disturbance, but they all had smiles on their faces. Mrs. Moto's presence in the library was a familiar one, and she was popular with the patrons.

"Shush, Sylvia is sleeping," I whispered to the calico.

Mrs. Moto sniffed Sylvia's hand and gave it a few licks. Then she laid down on the table and proceeded to give herself a head-to-toe bath.

I started to tip-toe away when Sylvia's eyes opened. "There you are Mollie. I must have dozed off."

She stretched her arms above her

head and yawned. Dr. McCoy mirrored her movements, yawning while he stretched his front paws out in front of him.

"Sit down," Sylvia said to me. "There's something I want to talk with you about."

As I set my stash of chocolate down on the table next to Mrs. Moto, Sylvia raised an eyebrow. "Is that all for you?"

"Oh, sorry, where are my manners? Please take one."

Sylvia shook her head. "I can't eat chocolate anymore. It gives me a rash in my armpits."

"That sounds itchy." I felt a sudden compulsion to scratch my own armpits, but restrained myself.

"Not as itchy as the rash on my feet I get when I eat jellybeans. But the worst one is the rash I get under my bra strap."

"Oh, let me guess, it's the laundry detergent you use."

"No, it's sardines."

"I can live without sardines and jellybeans." I wrinkled my nose. "But give up chocolate? No way. I'd rather deal with a rash."

"Be careful. Eat too much chocolate and you'll have a rash like me. Fortunately, hypnosis did the trick and I haven't had a problem with my armpits since."

"Wow, Hudson just mentioned hypnosis to get rid of my sugar addiction. I thought he was just kidding."

"Oh, no, it really works. You should try it. There's a fabulous hypnotist I know who lives in Coconut Cove." She gently moved Dr. McCoy to one side in order to reach her purse. Pulling out a business card, she said, "He's semi-retired, a former magician. You know I used to be his assistant back in the day. It was such a pleasant surprise to run into him. I hadn't realized that he had moved to Florida. His stage name is 'Hypnotist Hank.' Catchy, huh? Give him a call. He can help."

"I'll think about it," I said.

"Look, I know a lot of people don't believe hypnotism is real and there are a lot of quacks out there, but—"

I held up my hand. "No, I believe in it. It's a great technique for helping people remember things like alien abduction. I hear it's good for quitting smoking too. I'm just not sure if it's for me."

"Well, if you change your mind, give Hank a call." Sylvia reached into her purse again, then popped a piece of gum out of a foil packet. After putting it in her mouth, she opened a bridal magazine. "We should get down to business. I was thinking about these canapes for Anabel's reception."

"Is this why you asked me to come meet you here?"

"Of course. Anabel's wedding is our number one priority, right" She handed me the magazine. "Now, about these canapes."

I squinted at the photo. "Is that caviar?"

"And edible gold leaf. Almost too pretty to eat."

"I'm not sure that's really Anabel's style," I said, handing her the magazine back.

"Of course, it is. The problem with brides is that they're so excited and overwhelmed about their upcoming nuptials, that it's hard for them to make decisions." She patted her chest. "That's what makes wedding planners so indispensable. We can take that stress away from the young girls by making all the tough decisions for them."

There were a couple of major flaws with Sylvia's argument. First off, Anabel wasn't a young girl. I'm not saying she's old. We're about the same age, and when you're in your forties, 'young girl' is a fond memory, not reality. Second, I've known a few bridezillas who are crystal clear about precisely what they want. They don't need wedding planners to tell them anything. They hire wedding planners so that they have someone to blame when things go wrong.

Caviar and edible gold leaf—this was so not Anabel. Barefoot on the beach with flowers in her hair, totally her scene. I had to find a way to get Sylvia to focus on something other than Anabel's wedding.

"Did you know that Herbert is in Coconut Cove?" I asked.

That seemed to do the trick. Sylvia closed the magazine. "Herbert? Herbert is here?"

"Uh-huh. He's at the yacht club."

"Impossible." Sylvia stood abruptly, causing Dr. McCoy to tumble off her lap. "Come on, let's go."

"Where?"

"To the police station to go see Anabel's fiancé. Herbert Miller should be in jail." As Sylvia scooped up her purse, she added. "Bring that magazine with you. I have some ideas for what the groomsmen should wear that I want to run past the chief."

* * *

Thank goodness the chief was away at an office ergonomics training session. Sylvia tried to leave the bridal magazine with the receptionist, but Charmaine Buttercup wasn't having any of that.

"The last time I mentioned the wedding to the chief, he just about bit my head off," Charmaine said, tucking a lock of her strawberry blonde hair into her elaborate updo.

"Why's that?" I asked.

"I don't rightly know. All I did was tell him about when Dale and I got married and then, would you believe this, he pretended that his phone rang. The man had the nerve to have an entire fake phone conversation in front of me. Eventually, I gave up and left his office."

I bit back a smile. Charmaine was a sweetheart. Only she did have a tendency to ramble on, a trait which I knew drove the chief to distraction.

"Sylvia's exhausted," I said to Charmaine. "I should get her back to the bed-and-breakfast."

Sylvia wrung her hands. "I can't rest until I know that Herbert Miller is in jail."

"Mollie is right," Charmaine said. "You look plum worn out. Go get some rest, and I'll be sure to tell Chief Dalton all about this Herbert Miller fellow the second he gets back. Don't worry, the chief will know what to do."

Sylvia nodded, then tried again to give Charmaine the magazine.

Charmaine gently rebuffed the attempt. "Lunch later this week, Mollie?"

After picking a date, I ushered Sylvia out of the police station.

"I'm really not that tired," she said as we walked to the car.

"You've been through a lot," I said.

"You should rest. Your immune system will be weakened from the stress. You don't want to get sick."

On the drive back, Sylvia looked at pictures of Regency era style weddings on her phone. "How about having Anabel ride a white stallion down the aisle?"

"I think she's allergic to horses," I said.

"This stupid phone," she said. "It's turned itself off again. I need Anthony to look at it for me. Sometimes, I wish we still used paper and pencil. I'm not very good with technology."

"Must be tricky since you were married to a guy in telecommunications."

"Tell me about it," she muttered.

After dropping Sylvia off at the Honeysuckle Cottages, I checked my phone. Scooter had sent me a cryptic text, telling me to meet him at our friend Penny Chadwick's boat, *Pretty in Pink*.

I deposited Mrs. Moto at our boat, then headed to D Dock where Penny's boat was berthed. I was surprised to find Herbert sitting in the cockpit, chatting with Penny about options for relocating his boat from Cleveland to Coconut Cove.

When Penny saw me, she said, "There's some lemonade in the galley. Help yourself. Scooter's already down there."

Herbert gave me a quick hello, then turned back to Penny. For a man who might soon end up in jail, he seemed rather focused on how much it would cost to truck his boat to Florida.

"I see you found our number one suspect," I said quietly to Scooter as poured me some lemonade. "Did you get any useful intel out of him?"

"I sure did." Scooter glanced up into the cockpit to make sure that we wouldn't be overheard. "Herbert told me that Dominic is a loan shark."

"That makes sense," I said, remembering how Dominic had given

Fletcher money in exchange for his car keys and gold watch. "But why was he on the cruise? Who takes their own personal loan shark with them?"

"That part I don't know."

"Okay, Dominic is a loan shark. But I'm not sure how that's relevant."

"I figure Herbert told me that to throw us off the scent. He's trying to set Dominic up to be the fall guy."

"That fits the facts. If you kill someone, you try to shift the focus to someone else. Sometimes, you might even plant false clues. But trying to pin it on Dominic? No, I don't see it. Herbert is smarter than that. Sure, Dominic might have loaned Fletcher money, but how could he collect if Fletcher was dead? That's why we ruled out Dominic as a suspect back on the ship." I took a sip of the lemonade, then smacked my lips. "That's tart. I wonder if Penny has any sugar around here."

As I peeked in the canisters on the

counter, Scooter rubbed his hands together. "I haven't told you everything yet. Herbert says that he heard Dominic and Fletcher arguing earlier that evening. Dominic told Fletcher that he'd have to come up with the money he owed when they got back to port or else. Fletcher laughed, saying that you can't collect money from a dead man."

"Right, that's what I just said."

"But here's where it gets interesting." Scooter paused for dramatic effect. "Dominic's reply was, 'But I can collect from your widow.'"

"That *is* interesting. Now we have two fights—one between Fletcher and Herbert, and one between Fletcher and Dominic." I ran my fingers through my hair. "But there was a witness to Fletcher and Herbert's fight. Did Herbert say if anyone else heard Dominic threaten Fletcher?"

"No, he didn't." Scooter leaned against the counter. "Now that I think about it, it does seem like Herbert is lying. When I asked him if he had told the police about Dominic, he said he hadn't."

"Well, there you go then."

"But, on the other hand, Herbert told me that Dominic has some serious connections. Maybe he was afraid to go to the police. In fact, he made me swear that I wouldn't tell anyone what he told me."

I furrowed my brow. "I don't know, it sounds fishy."

Scooter took my glass from me and set it on the counter. "You're better with this sort of thing than I am. I think you should have a crack at questioning Herbert."

As we sat down in the cockpit, I tried to figure out how to tackle bringing up the subject of Fletcher's death.

"Are you okay, sugar?" Penny asked me. "You look lost in thought."

"Speaking of sugar, do you happen to have any that I could add to my lemonade?"

She smiled. "A little too tart for you? No problem, I'll get you fixed up."

After she went down below, I turned to Herbert and dived right in. "Scooter told me what you had said about Dominic."

"That was supposed to be between us."

"I can't keep secrets from my wife," Scooter said.

Herbert sighed. "I couldn't either."

"You have to tell the police what you heard Dominic say to Fletcher," I said. "If not for any other reason than to make sure no one tries to pin the murder on you."

I was proud of myself for this line of questioning. Herbert would relax, thinking we were on his side. Maybe he'd accidentally let something incriminating slip.

His eyes widened. "Who would do that?"

"Anthony?" I suggested.

"That punk has had it in for me from day one." Herbert clenched his fists. "He thinks I'm some sort of dinosaur. He's trying to push me to retire so that he can take over the company. You should hear the lies he told Fletcher and Sylvia about me. Wait until I see him—"

Someone rapped on the hull. "Penny, you there? I've got your order."

Penny came into the cockpit and leaned over the side of the boat. "Hi Melvin. Here, let me help you with that."

As Melvin handed Penny a couple of cartons, I blanched when I saw that Velma was standing next to him. What if Herbert realized who she was? What if he found out that she had witnessed his fight with Fletcher?

"Come aboard," Penny said to Melvin and Velma. "I've got some cold lemonade. Herbert, scootch over a little so that they can sit down."

Velma shot her uncle a nervous glance. Except he seemed oblivious to who the man she was sitting next to was. When Herbert smiled at her, she broke into tears. "I can't do this."

"Do what?" Melvin asked.

"He paid me to lie," she said in a shaky voice.

"Who paid you to lie?" Melvin nodded his head toward Herbert. "This man?"

"No, it was the other man. He told me he would give me money if I said that I saw them fighting. But there wasn't any fight."

I leaned forward. "You mean you didn't see Herbert fighting with Fletcher?"

Velma's chest heaved as tears streamed down her face. She was sobbing so hard that I couldn't make out her response, but from the emphatic shaking of her head, her answer was clear. Someone wanted to pin the murder on Herbert, and they had enlisted Velma's help to do so.

CHAPTER 9
TINY HAMSTER SWEATERS

"You lied?" Melvin pulled his niece to her feet. "You accepted a bribe? How could you? That's not how you were raised."

"Please, you have to understand." Velma placed her hand on her uncle's arm, but he shook it off.

"Understand what? What is there to understand?" The set of Melvin's jaw reflected the anger he felt, but his dark brown eyes hinted at something else. Shame, perhaps? Knowing a member of his family had done something that didn't sit right with his values would sting. "If your parents were still alive, they would be horrified."

Penny, Scooter, and I exchanged glances. Melvin had dealt with more than his fair share of family tragedy in the past. Hopefully, this wouldn't push him over the brink.

Velma collapsed onto the bench seat, tears streaming down her face. "I did it for Ashley. Her boy is really sick, and she can't afford the medicine he needs."

Worry creased Melvin's brow. Sitting next to his niece, he took her hand in his. "Why didn't you tell me about your sister? I would have helped."

"She made me swear not to tell you. She knows what you think about her husband."

Melvin scowled. "That no-good fool."

"You never could stand him," Velma said.

"He spends more time in police

custody then he does at home," Melvin said. "But you and Ashley still should have come to me. To take money and lie? I never thought you would have done such a thing."

"I was desperate. I spoke with Ashley right before the ship departed. She told me that her boy had taken a turn for the worse. When that man offered me money . . . well, it seemed like the answer." Velma took a deep breath, then continued, her voice quiet and flat. "I didn't know someone had been murdered. By the time I found out, I was in too deep."

Melvin groaned. "This is all my fault."

"It's not your fault," Velma said. "I should have told you about Ashley. I know that now."

"We need to fix this. Together." Melvin squeezed Velma's hand. "We'll go see Chief Dalton. He'll know what to do."

"We can go with you," I offered. "We were on the cruise with Velma."

Melvin shook his head. "I think it would be best if the two of us went on our own. The chief can follow-up with you afterward."

I nodded, then looked at Velma. "Before you go, can you tell us who the man was? Who asked you to lie for him?"

"I'd like to know that as well," Herbert said crisply. "You fabricated a story which implicated me."

Velma's eyes started watering again. "I'm sorry, sir."

"How about some tea, sweetie? Tea always helps," Penny said to the young woman.

While Penny went down below to rustle up refreshments, I handed my phone to Velma. "Have a look at this picture again. Can you show us which man it was?"

She pointed at Anthony. "It was him."

Herbert gritted his teeth. "I knew it. He'll stop at nothing to get what he wants, even if it means killing his uncle."

Velma gasped as she realized the implications of what Herbert said. "How could someone kill a member of their own family?" She averted her eyes from the image on the screen, then thrust the phone at me. "I almost helped a murderer get away with it."

"You didn't know," Scooter reassured the young woman. "It sounds like you were just trying to do the right thing for your family."

She looked down at the floor. "But it wasn't the right thing, was it?"

"Anthony may not have been the killer," I pointed out.

Velma furrowed her brow. "But why else would he have asked me to lie for him?"

"I'm not sure. Maybe if you tell us more about what happened that night, we can try to figure it out."

"Go on," Melvin said. "You can trust these people."

Herbert folded his hands in his lap and fixed his gaze on Velma. My stomach twisted in knots. Could we trust Herbert? Until now, there had been a strong possibility that he had killed Fletcher. Velma's confession now pointed the finger at Anthony, but maybe there was another reason why Anthony had asked her to lie. Herbert could still be the killer.

As if sensing my thoughts, Scooter said to Herbert, "Maybe we should wait down below with Penny. Velma might be more comfortable talking with just Mollie."

"No, it's fine," Velma said. "I don't mind."

I took a deep breath. "Okay, why don't you start with when you arrived at the casino?"

"I wasn't supposed to be working at the casino that night, but one of the other girls got sick, so she asked me to cover for her. At first, my manager had me working in the main room."

"You were working there as a waitress, right?" Herbert asked.

"Yes, sir, that's right. Drinks, mostly. Occasionally some chips or pretzels, that kind of thing. They served food in the VIP Room. That's where the man . . . what was his name again?"

"Anthony Wright," Herbert spit out.

"That's where I first saw Mr. Wright."

"Let's get back to the VIP Room in a minute," I said. "Can you tell us who you saw first in the main casino that night?"

I handed her my phone again. She took a deep breath, then scrolled through the pictures. When she reached one of Fletcher, she said softly, "This is the man who died."

"God rest his soul," Melvin said.

"He didn't treat your niece very well," I said. "He was rude to her at dinner."

"It was probably the drink talking." Scooter pursed his lips. "Although that's no excuse for his behavior."

"Well, he certainly got drunker at the

casino and ruder. Yet, everyone working there kept putting up with it and smiling," I said.

Velma shrugged. "It comes with the job. Most of the passengers are nice."

"Who else did you see that night?" Scooter asked.

"There was that huge guy. He looks like he's into bodybuilding." Velma turned to me. "You were playing craps with him."

"I'm not sure I have a picture of him, but that sounds like Dominic."

"Hang on a minute." Scooter helped Penny pass steaming mugs of tea to everyone.

As Penny set a plate of gingersnaps onto the cockpit table, she asked, "What did I miss?"

"A lot," I said. "Velma is being a huge help."

"Am I?" Velma's voice wavered.

"Definitely," I said.

"Herbert, remember what you told me

at the yacht club about how Dominic threatened Fletcher?" After Herbert nodded, Scooter turned to Velma. "Did you see any sort of altercation between Dominic and Fletcher that night? Did they have a fight? Did Dominic seem angry?"

Velma shook her head. "No. The only thing I remember about him is that he asked me for some rutabaga juice."

"Rutabaga juice? What a strange thing to order," Herbert said.

"He told me that it was for a diet he was on. Ruta … rutasomething."

"Rutamentals," Scooter and I said at the same time.

"I can't believe people still think rutabagas are the secret to weight loss." I creased my brow. "Strange that a bodybuilder would be trying to lose weight. Aren't they always trying to bulk up? Uh … Sorry, I'm getting us off track."

Velma smiled faintly. "When I told him

we didn't have any, he asked for spicy tomato juice with a celery stick."

"Oh, a Bloody Mary," Scooter said.

"No, just plain juice."

"If you make a virgin Bloody Mary right, you won't even know that it doesn't have vodka in it," Herbert said.

"You tried to get Fletcher to stop drinking that night, didn't you?" I asked.

Herbert frowned. "As usual, he didn't listen to me."

Melvin looked at his watch, then glanced at his niece. "Maybe we should get going."

"But she hasn't told us what happened between her and Anthony yet," Scooter said. "That's the crucial part."

Penny offered Melvin a gingersnap. While he dunked it into his tea, he nodded at Velma to continue.

"You want me to tell you about the VIP Room?" she asked.

"Please," Scooter said.

"They moved me in there around ten.

It was really busy. We had lots of high rollers that night, and needed extra help."

"What time were you there until?" I asked.

"My shift didn't end until midnight."

Scooter helped himself to a cookie, then asked, "Were there a lot of people in the VIP Room?"

"There were a number of poker games going on. Let's see, there was a table of older Japanese gentlemen in one corner. They were very quiet and polite. There was another table of young guys going to the Bahamas for a bachelor party. They were having quite a good time."

"Rowdy, huh?" Scooter asked.

Velma smiled. "I had to ask them a few times to keep it down."

"Tell us about the other players," I said.

Velma looked upward as she tried to recollect that night. "Let's see, there were two other tables in the middle of the room. Nothing out of the ordinary with them. Then there was the table that Mr. Wright was playing at. That one was located in the front of the room, next to the bar."

Scooter raised his eyebrows. "So was Anthony there the entire night?"

"No, he left at ten-thirty."

"How can you be sure of the time?" I asked.

"I had already worked one shift that night, but with some of the crew sick, they asked me to do a double shift. I was so exhausted that I kept checking my watch all evening. I wanted my shift to be over so that I could go to bed." Velma hesitated for a moment, then looked at Herbert. "You were in there as well, sir."

Herbert straightened his shoulders. "Yes, I came in to check on the potential investors. There's nothing wrong with that."

"No, of course not." Scooter held up a placating hand. "We're just trying to piece together what happened that night. How long did you play poker with the guys?"

"I don't gamble," Herbert said.

"Smart man," Melvin said. "Gambling is a vice."

"Didn't I see you with a scratch card the other day?" I teased.

"Well, that's different," Melvin said.

Herbert cleared his throat. "For most people, the occasional flutter or scratch card isn't a problem. But for others, it can be an addiction."

I gave Herbert an appraising look, then turned back to Velma. "So, to the best of your recollection, Anthony wasn't in the VIP Room between ten-thirty and midnight."

"No, ma'am," she said.

Scooter cocked his head to one side. "When did Anthony ask you to lie for him?"

"It was early in the morning. I only got a few hours of sleep before I had another shift. I was in the lounge, tidying up the coffee station when he came up to me. He asked me if I remembered him from the VIP Room and I said yes. Then he said that he needed my help. His girlfriend thought he was cheating on her."

"Wait a minute, this was all supposed to be a cover story for Madison?" I asked.

"Don't fall for that," Herbert snapped. "This is all typical Anthony. One lie wrapped around another lie. He was too busy killing his uncle to be cheating on Madison."

I shot Herbert a glance, then looked at Velma. "Can you finish telling us what happened?"

"That's it, really. He said that if anyone asked, I should say that he was in the VIP Room the whole night. I assumed he was referring to his girlfriend. When he shoved a wad of cash in my hand, I agreed."

"When did you realize that there was more going on?" I asked.

"When my manager asked to see me. I went to her office, but before I could knock on the door, Mr. Wright pulled me aside. He handed me more money, double what he had given me earlier, and told me to go along with what he said. Then he went into my manager's office with me."

"Didn't your manager think it was odd that he accompanied you?" I asked.

"She seemed a little flustered at first, but then she explained that it was Mr. Wright who had suggested that she speak with me. After explaining to me that there had been a terrible accident with Mr. Wright's uncle, she said that the assumption was that he had been inebriated and fallen overboard. She just needed me to confirm that he had been intoxicated. I said that he had been drunk, and that's when Mr. Wright jumped in." Velma took a moment to gather her thoughts, then continued, "He described the fight—"

Hebert interjected, "The fight that never happened."

"Let the young lady speak," Scooter said.

"I started to say something, but the way Mr. Wright looked at me made me think twice. And it was so much money. I just went along with it." She wrapped her arms around herself. "My manager excused me and as I was walking to the door, Mr. Wright complimented me on being such a hard worker. He told my manager how he had been in the VIP Room the whole evening. That's when he nodded at me and I realized he wanted me to back-up his story, which I did. At the time, I thought it was still about his girlfriend. How could I be so stupid?"

As Velma put her head in her hands

and sobbed, Melvin patted her knee. "It's all right. The important thing is that you're going to make amends. Come on, now … let's go see Chief Dalton."

"Poor thing," Penny said after they left. "We've all made mistakes that we're ashamed of."

As we all nodded in agreement, I wondered what kind of mistakes Herbert was ashamed of. Did any of them include murder?

* * *

After we all spent a few moments reflecting on the mistakes we had made in our past, Herbert made an observation about how calmly we had discussed Fletcher's murder.

"This isn't the first time that Mollie has been involved in this sort of thing," Penny said wryly.

"Scooter seems to have ice in his veins too," Herbert said.

Penny looked at Scooter. "Hey, he's right. You're as cool as a cucumber. Usually, you look like you're going to pass out when anyone so much as mentions blood, let alone murder. What's happened?"

"I'd like to know the answer to that too," I said. "I bought tons of chocolate at the library, and he's barely touched it."

"That's a sure-fire sign that your husband has been replaced," Penny joked. "I've never known Scooter not to consume chocolate like it's going out of style when you're investigating a murder."

"You do this professionally?" Herbert asked. When I shook my head, he said, "Then why are you involved?"

"That's a good question," I said. "To be honest, Scooter is the one who has been leading the charge on this one."

Scooter arched an eyebrow. "Hey, you were the one who wanted to go on the cruise so you could find out what happened between Herbert and Fletcher."

"Going on the cruise is different from investigating murder," I pointed out.

"Hang on a minute," Herbert said. "What did you mean when you said you wanted to know what happened with Fletcher and me?"

Scooter and I exchanged glances. When we both started to speak at the same time, Scooter smiled. "Ladies first."

"Well, there were all these rumors that Fletcher had embezzled money from your company."

I paused, waiting to see how Herbert would respond. When he didn't say anything, Scooter jumped in. "Mollie was surprised when she found out that the two of you were still partners."

Herbert nibbled on a gingersnap. "These are good," he said to Penny.

"I got them at the Sugar Shack," she

said.

"Oh, yeah? I'll have to check it out."

"It's on Main Street—" Penny started to say.

Frustrated with the change of topic, Scooter interrupted. "Basically, Mollie wanted to find out why you were still working with someone who stole money from you. She couldn't understand why you would work with someone as crooked as Fletcher. Unless . . ."

"Unless I was crooked too?" Herbert said dryly.

"No, that's not what I'm saying," Scooter said.

"You wouldn't be the first person to think that. My reasons for sticking with Fletcher are complicated. They're also private." Herbert stood and brushed crumbs off his pants. "I think it's time I went."

"We're not trying to pry," I said.

"Really? Isn't that exactly what you're doing?" Herbert asked sharply before looking at Penny. "Thank you for your hospitality."

"Sure thing," she said. "Let me know if you want any more information about moving your boat to Coconut Cove."

Herbert fixed his gaze on Scooter and me. "I'm not sure if that's on the agenda anymore."

"Okay, well if you change your mind, you know where to find me," she said.

He nodded, then stepped off the boat onto the dock. Before he walked away, he added, "At least one good thing has come out of this. Anthony is going down for the murder of his uncle. It couldn't happen to a nicer guy."

* * *

"We never even got a chance to ask him what he saw that night," I said after Herbert left.

"Even if we had, I don't think he would have been very forthcoming," Scooter said as he cleaned his glasses.

"Okay, you all are going to have to fill me in from the beginning. All I knew is what Nancy told me, then that poor girl confessed to lying about who was where and when. What exactly is going on?" Penny asked.

"I'm not sure I actually know at this point. There have been a lot of twists and turns." I ran my fingers through my hair. "What did Nancy say? Let's start from there."

"Not much. She called me earlier today and told me that someone was killed on your cruise. It wasn't a very detailed account. I didn't even know the victim's name was Fletcher until now."

"That's pretty surprising considering the fact that Nancy practically runs the Coconut Cove grapevine. I would have thought she would have told you Fletcher's full name, date of birth, and other vital statistics."

Penny chuckled. "True. But she

seemed more interested in telling me about your plans for Anabel's bachelorette party."

"Let me guess, she told you I didn't have a plan."

"Okay, there was a little bit of that. You know how she is."

"So, what do you think of the idea? Are you still up for sailing to Destiny Key on *Pretty in Pink*?"

"Sure, it will be fun." Penny smiled. "I'm really excited for you. This will be the first time you're captaining *Marjorie Jane* on your own."

My heart started beating faster, and I gripped Scooter's hand. "I'm not sure I can do this without you."

Scooter smiled. "Of course, you can. I have every faith in you."

"He's right," Penny said. "You've come such a long way since you first started taking sailing lessons with me. You're more than ready for this."

Scooter winced as I squeezed his

hand. "You've got this, my little commodore."

"My little commodore … I might be able to live with that pet name," I said.

"It ranks above a captain, but below an admiral, because we both know that Mrs. Moto is the admiral of our boat," Scooter said with a chuckle.

"Are you bringing Mrs. Moto to Destiny Key?" Penny asked.

"Of course. She's one of the girls," I said.

"Well, then you don't have a thing to worry about. She'll tell you if you're doing anything wrong. And don't forget, I'll be on the other end of the VHF radio if anything comes up." Penny checked her phone. "Darn, I have to show someone a boat. But I want to hear more about this case you guys are working on. Promise to fill me in later?"

After giving her our assurances, Scooter and I walked back toward our boat.

"Herbert did raise a good point," I said. "Why are we investigating Fletcher's murder?"

"We saw the man die. If that's not good enough a reason to get to the bottom of things, I don't know what is."

I took a deep breath. "Okay. I guess we need to regroup and figure out what our next steps are."

"Where's your notebook?" Scooter asked.

"I left my purse on the boat when I dropped Mrs. Moto off."

Scooter tapped the side of his head. "I'll try to remember everything until we get back. By the way, do you think we could get a more manly notebook and pen? I feel a little silly writing in something with unicorns on it. Not to mention the glitter pens. Should notes about murder investigations really be sparkly?"

"I know plenty of guys who use glitter pens."

"Really? Who?"

"Um . . . Alan Simpson."

Scooter chuckled. "Okay, I can see that. Alan's the creative type. The man knits sweaters for hamsters."

"They're selling like gangbusters."

"You're kidding? People are buying hamster sweaters?"

"People will buy anything, especially if it's tiny and adorable."

"Obviously, I need to put more effort into our online shop."

I held my hand up. "It's not *our* online shop. That is all you, buddy."

"It's really Mrs. Moto's shop. Her YouTube followers really like buying merchandise with her image on it, especially since the proceeds go to the non-kill animal shelter. The t-shirts have been doing well. Maybe sweaters would be popular too." He paused to wave at the owners of *Mistletoe*, a large catamaran which was tying up at the fuel dock. "You know what would be fun? Ugly Christmas sweaters for cats."

"I think you should branch out and make ugly Christmas sweaters for dogs too. Frick and Frack would look cute in them. Actually, you know what would be even better? Matching sweaters for the humans. Anabel and the chief could match their dogs, and we could match our cat. We could all wear them to the Christmas parade."

"That does sound fun," Scooter admitted. "But which one of us is going to learn how to knit."

"I nominate Mrs. Moto. She can play the ukulele, why not knit a sweater too?"

When we reached our boat, Scooter said, "This probably sounds bad, but investigating a murder is kind of fun too. It's like a puzzle."

"That's an apt description. Let's figure out what pieces we do have and which ones are missing."

"We have three suspects—Anthony, Dominic, and Herbert. Sylvia and

Madison both have an alibi."

"But so did Anthony," I pointed out.

"Yeah, but theirs is different. They were at the magic show together. I can't see both of them lying, can you?"

"It's not outside the realm of possibility."

"But we need to prioritize," Scooter said. "I say we start with the three guys. We need to find out exactly where they were when Fletcher was killed."

"Okay, I think we should tackle Anthony first. He's now our number one suspect. And even if he didn't kill his uncle, I want to know why he lied."

"And why he coerced Velma into lying for him," Scooter added. "This is going to ruin the girl's life."

"I think we should give Herbert some space. He's not exactly eager to talk with us, so we'll need to figure out the best way to approach him."

Scooter nodded. "Makes sense. What about Dominic? We don't even know where he is."

"Sylvia might know. Why don't I give her a call?" Before I could pull my phone out of my pocket, I felt a furry paw tap me on the side of my face. I laughed as Mrs. Moto yowled in my ear. "We might need to feed the cat first."

CHAPTER 10
RESERVATIONS REQUIRED

After feeding Mrs. Moto, Scooter and I headed to one of Coconut Cove's popular seafood restaurants—Chez Poisson. I had called Sylvia while Scooter opened up a can of Frisky Feline Ocean's Delight, and she had told me that Anthony and Madison had gone out for a romantic dinner.

"I think he might be popping the question," Sylvia said. "It will be fun having another wedding to plan."

"That's where the chief proposed to

Anabel," I said.

"Really? Chez Poisson is a fancy restaurant. I told you that I have a sixth sense about brides. If Anabel likes Chez Poisson, then she's going to love those canapes with caviar and gold-leaf."

"Well, the chief did wear an Elvis costume when he proposed. So I guess they put their own spin on fine dining."

"An Elvis costume," Sylvia spluttered. "Surely, you're joking."

"Nope, not joking at all. Hmm . . . the King of Rock and Roll. That would make a great wedding theme, don't you think? The chief could wear his Elvis costume. Maybe the white one with the red and gold trim. Although, I suppose that would clash with the bride. His sequined royal blue one is nice though. And it has a cape that goes with it."

"Chief Dalton has more than one Elvis costume?" Sylvia's voice had raised at least an octave by this point.

"Uh-huh. And you could serve peanut

butter, bacon, and banana sandwiches at the reception." I was just warming up to the subject. Finally, I had found a way to get Sylvia to withdraw her services. There was no way that she would want to be associated with a theme as tacky as this one.

After a beat, she said, "Oh, I get it. You're pulling my leg. You're such a card, Mollie."

"No, really, I'm serious. Elvis is definitely the way to go."

She hemmed and hawed for a few moments, then unfortunately came around to the idea. "I suppose peanut butter, bacon, and banana sandwiches wouldn't be so terrible. We could cut the crusts off and make them look more like the little sandwiches you get at high tea. The bridesmaids could even wear blue suede high heels. It's a stroke of genius. So kitschy that it's classy. Okay, dear, I have to run. I have a million things to research."

When we walked into Chez Poisson, the maître d' seemed incredulous that anyone would turn up without booking a table in advance. Giving a Scooter a meaningful look, he consulted his leather bound reservation book. Scooter hated this sort of thing, but he reached for his wallet.

With the skill of a magician, the maître d' took the folded bills from Scooter and made them disappear. One second the money was in his hand and in the next second it was gone. He snapped his fingers. A waiter rushed over, the maître d' had a whispered conversation with him, then turned back to us.

"I'm sorry, sir, but we can't accommodate you tonight. We are completely full. Perhaps you and madame would like to have a drink at the bar instead."

Scooter clenched his fists, then did that calming ritual of his. Apparently, it helped keep you from losing your temper as well as coping with murder.

As we sat at a small table in the corner of the bar sipping on gin and tonics, I said, "I don't think this is going to work. The idea was to casually run into Anthony and Madison. We can't even see the dining room from here."

"We can pretend to be going to the restroom," Scooter suggested.

"That's a great idea, but unfortunately they're located in the lobby by the entrance. The maître d' would notice if we tried to sneak past him into the dining room."

Scooter sighed. "This isn't going well."

I patted his hand. "Things don't always go to plan. We'll figure something out."

Turns out we didn't need to worry about how to accidentally run into the couple. They made it easy for us.

Hearing a commotion, I leaned sideways and peeked through the arched doorway which led into the lobby. I tugged on Scooter's sleeve.

"Madison is out there."

He shifted his chair over so that he had a better view. "She doesn't look happy."

It was true. Madison had her arms folded across her chest and was tapping her foot on the marble floor. "Get my coat," she barked at the maître d'.

Anthony grabbed his girlfriend's arm. "You're embarrassing me."

"It's all about you, isn't it?" She put her hands on her hips. "You're just like your uncle."

Anthony narrowed his eyes. "What does my uncle have to do with this?"

"Stop changing the subject."

"Me? You're the one who mentioned him." Anthony's jaw tightened. "There was something going on between the two of you, wasn't there?"

"You're disgusting."

"Oh, don't act so high and mighty. Don't forget how I met you. You were the type of beauty pageant contestant who would do anything to get what they wanted. Stealing that girl's hairspray and blow dryer? That was really low."

Madison stamped her foot. "I've wasted enough time on you. It's over."

Anthony threw his hands in the air. "Fine with me."

"Fine with me too." Madison hesitated for a moment, then strode toward the door. She paused only long enough to snatch her coat from the maître d'.

Anthony murmured something to the maître d', then slipped him some money.

"Wow, dinner and a show," I said under my breath. "Well, not really dinner since we couldn't get a table, but the show sure was something."

Scooter shifted his chair back to its original position. "Shush, he's coming in here."

"Scotch on the rocks," Anthony told the bartender.

After taking a sip of his drink, Anthony

turned around and surveyed the room. The other patrons avoided his gaze, chatting quietly about what had just happened.

I took the opposite approach, locking my eyes with Anthony and waving him over.

Anthony drained the rest of his scotch. After the bartender refilled his glass, he walked over to our table. "Sorry you had to see that."

"All couples fight from time to time," Scooter said diplomatically.

Anthony rubbed his finger around the rim of his glass. "Yeah, but not like that."

"I'm sure you guys will make up," I said.

"She'll come around. She always does. I'll give her some time to cool off before I head back to the bed-and-breakfast." He patted the pocket of his jacket. "You know, the funny thing is that I was going to . . ."

I leaned forward. "Going to what?"

Anthony shook his head. "Never mind. It isn't important. What about you two? Are you waiting for your table?"

"No, we just popped in for a drink," Scooter said.

"It's a nice place. Shame I didn't get to try the food before Madison threw one of her fits."

"Why don't you eat with us?" I suggested. "The bar menu looks good."

"I thought you were just having drinks," Anthony said.

I patted my stomach. "I guess I'm hungry after all."

Scooter chuckled. "When aren't you hungry?"

After ordering appetizers to share, Anthony raised his glass. "I'm glad I ran into the two of you. It's nice to see a friendly face, especially after the past few days."

"Good thing Herbert didn't join us then," I said. "I understand that he wouldn't exactly be a friendly face."

Anthony tightened his grip on his glass. "Why's that? Because he's practically ruined the company or because he killed my uncle?"

Scooter cleared his throat. "I saw Herbert earlier today. He was adamant that he didn't have anything to do with Fletcher's death."

"He'd say anything to save his own skin, wouldn't he?" Anthony took a sip of his drink. "It's only a matter of time before he's arrested. The only reason they haven't done so yet is because that fool of a captain is still insisting that it was an accidental death."

"Herbert said something interesting," I said.

"Oh, yeah, what's that?"

"He thinks you killed Fletcher."

Anthony slapped his hand on the table and roared with laughter. "He better come up with a better defense than that. I have an alibi."

"But you—"

Scooter gripped my hand tightly and shot me a warning glance.

"But I what?" Anthony prompted.

"Um, you have a spot on your shirt," I said.

Anthony looked down and scowled. "Madison was drinking red wine. She slammed her glass on the table, and some of it must have sloshed out. Excuse me for a minute while I try to get this out."

As he walked to the men's room, I gave Scooter a questioning look. "Why did you stop me?"

"If he killed Fletcher, what do you think he'd do to Velma if he found out she confessed to faking his alibi?"

I put my hand to my mouth. "Oh, my gosh, you're right."

"We have to find another way to find out what he was really doing that night. We can't ask him directly."

"When did you get so good at this kind of thing?"

He pecked my cheek. "I learned from the master."

* * *

Scooter and I kept the conversation light once Anthony returned to the bar. Anthony didn't seem eager to go back to the bed-and-breakfast and face Madison, so we stayed late, listening to him talk. We learned a few interesting things—Madison's talent in her beauty pageants was twirling batons that lit up (she was an electronics whiz and had done all the wiring herself), Sylvia had spent a month in Alaska in search of a cure for the dry patch on her right elbow (sadly, instead of coming back with a cure, she came back with a severe case of frostbite), and Anthony loved listening to audiobooks while in the tub (long, hot baths in the morning was his favorite ritual to pamper himself)—but nothing that helped with our investigation.

The next morning, I headed to the police station to share our concerns about Velma's safety. One of Scooter's molars was causing him a lot of pain, having kept him up all night, so he had ended up making an emergency dental appointment. When he suggested canceling so that he could join me, I told him that taking care of his tooth took precedence. He reluctantly agreed.

Charmaine Buttercup greeted me enthusiastically, offering me not one, but two kinds of homemade fudge. "Go on, try them. Tell me which one you like better."

"Definitely the one with peanut butter."

"Good. That's the one I'll make for Anabel's bachelorette party. I'll whip up a huge batch."

"You're bringing something?"

"Well, sure. It isn't a party without fudge." When she saw the expression on my face, she said, "Is that okay? I assumed everyone was bringing a dish to share."

"No, that's absolutely perfect," I reassured her. "It's just that I haven't even thought about food for Anabel's party. I have so much to get done before this weekend. Catering, party games, picnic blankets . . . and everything else I can't think of."

Charmaine smiled. "Don't forget the music. Gotta have music to dance to."

I ran my fingers through my hair. There was no way I was going to be able to pull this off. Nancy was right—I was a party planning failure.

Charmaine came around the front desk and gave me a hug. "Honeybell, what's wrong?"

"I have a murder to plan and a party to investigate."

She chuckled. "I think you have that backward."

"Huh?"

"You have a party to plan and a murder to investigate, right?"

I groaned. "Did I say I had a murder to plan?"

"You sure did. And while I know you could plan yourself a fine murder with all the bells and whistles, you probably don't want to go around telling everyone that. Now, don't you worry. You focus on the murder investigation."

"But the party—"

"Shush, now. While you're in with the chief, I'll start on a list of what needs to be done for Anabel's party. Once everything is down on paper, it won't seem nearly as overwhelming as it does right now. Then together we can go through it one by one and figure out how to get it all done. I'll be right by your side to help you every step of the way."

"You're a lifesaver."

She grinned and handed me a large piece of peanut butter fudge. "Shoo, now. The chief is waiting for you."

"Don't eat in my office," Chief Dalton grumbled without even looking up from the papers on his desk. "You'll get crumbs everywhere."

"It's fudge, not toast. Crumb-free. Want some?"

The chief leaned back in his chair. "Is it the one with peanut butter swirls?"

"Sure is." I split the fudge in two, then handed him half.

"I've gained weight since Charmaine started working here." He patted his belly. "I'm not sure if my tux is going to fit."

"You're going to wear a tux to the wedding?"

The chief scowled. "That wedding planner of yours told me I have to."

"She's not my wedding planner."

"You introduced her to Anabel. Case closed."

"When exactly is the last time you wore this tux of yours?"

"Sometime in the last century."

I bit back a smile as visions of a powder blue tux paired with a ruffled white shirt filled my head.

He sighed. "Yeah, it's never going to fit. I don't know why Anabel wants such a fancy wedding. I thought we'd do something simple."

"I'm not so sure she wants anything fancy either."

"Then why does your wedding planner keep dropping off magazine articles about floral centerpieces, champagne fountains, and fancy food like caviar and gold leaf canapes. I don't even know what canapes are."

"They're hors d'oeuvres."

"Why would anyone eat food covered in gold? What's wrong with chicken wings?"

"She's trying to distract herself. It's a way of coping with her husband's death."

"Fair enough," he said. "But can't she find a way to distract herself without making me wear a tux or eating metal?"

"Let me talk to her."

The chief nodded, then opened a file folder and examined the contents.

I cleared my throat. "Ahem, I'm still here."

"I thought we were done," he said as he scrawled his signature on a form.

"No, I came in to talk with you about Melvin's niece. I'm worried about her."

"The girl will be fine," the chief said. "No one is going to press any charges. I think she's learned her lesson."

"That's not what I'm worried about."

The chief glanced at me. "Oh, you're worried she might lose her job when the cruise line finds out that she lied."

My shoulders slumped. "I hadn't even thought about that. I hope that doesn't happen."

"Then what are you worried about?"

"That she could be in danger. If Anthony Wright finds out she's admitted to lying about his alibi, he might come after her."

"He might be angry, especially if his

girlfriend finds out that he was with another woman. But I don't think he'll take it out on Velma."

My eyes widened. "Wait a minute, I get what's going on here. You don't think that Fletcher Tolliver was murdered."

The chief rubbed his temples. "Mrs. McGhie, why must you think that every single death is sinister? Mr. Tolliver fell overboard. It's tragic, but not criminal."

"But that's not what happened. Scooter and I witnessed the whole thing."

"You saw a man fall overboard, right?" The chief asked. "Did you see anyone push him?"

"You don't have to see someone be pushed to know that he was pushed."

"I have it on good authority that it was an accident. Case closed."

"Then why is Fletcher's nephew saying that it's murder?"

The chief shrugged. "People say crazy

things when they're upset."

I leaned forward. "The captain of the cruise ship is covering this up. I'm positive."

"I'm going to be brutally honest with you, Mrs. McGhie." He waved his hand at the stacks of paper covering his desk. "I have enough to deal with in terms of real crime in Coconut Cove. I don't have time to worry about hypothetical crimes on the high seas."

"The high seas," I mused. "How exactly does that work?"

"What do you mean?"

"If someone commits murder in international waters," I held up a hand. "Hypothetically speaking, of course. Who has jurisdiction?"

"Well, it falls under the scope of maritime law. It would be up to the captain of the ship to decide if someone should be incarcerated if they're suspected of committing a crime."

"That's it? The captain gets to decide

what happens?"

The chief drummed his fingers on his desk. "It's not as simple as that. The laws of the country in which the boat is registered would apply. There's also the 'passive personality principle.'"

"How does personality type figure into this?"

"No, not personality type. It refers to the jurisdiction of the country that the victim is from."

"Fletcher was an American citizen. So this is an American matter." I cocked my head to one side. "So, hypothetically speaking who would be in charge of the investigation? The FBI? Do you have their number?"

The chief suppressed a smile. "No, but I'm sure you can find it online. Make sure you tell them about how your cat sometimes helps you with your investigations. They love that kind of thing."

* * *

I was on hold with the FBI for forty-five minutes before I hung up. Sylvia had insisted that Anabel and I meet her at Sailor's Corner Cafe for a late breakfast to continue the flurry of wedding planning that she had unleashed ever since meeting Anabel. I was running late, and the thought of poor Anabel trying to fend off Sylvia's ideas without support made me anxious.

As I was rushing down Main Street, Nancy bellowed from across the road. "Mollie, wait up." Instead of crossing at the crosswalk—which surprised me as usually she was a strict rule follower—she walked briskly through traffic. Of course, all the cars came to a screeching halt when they saw Nancy. Her force of personality made crosswalks unnecessary. Why wait for a light to change when you want to give someone a scolding? Especially when that person was me.

She scowled. "You haven't sent out an updated invite to Anabel's bachelorette party yet. All the guests still think it's taking place at the Tipsy Pirate."

"Everyone that's coming is from Coconut Cove," I said. "So, they all know that the Tipsy Pirate is shut down."

"Humph." Nancy pursed her lips. "But they don't know where the party is going to be held. If you had created a spreadsheet, like I suggested, then you wouldn't be in this predicament. You would have been organized and promptly informed people about the change in venue."

Okay, she had a good point, but I wasn't going to let her know that. "Of course they do. Didn't you get my email telling everyone about the change of plans? Maybe it went into your spam folder."

"Why did you send it to my spam

folder? That's poor planning on your part. Invitations should be sent by postal mail, preferably, but if you are going to email . . ." she paused to make sure that I realized that the emailing of invitations was not really acceptable in her etiquette handbook, "then you should send your emails directly to everyone's main email inbox."

"I don't control how email servers operate," I said. "If I did, I wouldn't get regular emails from people in Nigeria promising me a huge commission if only I'd help them by transferring funds on their behalf. I probably wouldn't get emails about updates to the marina rules and regulations either."

Nancy furrowed her brow. "Hang on a minute, I send you the marina emails. And you never respond in a timely fashion."

"See what I mean? You can't control email servers." Before she could figure out that her emails go into a special folder, otherwise known as my trash, I told Nancy that I was late.

"Are you having breakfast at the cafe? Do you know if they have any rutabaga specials back on the menu?"

I groaned. "Don't tell me you're back on that Rutamentals diet."

"Goodness, no. It's for a gentleman I met at the marina. He swears by Rutamentals. Says it's helped him build muscle without gaining fat. He actually stopped by looking for Herbert. He said that he's a friend of his."

"Let me guess. Large guy? Lifts a lot of weights. Name of Dominic?"

"Yes, that's him. Did you meet him on the cruise?"

"Sure did. I hung out with him at the casino. He called me his Lady Luck."

"Humph. You'll be lucky if you pull off Anabel's party this weekend." Having said that, she scurried off to check her spam folder while I sent Scooter a quick text.

Guess who is in town? Your favorite rutabaga-loving loan shark.

CHAPTER 11
BOB NEWHART IS CALLING

When my phone rang, I smiled. Scooter had added a new ringtone for me. It sounded exactly like Bob Newhart saying, "It's your wonderful hubby calling. Please answer the phone." The deadpan delivery and slight stammer were so cute that I listened to it twice before picking up.

"Hang on a sec," I said. "Let me go somewhere quieter so I can hear you." Realizing I was right outside of the peaceful courtyard that housed the town's rose garden, I pushed open the gate. I nodded at Mrs. McDougall, who was sharpening her pruning shears, then put the phone back to my ear and said to Scooter, "Okay, shoot."

"Waa djw ceef se?" Scooter asked.

"Huh?"

"Waa djw ceef se?" he repeated slowly, emphasizing each word. The emphasis didn't help. I still didn't have a clue what he was trying to convey.

"I can't understand you."

"E aat wut kanna."

This felt a bit like trying to figure what Mrs. Moto was trying to communicate when she meowed insistently at us. Usually she wanted food, scratches behind her ears, a game of laser pointer, or sometimes catnip. But what was Scooter trying to say? I assumed his topic of conversation was slightly more complex than needing a can of wet food opened immediately.

I pressed the phone closer to my ear.

"Come again?"

"Lwakane," he said.

"Oh, I get it. You're trying to speak Klingon." I cleared my throat, then switched to speaking the famous *Star Trek* warrior species' language. "TlhIngan QaQwI"e'," I said, complimenting him.

To be honest, his Klingon wasn't all that good, but I appreciated him making an effort. He knew how much I loved the *Star Trek* franchise. Though to my surprise, Scooter hung up. A few moments later, a text came through from him.

I wasn't speaking Klingon.

I scratched my head. What other *Star Trek* languages could Scooter possibly know? I shot him back a quick reply. *What was it? Vulcan? Ferengi?*

It was English. I had an emergency root canal. The tooth was badly infected. The lidocaine hasn't worn off yet. Makes it hard to talk.

So that was why his tooth had been causing him so much pain. *You poor thing. Does it hurt? Are you okay?*

While I waited for Scooter's reply, I watched Mrs. McDougall spread fertilizer underneath the velvety red roses climbing up the brick wall. Then I looked back at my phone. You'd think a guy who works in telecommunications would be faster at texting.

My phone pinged. *I'm fine. Back at the boat. What did the chief say?*

After trying to figure out how to sum up my less-than-helpful conversation with Chief Dalton, I finally settled on a rolling eye emoji.

That good, huh? Scooter replied.

Basically, we're on our own unless we can get the FBI to help. Going to the library to research maritime law.

I'll try to track down Dominic. Catch up later, Scooter texted back, along with several sailboat emojis.

On my way out of the garden, I

stopped to chat with Mrs. McDougall. "What kind of rose is that? It's taking off like wildfire. I bet it will cover that entire wall soon."

"Pretty, isn't it?" she said. "It's called 'Don Juan.' Definitely a bit of a show-off. Still, you can't help but fall in love with it."

"Kind of like its namesake," I said.

She laughed. "Yes, be careful it'll seduce you with its good looks."

While I helped Mrs. McDougall carry some bags of fertilizer from her car into the garden, I thought about Madison. She was a stunning woman. It was no wonder that she had competed in beauty pageants. Had she also used her looks to seduce men? I remembered the conversation I had overheard between Fletcher and Madison on the cruise ship. Fletcher had threatened to tell Anthony something about Madison. What was that secret? Had she been cheating on her boyfriend?

Cheating on her boyfriend . . . I played this scenario over and over again in my mind, then I gasped. At Chez Poisson, Anthony had practically accused Madison of sleeping with his uncle. She had denied it, but really, would she have admitted it to Anthony if she had? Scooter and I had found that pink cigarette butt at the crime scene. Had Fletcher and Madison argued that night about their affair? An argument that had become so heated that she took the opportunity to make sure he could never reveal her secret by pushing him to a watery grave.

Mrs. McDougall interrupted my train of thought to give me some tips on what herbs would grow well on our sailboat. After I said goodbye to her, I realized that I was supposed to be meeting Anabel and Sylvia at the cafe. When I rushed in, Anabel was sitting at a table by herself.

"Sorry I'm late," I said. "Did I miss Sylvia?"

"She was only here for a second. She dropped off some more bridal magazines and told me she couldn't stay."

"Did she say why?"

"Mentioned something about going to see a guy named Hank."

"Hank? Oh, that hypnotist she told me about. She must have a new rash."

Anabel sighed. "I think I'm going to start breaking into a rash if I have to look at one more picture of place settings, wedding arches, or boutonnieres. I told Tiny last night that we should elope."

"Eloping sounds romantic."

"I guess." Anabel absentmindedly traced her finger on the cover of one of the magazines. "But I really want all our friends to be there."

"Let me talk to Sylvia," I said. "You should be excited about your wedding, not dreading it."

"Do you mind? It's not that I don't appreciate her help, but it's so . . ." she chewed on her lip as her voice trailed off.

"Overwhelming?"

"Exactly. Just tell her that I want to put the wedding planning on hold, at least until after my bachelorette party on Sunday. I have a commission to work on this week, which is going to take all my focus. And then I want to enjoy the party without stressing about anything else."

After reassuring Anabel that I would take care of everything, I grabbed the stack of magazines. "I'll give these back to Sylvia and explain the situation." Then with more confidence than I actually felt, I added, "And don't worry about your party. I've got everything organized. It's going to be lots of fun."

Making a mental note to catch up with Charmaine Buttercup about the to do list she was working on, I headed to the library. First things first, the murder, then the party.

* * *

Hudson smiled at me when I walked into the library. "Back for more chocolate?"

Remembering what a struggle it was to button up my jeans this morning, I shook my head. "I'll pass."

"Really? You're giving up chocolate?" Hudson nodded approvingly. "I told you seeing a hypnotist would help."

"Whoa, I never said I was giving it up. Just cutting back a little."

Dr. McCoy hopped onto the counter and snaked a paw into the box of chocolate bars. With a bit of effort, he pushed one out. When it landed on a stack of books, he meowed at me.

Hudson stroked his fur, then placed the bar back in the box. "Don't tempt the lady."

Locking his eyes on me, Dr. McCoy meowed again.

"That time, I think he was asking where Mrs. Moto is," Hudson said.

"Sorry, she's back on the boat," I said. "I'll bring her in next time."

"Dr. McCoy sure is going to miss her," Hudson said.

"Miss her? Why?"

Hudson leaned across the counter and lowered his voice. "Can you keep a secret? I'm dying to tell someone."

"Of course. I'm great with secrets."

He tapped his fingers on the counter for a moment, then said, "I have an interview for a head librarian position lined up."

"Where's Janice going? She's too young to retire."

"No, the position is at another library." He grinned. "I couldn't believe it when they called."

"You're leaving Coconut Cove?" I glanced at Dr. McCoy. "You're both leaving?"

Hudson held his hands up. "It's not a done deal. They're interviewing two other candidates."

"Wow. That's big news. The library won't be the same without you. Is it far away?" When Hudson nodded, I said, "Your family will really miss you."

"They don't know yet. And you have to promise not to tell anyone, especially Aunt Nancy. If she gets wind of it, well, all heck will break loose."

"Understood. I know what the Coconut Cove grapevine is like."

"Thanks, Mollie. I've been bursting to tell someone, and you happened to come around at just the right time."

"I'll keep my fingers crossed for you. If anyone deserves to be a head librarian, it's you. Your nautical book club has been a big hit. Of course, now that I've read *Moby Dick*, I'm little anxious about running across a whale in our travels."

"Don't worry. If a whale approaches

Marjorie Jane, Mrs. Moto will scare it off."

I laughed. "Knowing that cat, she'd jump in the water. She loves swimming. She'd probably think the whale was a giant dolphin which had come just to play with her."

"Dr. McCoy doesn't like to go in the water, but he does like walking along the beach. If I do get this job, I hope Dr. McCoy can adapt. The weather will be quite different."

"How so?" I asked.

"Let's just say that I'll need some serious cold weather gear."

"After living in Florida, I don't think I could do winter anymore." I mentally shook myself when my eyes drifted to the box of chocolate. I could swear it was whispering to me, *Resistance is futile*. Averting my gaze, I said, "I need to do some research on maritime law. Can you point me in the right direction?"

"Of course. We have a number of

books on the subject."

Dr. McCoy followed us to the reference section. He stretched up on his hind legs and sniffed at a set of large leather-bound books.

"He's my secret weapon," Hudson said. "Who needs a card catalog when Dr. McCoy knows exactly where what you need is shelved."

"Does the library that's interviewing you know that you have a cat who comes to work with you?"

"Not yet. I thought I'd wait and see if they make an offer before I bring that up." Dr. McCoy tapped one of the books with his paw, and Hudson pulled it off the shelf. "What do you want to know about maritime law specifically?"

"What happens when someone is murdered in international waters," I said.

"Still on the case, huh? Why don't you start with this one?" he suggested, placing the book in my hands. "Dr. McCoy usually has a sixth sense about these sorts of things."

As I sat at one of the tables reading through overly dry paragraphs of legal jargon, my eyes began to glaze over. Maritime law is one of the oldest bodies of law that still operates in the world. Maybe the fact that it was developed back in ancient times was why it was so dull. Despite the excruciating boredom, I continued to plow through the book. Unfortunately, most of what I read seemed to apply to people such as offshore oil workers, international seamen, and ferry boat workers. Nothing jumped out at me that pertained to folks who went on a cruise ship for pleasure.

In between yawns, I mentally filed away a few tidbits in case the Tipsy Pirate reopened. Their pub trivia nights had been one of the highlights of my week. If they started back up, I would be able to belt out the fact that maritime law is also known as admiralty law. I smiled, thinking about what Mrs. Moto's reaction would be if I told her about admiralty law. As the honorary admiral aboard our boat, she would assume that meant she was entitled to pass judgment on us. Not that she doesn't do that already. She's a cat. Cats are always judging their humans and finding them lacking.

When I reached the section about wrongful death, I perked up. The captain of the cruise ship had refused to label Fletcher's death as murder. Despite that he still had to be investigating the incident, didn't he? The killer had opened the gate and then pushed Fletcher through it. Shouldn't the gate have been locked to begin with? What if some kids had been up on that deck, messed around with the gate, and one of them had fell overboard? That would have to be negligence on the cruise ship's part.

I leaned back in my chair and

considered the implications of the unlocked gate. Pushing someone through an open gate was one thing. However, lifting Fletcher up and shoving him over the railing? That would have been much harder. Someone like Dominic, with all of his muscles, probably would have been able to toss Fletcher overboard easily. But I wasn't so sure about Herbert and Anthony. They were both on the scrawny side, their physiques indicating that they spent more time behind a desk than in the gym.

Then there was Sylvia and Madison. Would either of them be strong enough to push Fletcher overboard? It didn't seem likely, but Fletcher had been drunk. Both of them had alibis, but I didn't want to rule them out completely. There was also the pesky question regarding the cigarette butt that we still needed to get to the bottom of.

I snapped the book shut and ran my

fingers through my hair. Why was I engaging in hypothetical scenarios? Sure, if the gate had been locked, maybe Fletcher would still be alive. Except it hadn't been, and Fletcher was dead.

Then I cocked my head to one side. There was something else strength-related to take into consideration—the gate. I had tried and couldn't unlatch it. Scooter was the one who had opened it when we were inspecting the crime scene.

Drumming my fingers on the table, I thought about all the suspects. The gate would have been child's play for Dominic, and probably not have presented a problem for the other guys. Or would it have? On the cruise, Anthony had struggled to open a jar of jam and Madison opened it for him. At the time, he joked that he had loosened it up for her. But had he? Or was Madison the one with the muscle in their relationship?

That brought me to Sylvia. I shrugged, not really knowing if she had the capability to open jars, let alone sticky gates. Then I remembered her special badminton exercise regime designed to strengthen her hands and forearms. The gate would have been a cinch for her.

Dr. McCoy hopped up on the table to lay down on the maritime law book. "Are you saying that's enough research for today?" I asked him. Dr. McCoy meowed, and I scratched his head. "I didn't learn too much from it, but it did confirm the 'passive personality principle' the chief told me about. Basically, it means that the federal authorities need to get involved, because Fletcher was an American. Even if they don't believe that it was murder, they should still investigate it as a wrongful death, don't you think? That gate shouldn't have been left unlocked."

Soft snoring was the only response I

got from Dr. McCoy. Gingerly removing my hand from underneath his head, I walked into the lobby to try phoning the FBI again.

While on hold, I checked out the community bulletin board. Mrs. McDougall had posted a sign-up sheet for volunteers to work in the rose garden. If we weren't leaving for the Bahamas after the holidays, I would have added my name to the list. The high school marching band was holding a pancake breakfast to raise money for new uniforms. I made a note of the date. Pancakes and a good cause? Count me in. My mouth was salivating in anticipation of light, fluffy pancakes drenched in maple syrup.

Tapping my foot along with the cheesy hold music, my eyes caught sight of a bright orange flier tacked to the corner of the bulletin board. I could hardly believe it. Trixie Tremblay, the founder of the Rutamentals program, was back in town. She was even holding a cooking seminar tonight at the community center. Dominic was a fan of Rutamentals. Was it possible that he would be attending Trixie's seminar this evening?

I sent Scooter a quick text—*Hope you're able to chew by tonight. Rutabagas are on the menu*—then scowled when my call to the FBI got disconnected.

* * *

The upside about Scooter's lidocaine wearing off is that he was able to talk. The downside was that now he could feel the pain from where the root canal had taken place. He tried to insist that he was fine, wanting to go with me to the Rutamentals seminar. Though the way he rubbed his jaw, and the agony etched on his face, made me insist that he take a couple of pain pills and crawl into bed.

After kissing him on the forehead, I said, "Don't worry, I'll call you if I find out anything interesting from Dominic."

"Be careful," Scooter said. "Don't let Dominic know you think he's a suspect."

"I'll be fine. The event is taking place at a public place so there will be lots of people around. Besides, Dominic isn't the brightest turnip to fall off the truck. Or should I say the brightest rutabaga? Honestly, I could probably ask him straight out if he killed Fletcher and he still wouldn't have a clue."

Scooter squeezed my hand. "Promise me you won't ask him that. Try to be more subtle with your questions."

"Subtle? Not a problem," I said, smiling brightly. After giving Mrs. Moto and Scooter a final kiss goodbye, I headed to the community center. The lot was full, and I ended up having to park my car on the street. It always amazed me that so many otherwise intelligent people thought that a diet based on rutabagas was a good idea, despite the, ahem, digestive issues it caused. Still, I had to hand it to Trixie Tremblay. She had managed to transform a humble root vegetable into a vast business empire.

When I walked into the center, I realized that Rutamentals wasn't the only show in town. Trixie was competing with a knitting workshop, a master gardener seminar, and an alcohol addiction recovery meeting.

Alan Simpson cornered me by the coffee urn and tried to convince me to attend his workshop. "Don't you want to learn how to make tiny sweaters for hamsters?" he asked. When I reminded him that I didn't have a hamster, he said, "They work for gerbils and guinea pigs too. Well as long as you adapt the pattern."

"What about something cat-sized?" I asked. "I want to make Mrs. Moto an ugly Christmas sweater."

"Sorry, no can do," Alan said. "My needles are too small to work for feline apparel. But I can give you some pointers."

After arranging to catch up for a knitting lesson the following week, I helped Mrs. McDougall carry some boxes of heirloom seeds into her classroom. When Trixie Tremblay's theme music started blaring from the room next door, Mrs. McDougall and I exchanged glances.

"I can't believe that woman is back in Coconut Cove. The only thing rutabagas are good for is ground up as fertilizer," the older woman muttered.

"I don't know. That seems kind of cruel to the other plants," I joked, taking my leave.

It appeared to be standing room only at the Rutamentals seminar. Somehow, as I weaved my way through the crowd, I spotted an empty seat right next to

Dominic. It was like the universe knew I needed to speak with him.

As I sat down, I realized why no one was in that spot. Dominic's legs were so muscular that his left thigh spilled onto half of the chair I was attempting to sit on.

He grinned when he saw me, his tiny baby teeth glinting in the overhead lights. Tapping the arm of the man sitting on the other side of him, he pointed at me. "Lady Luck," he said.

The man nodded, then went back to looking at his Rutamentals catalog.

I perched on the edge of my seat and attempted to have a conversation with Dominic, but the pounding music made it impossible. Impatient to get the show started, the crowd clapped their hands and chanted Trixie's name. A woman wearing a purple leotard, stiletto heels, and her trademark leg warmers bounded to the front of the room. Everyone rose to their feet and cheered, except me. That's because I had ended up on the floor when Dominic stood, his massive frame pushing both of our chairs backward.

By the time I got to my feet, everyone else had taken their seats again. Assuming that I was standing up because I was eager to ask a question, Trixie pointed at me. "Tell everyone your name," she said, in her high-pitched and annoyingly chirpy voice.

"Uh, Mollie." My face grew warm as everyone turned to look at me.

"Tell everyone why you're here, Mollie," Trixie said.

I glanced down at Dominic. I couldn't very well tell Trixie and everyone else that I was here to investigate a murder. So, I blurted out the first thing that popped into my head. "I want to give up chocolate."

A few people gasped. Probably folks who knew me and were all too aware of my torrid love affair with all things chocolate. I gasped too. Why did I say that? Was my subconscious trying to tell me something? Since I know my conscious mind in no way, shape, or form ever wanted to give up chocolate.

"You've come to the right place, Mollie. Within one week of being on the Rutamentals program, I guarantee you won't want to eat chocolate again."

She gave me an appraising look, then continued. "I can't help but notice that your upper arms are a little flabby." I arched an eyebrow, and she held up her hand. "Don't worry. It happens to most women when they reach your age. But Rutamentals will help transform that flab into muscle. Look at the gentleman sitting next to you. Before he embraced a diet of rutabagas, he was scrawny. He could barely lift a ten-pound weight. Now he can easily bench press two hundred pounds."

As the room broke out in applause, I hastily took my seat. Or my half a seat.

When Trixie held up her hands for silence, Dominic put his arm around me and said, "Lady Luck."

Trixie smiled. "She certainly is a lucky lady. Lucky that she's discovered Rutamentals."

All I can tell you about the following hour is that it was one of the longest of my life. I had to endure a presentation on ten little-known facts about rutabagas, taste test a new line of iced rutabaga teas, and do chair yoga. When the seminar finally ended, I managed to engage Dominic in conversation.

Okay, it wasn't really a conversation. I asked questions and Dominic gave what could charitably be called 'concise answers,' some of which made no sense.

I started with the note that someone had sent Dominic on the cruise ship. Since he had eaten it after reading it, the only thing I knew about it was that it mentioned extortion and financial records. Maybe I could get him to reveal what it had said and who sent it to him.

"Is someone trying to extort money from you?" I asked.

Dominic furrowed his brow. "Extort?"

Remembering that he had been stumped by the term "extortion" in the note and had to ask an elderly couple what it meant, I explained, "You know, like when someone threatens you unless you pay them."

He flexed his biceps. "Threat. No threat."

"Okay, gotcha. No one in their right mind would threaten you with bodily harm, but they could threaten you with something else. Perhaps by revealing a secret of yours?"

He gave me a toothy grin. "Secret. I keep secret. I no tell secret."

"I'm good at keeping secrets too." I put a hand to the side of my face and whispered, "Why don't you tell me one of your secrets and then I'll tell you one of mine. For example, maybe you could tell me if Fletcher owed you a lot of money. That would be a fun secret to share."

Dominic nodded, and I leaned forward, eager to hear the answer. "Fletcher not lucky."

I rubbed my hands together. Now we were getting somewhere. "Fletcher lost money gambling, so you loaned him money, right?"

"Yes. Gave him money." Dominic pulled out his wallet and handed me a piece of paper. "I got this."

I unfolded the paper, then said, "Oh, this is a check. A check drawn on Fletcher and Herbert's company account."

"Check," Dominic said.

"But it's postdated. You can't cash it until January of next year." I cocked my head to one side. "That's odd. Why would Fletcher give you a postdated check?"

Dominic stared at me blankly, then tried to take the check back.

"Hang on a second, let me take a picture of it first." After I returned it to him, he carefully folded it back up and placed it in his wallet. "When did you get this?"

"Got it on cruise," Dominic said.

"But when on the cruise? What time?"

Dominic pulled up his sleeve and squinted at his watch. "Nine."

"Yes, it's nine o'clock now. But what time did Fletcher give you this check? Did he give it to you at the casino?"

Dominic held his wrist up to my face. "Nine."

That's when I noticed that his watch had a plain black leather strap. It wasn't the flashy gold watch that I had seen Fletcher hand Dominic that night. When I asked him what had happened to Fletcher's watch, he gave me another blank look. I decided to try another tack.

"Remember how you were watching

Fletcher play craps at the casino?" Dominic nodded. "Then I left." This earned me another nod. "Did you stay at the casino after I left?" When Dominic nodded for a third time, I felt elated. My questions were getting through to him. "Did you stay at the casino the entire night?"

Dominic shook his head. "Casino. No."

"Where did you go? Did you go outside onto the deck?" I know that Scooter had urged me to be subtle in my questioning. However, I had thrown that strategy out the window a long time ago when even straight-forward questions proved challenging for Dominic. "Were you outside with Fletcher?"

"No. No outside. Magic."

I furrowed my brow. "Magic?"

"Big spiders. Magic."

"You went to the magic show?"

Dominic nodded vigorously, then abruptly stood and walked toward the front of the room where Trixie was selling Rutamentals merchandise.

Realizing that was probably as much information as I was going to get out of Dominic for the night, I decided to head back to the boat to debrief Scooter. As I walked out into the hallway, Mrs. McDougall waylaid me. "Can you help me carry some pruning shears to my car? They're on the table in the classroom."

As I went to retrieve them for her, I noticed two familiar men in the room next door. I could understand why Herbert had attended an alcohol addiction recovery meeting, but I was surprised to see Anthony there as well. I was even more surprised to see the two of them speaking in what appeared to be a civil manner. They detested each other.

The room was empty except for the two of them, and they were speaking quietly so I wasn't able to eavesdrop inconspicuously on their conversation. Instead, I leaned against the door frame, trying to decipher what they were saying through body language alone. Unfortunately, my ability to understand body language was worse than my ability to understand Klingon, so I had no idea what they were talking about.

After a few moments, they rose from their chairs and shook hands. When they saw me, they both did a double take.

"What a pleasant surprise. Are you here for the knitting workshop?" Anthony asked smoothly.

"No, I was at the Rutamentals seminar," I said.

Herbert wrinkled his nose. "Rutabagas?"

I nodded, then asked, "What are you two up to?"

Anthony clapped Herbert on the back and said in a jovial tone, "Just talking about my uncle's unfortunate death and how we should take the company forward from here."

Herbert's smile was more forced. "Yes, it's sad that we'll no longer have Fletcher at the helm, but Anthony will do a fine job taking over the company reins."

My eyes widened. "Anthony is taking over? That's certainly a surprise."

"Yes, I've decided to retire and sell the company to Anthony," Herbert said. "When you see how a tragic accident can end your life, like it did with Fletcher, it makes you reconsider things."

"Tragic accident," I spluttered, looking back and forth between the two men. "But it wasn't a tragic accident. It was murder."

"Murder?" Anthony frowned. "It wasn't murder. My uncle drank too much and fell overboard."

"But both of you were convinced that it was homicide," I said, leaving out the part that each of them had accused the other one of killing Fletcher.

Herbert shook his head. "That was just grief talking. Anthony lost his beloved uncle, and I lost my dear friend. When something like that happens, you want to lash out and blame someone, anyone really."

Anthony fixed his gaze on me, his eyes turning steely. "It was an accident. A tragic accident."

After the two of them left, apparently best buddies now, I slumped onto a chair in shock. It had only been a few days since Fletcher had been killed. Anthony and Herbert had been mortal enemies, and now this? Now they were suddenly united not only about the leadership of the company, but also about the cause of Fletcher's death? Something was going on and I was determined to get to the bottom of it.

CHAPTER 12
INTERNATIONAL BAGEL DAY

It was obvious that Anthony and Herbert had made some sort of pact to cover up the truth. On the surface, it looked like Anthony had come out ahead. He was going to take over the company. Apparently denying that his uncle had been murdered was the price Anthony was willing to pay in order to become CEO.

What I couldn't figure out was what Herbert was getting out of it. Previously, he had been adamant that he had no intention of retiring. Work had been everything to him. Now he was making plans for all the free time he was going to have on his hands. Had Anthony paid him off? Offered him some sort of financial incentive to retire early? Or had he blackmailed him? Threatened to reveal something if Herbert didn't play ball?

These are the kinds of questions that Scooter and I mulled over that night. I even called Sylvia to get her take on the matter. She was firmly in "Team Accidental Death," parroting the same party line as Anthony and Herbert.

In the end, we decided to let the whole matter drop. As Scooter pointed out, no one believed that it was murder. Or, at least, they weren't admitting it out loud. The FBI had given me the runaround, Chief Dalton was disinterested in the case, and even the captain of the cruise line was sticking to the story of accidental death.

Rather than fight an uphill battle, we got back to more important things—our boat project list and planning Anabel's party. While Scooter focused on installing new water tanks, I organized catering, put together a playlist of fun beach party tunes, made party favors, picked up decorations, and helped Charmaine make several batches of fudge.

I'd have to say that I definitely got the better end of the deal. Replacing our old, leaking tanks involved crawling into tight spots, disconnecting hoses, and cutting through fiberglass. None of it very pleasant, but being able to carry enough water for drinking, cooking, and washing up would be essential when we were in the Bahamas. For a while there it was touch and go when it looked like the new tanks we had purchased wouldn't fit. Somehow, Scooter managed to squeeze them in, finishing with plenty of time to spare before

Anabel's party.

When I got up on Sunday morning, the first thing I did was run the bathroom tap, squealing with joy at the water coming out of it. Then I swung by Charmaine's house to pick her up. Her husband, Dale, stowed two large trays of fudge in the trunk. Charmaine planted a kiss on his cheek, leaving a smear of bright pink lipstick behind. He smiled, then swatted her rear as he opened the passenger door for her.

"That man sure is a keeper," Charmaine said as we pulled out of the driveway. "There were a dozen red roses waiting for me next to the bed when I woke up this morning."

"Don't tell me I missed your birthday," I said.

"No, that's not for ages."

"It's your anniversary then?" When she shook her head no, I asked, "Then why the roses?"

"He told me that it's to celebrate

International Bagel Day."

"Bagels?"

"Uh-huh, I love bagels, but I can't eat them on account of this new diet I'm on."

I groaned. "Please don't tell me you're doing Rutamentals."

"Gosh, no." She wrinkled her nose. "I'd rather eat Styrofoam packing peanuts than eat a rutabaga."

"Then why no bagels?"

"Cream cheese. Ever since I stopped being a vegan, it's been my downfall. I can't eat a bagel without spreading a lot of cream cheese on it. And I mean a lot." She sighed. "So I had to give up bagels. Dale knew that today would be tough for me, so he got me flowers to cheer me up."

"The two of you are a great couple," I said.

"Oh, honey, we're just like any other couple. Sometimes we fight like cats and dogs."

As I turned onto Main Street, I said, "Scooter and I had a huge fight recently. It was our first one in ages."

"But everything's better now, isn't it?"

"Uh-huh. We had a really good talk. I don't know if I told you this before, but I offered to take over managing our finances so that I could be more involved in things. I knew Scooter always worried about money, but I didn't realize how bad it was until there was this little issue with the password to our online account. And then he had wanted to invest in Fletcher's business opportunity. The whole thing was a nightmare."

"I didn't know the two of you had money problems," Charmaine said. "Can I do anything to help?"

I pulled into the Sugar Shack's parking lot, then turned to her. "No, it's nothing like that. I didn't realize how bad his anxiety was about the possibility that we might not have enough money one day, not that we have money problems now. We're fine financially. Scooter does well with his business, and I've been bringing in a little extra."

"So, what's the problem?" she asked.

"Scooter has really been looking forward to taking time off and going sailing. I know you don't have a sailboat, but they can be real money pits. He wants to make sure we have enough of a cushion so that we don't have to stress about it when things break." I unbuckled my seatbelt, then added, "Sailing has been his dream for years. I really hope the reality of it lives up to his expectations. That's why I keep trying to rein him in."

Charmaine chuckled. "I can't imagine that's easy. His face lights up when he talks about *Marjorie Jane*."

"Oh, don't I know it," I said. "I keep telling him that we need to take baby steps. Let's get to the Bahamas, then we can decide if we really want to keep going onward from there or come back to Florida."

"What's he going to do about his business while you guys are in the Bahamas?"

"We're both going to try to work remotely and see how it goes. He's mentioned the possibility of bringing on a partner. But having seen what happened between Fletcher and Herbert, I'm not so sure that's a good idea. Someone could wind up dead." When I saw the expression on Charmaine's face, I said, "Sorry, that was a bad joke, I know."

"You still think it was murder, don't you?"

"I know it was. But apart from Scooter, no one else seems to agree with me, so I'm washing my hands of the matter. In fact, I'm going to stop sticking my nose into things which don't concern me. From now on, my only investigations are going to be about alien abductions, not murder." I snatched my purse from the backseat. "Come on, let's grab Penelope and the catering, then head back to *Marjorie Jane*. The other ladies are going to be there soon. Then it will be time to set sail for Destiny Key and party."

* * *

When I spotted Sylvia and Madison sitting at one of the tables on the marina patio, I stopped in my tracks. "I wonder what they're up to," I said under my breath.

Charmaine shifted the trays she was carrying in her arms. "Are they here for Anabel's party?"

"Not that I know of," I said. "Maybe Anabel invited Sylvia, but she doesn't even know Madison, so I don't know why she would come."

Penelope put a hand over her eyes to shield them from the sun. "Are you talking about those two ladies?"

"Uh-huh. Sylvia is the older woman. She's the widow of the man who died on the cruise ship. The other woman is the girlfriend of Sylvia's nephew."

"I've seen the younger woman before," Penelope said. "I was at the jewelers. She wasn't happy. Though I'm not sure what they did to upset her."

Charmaine nudged me. "They're headed this way."

Sylvia gave me an air kiss, then said, "We weren't sure where your boat was docked. I was worried that we were late, but it looks like we came just in time."

I furrowed my brow. "In time?"

"For the party, silly." Sylvia looked at our carts, which were laden with coolers and boxes. "What's all that?"

"The catering. Sandwiches, quiche, salads, and of course ..." I smiled at Penelope, "the most delicious pastries you'll ever taste in your life."

Sylvia frowned. "You're schlepping that all to your boat? I don't know what kind of third-rate caterer you're using, but they should have delivered this, then set everything up for you."

I cleared my throat. "Sorry, I should have introduced you to Penelope. She owns the Sugar Shack."

"Sugar Shack, that's a cute name for an ice cream parlor," Sylvia said dismissively.

Penelope arched an eyebrow, but bit her tongue.

"It's not an ice cream parlor," I said. "It's primarily a bakery, but they also do light lunches. They're the ones doing the catering for Anabel's party."

Sylvia looked back and forth between me and Penelope, then said, "Oh, you're such a card, Mollie. Isn't she a card, Madison?"

Madison bit back a smile, then shook Penelope's hand. "It's lovely to meet you," she said. "I'm sure the food will be delicious."

It all seemed to go over Sylvia's head.

I put it down to fatigue. There were dark circles under her eyes. I couldn't imagine that she had been sleeping well. When you're exhausted, you can't think properly and sometimes even say tactless things.

"Here, let me help you with that." Madison grabbed one of the trays Charmaine was carrying. She smiled brightly and looked at me. "Which way to your boat?"

Penelope and I led the way, pulling the carts behind us. The others followed, chatting away about wedding dresses.

When Sylvia started describing the latest trends in wedding veils, I gulped. Earlier in the week, I had spoken with Sylvia and told her that Anabel wanted to put wedding planning on hold for the time being. Apparently, I had been too subtle in my approach since Sylvia was practically gushing about handmade Italian lace.

When we reached *Marjorie Jane*, I pulled Sylvia aside. "I don't think Anabel is planning on wearing a veil. In fact, she and the chief are thinking of eloping. So maybe today, we could focus on just having fun, and not talking about wedding planning?"

"Eloping? Oh, that would be a shame, but I understand." She looked in Madison's direction. "I'll tell her to keep the talk about wedding planning to a minimum."

"Is Madison helping you with your wedding planning business?"

Sylvia lowered her voice. "No, I'm helping Madison plan her wedding. I think she'd look gorgeous in a full wedding veil, don't you?"

"The woman is stunning. She'd look gorgeous in a garbage bag," I said.

Madison walked over to us, wagging a finger playfully. "What are you two whispering about?"

"You know how terrible I am at

keeping secrets," Sylvia said. "I told Mollie about you and Anthony."

"Well, hopefully Mollie is better at keeping secrets than you are," Madison said. "I don't want Anthony finding out that I know what he has planned."

I held my hand up. "Wait a minute, I'm confused. Did Anthony propose?"

"Madison found an engagement ring." Sylvia couldn't contain her glee. "Anthony told her that he has something special planned for her tomorrow. She saw a brochure for hot air ballooning peeking out of his briefcase. He's going to propose while they're up in the air, I just know it."

I recalled how Anthony had seemed poised to pop the question to Madison that night at Chez Poisson. Despite their very public blow-up, he had seemed confident that they would make up. It looked like things were back on track for the two of them to get engaged. Smiling at Madison, I asked her when she had found the ring.

"Yesterday," she said breezily while she pulled a pack of cigarettes out of her tote bag.

"I'm sorry, but you can't smoke aboard the boat," I said. "It's a fire hazard."

Madison waved a hand around the dock. "Is it okay if I smoke here?"

"That's fine. But maybe over there so that you're downwind of us?"

Madison nodded, then plucked a cigarette out of the pack. "No problem."

"You're the first person I've met who smokes pink cigarettes. I've only ever seen the white ones before," I said. "Yours are, uh, quite distinctive."

"Sylvia gave them to me," Madison said.

"They're from Paris," Sylvia said as she dug around in her purse. After finding the gum she had been looking for, she added, "If you're going to smoke, you might as well do it in style."

"It must be hard these days since so

many places don't let you smoke," I said.

"It's understandable," Madison said with a shrug.

"Did they let you smoke aboard the cruise ship?" I asked.

"The smoking areas on the ship were dreadful," Sylvia said. "Just because you're going to have a cigarette doesn't mean you want to breathe in everyone else's secondhand smoke."

Madison chuckled. "I know some ex-smokers who enjoy secondhand smoke on occasion."

"Is that where you smoked?" I asked the young woman. "In the designated smoking areas?"

Madison chewed on her lip for a moment. "Actually, I found a quiet spot that no one else seemed to know about. I probably shouldn't have smoked there, but . . ." Her voice trailed off as she looked at the cigarette in her hand. Then she smiled brightly. "Speaking of, let me go have that smoke."

As she walked to the end of the dock, puffing on her cigarette, I wondered if finding the pink cigarette butt at the crime scene had been innocent after all. Maybe that was the quiet spot she had found to smoke at. I shrugged. That had to be the explanation, didn't it? After all, she was with Sylvia at the magic show the night Fletcher was killed.

Oh, my gosh, stop it, I told myself. *You are not investigating a murder. Who cares where you found a cigarette butt? Who cares who killed Fletcher?*

Then a little voice inside me replied, *You, that's who.*

* * *

The sail to Destiny Key was amazing. At first, I battled my nerves and self-doubt. Scooter and I considered ourselves co-captains, but this was the first time I had captained the boat on my own. It was incredibly daunting. But after a while, I relaxed, enjoying the feeling of being in charge. Of course, Mrs. Moto kept me on my toes, meowing whenever she thought the sails weren't trimmed properly.

Pretty in Pink was sailing on a parallel course off to our port. Penny had half the guests on her boat, while I was ferrying the rest of the ladies. Anabel was aboard my boat, lounging in the cockpit with her two dogs, Frick and Frack, curled up at her feet. At first, she had been surprised to see Sylvia and Madison, but she quickly made them feel welcome. To her credit, Sylvia didn't mention Anabel's wedding, probably because she was too busy taking care of Madison, who was feeling seasick.

After we anchored, a dinghy raced toward us. As it neared *Marjorie Jane*, Ben cut the engine and called out, "Ahoy there, matey!"

Scooter was seated at the bow. He grabbed hold of the side of *Marjorie*

Jane, then tied the dinghy up. Once it was secure, he gave me a mock salute, "Good job setting the hook, Cap'n."

I smiled, reflecting on the fact that a year ago I would have thought any mention of a hook meant some sort of pirate with a peg leg, parrot on his shoulder, and a hook to replace a hand that a shark must have bitten off at one point. Now I knew that it referred to making sure the anchor was secure.

Scooter pointed back at the beach. "We have everything set up for you ladies. Tables for the food, a volleyball net, picnic blankets, and lots of throw pillows to lounge against."

"What is it with women and throw pillows?" Ben scoffed.

"They make things more homey," I said. "And they're cute. Everyone loves cute things, don't they?"

Scooter grinned at our young friend. "When you meet the right woman, you'll happily let her fill your boat with throw pillows."

Ben frowned. "Yeah, I'm not having much luck with the ladies these days."

Scooter and I exchanged glances. The poor guy had had his heart broken so many times in the past year. Almost as many times as I had stumbled across dead bodies.

"Have you met the crew of *Orangutan* yet?" I asked tentatively.

"*Orangutan*? That's a funny name for a boat," Ben said.

"It had an orange hull, go figure," Scooter said.

I rolled my eyes. Scooter never had been fond of any shade of orange. "Anyway, I happen to know one of the girls on board is single, and she's really into pirates."

Ben's eyes lit up. "A lassie who likes sailing and pirates? Timber me shivers. I'll have to introduce myself."

"Just take it slow," Scooter cautioned Ben before turning to me. "Want us to take the food over in Ben's dinghy? Then you could start ferrying the ladies over in our dinghy."

I ended up making four trips to the island, shuttling all the guests and their belongings. On my final trip, Scooter helped me pull the dinghy up onto the beach. "The guys and I are going to check out Warlock's Manor."

"Be careful," I said. "Remember what happened last time we were there."

"Things have changed on Destiny Key since that whole thing with Chief Tyler," Scooter said. "The islanders are a little bit more receptive to outsiders."

"'Little bit' being the key phrase there," I said wryly.

"Don't worry, Cap'n," Scooter said as he kissed me on the cheek.

"Cap'n," I repeated. "That might be the best pet name you've had for me so far."

"It's a title, not a pet name," he teased. "We'll meet you back here later to help clean up. Have fun."

It wasn't long before the ladies started digging into the food. I piled a slice of quiche, a curry chicken sandwich, and a few lemon bars on my plate, then joined Sylvia and Madison on a blanket underneath a palm tree.

"These sandwiches are delicious," Sylvia said. "You must tell me the name of your caterer."

Madison chuckled as I pointed at Penelope. "That lady there. She owns the Sugar Shack."

"Oh, yes, the ice cream parlor," Sylvia said.

While Sylvia munched on another sandwich, I turned to Madison. "When are you thinking of getting married?"

"I'd love to have a spring wedding, but that's probably not enough time to organize everything." She smiled at Sylvia. "Even with the best wedding planner in the world."

Sylvia beamed at the compliment. "I

think an autumn wedding would be nice. We could do an enchanted forest theme. Moss table runners, fairy lights, greenery everywhere."

"The wedding arch could be made out of vines," Madison said.

"I can picture you in an exquisite gold lace gown," Sylvia said.

Madison got a faraway look in her eyes. "I always thought I would wear a white dress." After a beat, she grabbed her plate. "I'm going to get another slice of that quiche."

As Madison walked toward the buffet table, Sylvia said, "An autumn wedding would be best. Anthony is going to have a lot on his plate. They don't need to rush things."

"I suppose he'll be quite busy learning the ropes of running a business."

"Nonsense," Sylvia snapped. "He's a smart boy."

I held up my hand. "Don't get me wrong. I'm sure he's very smart. What I meant was that the transition is happening sooner than planned."

Sylvia relaxed. "Yes, that's true. Fletcher's passing was unexpected. But Anthony had worked closely with him, so he's up to speed on everything. You and Scooter should reconsider investing. Anthony has had lots of inquiries from people who are eager to sign up. This opportunity won't be around forever."

"Oh, have the guys who were on the cruise decided to invest?" I asked.

"They'd be fools to pass it up," she said, deftly giving me a non-answer.

"What about Dominic?" When Sylvia furrowed her brow, I said, "I thought he was a potential investor. Wasn't that why he was on the cruise?"

Sylvia took a deep breath. "I suppose it's okay to tell you the truth now. Dominic wasn't a potential investor. He's a distant cousin from Bratslavia."

"Bratslavia? I've never heard of that

country. Is that one of the former Soviet socialist republics?"

"Oh, maybe I'm thinking of bratwurst," Sylvia said vaguely. "Anyway, Dominic is an ex-convict. Fletcher has been looking out for him. He's actually a sweet guy, just not very bright. And his English isn't very good. Fletcher thought it would be nice to bring him on the cruise, but he didn't want anyone to know about his criminal background."

"So he made up a story about him being an investor?"

"Well, Dominic does have a lot of money," Sylvia said. "He won the lottery last year. He may be dumb, but he sure is lucky."

I smiled. "And here I thought I was his Lady Luck."

"What's that?" Sylvia asked.

"Oh, nothing, it was something he said to me on the cruise ship."

Sylvia's face clouded. "I don't think I'll ever want to go on another cruise again.

Too many sad memories."

I didn't know how to console her, so I simply squeezed Sylvia's hand. She gave me a faint smile. "I think I'm going to go for a walk. Tell Madison where I went, won't you?"

After her walk, Sylvia was more like her usual self, chatting with the other women about beach-themed weddings. The rest of the afternoon went off without a hitch. Some of the women played volleyball, while others went swimming. Other ladies, myself included, chilled out on the beach blankets and listened to music.

"These throw pillows make all the difference," I said.

"You can never have too many throw pillows," Anabel said. "Tiny is steeling himself for when we move back in together after the wedding. He knows I've bought tons more pillows since the divorce."

Penny piped up. "I just ordered some

new ones with anchors on them."

"Let me guess," I said. "They're pink."

She laughed. "Is there any other color?"

"Hey, what are they doing here? Don't they know it's girls only?" Anabel smiled at the Yorkies nestled in her lap. "Present company excepted."

I lifted my head and saw Scooter and the other guys walking toward us. "They must be heading back to Ben's boat. It's getting late. We should probably get moving too."

Penny pointed at the other end of the beach. "But Ben's dinghy is over there."

"I think something is wrong," I said, noting the grim expression on Scooter's face.

"Did someone get hurt?" Anabel asked, rising to her feet. "Is Tiny alright?"

"They all look okay," I said. "It must be something else."

"Do you know where Mrs. Tolliver is?"

Chief Dalton asked as he approached us.

"Sylvia? She went for a swim with Madison." I pointed at a cluster of palm trees which shielded a small protected cove.

The chief nodded, then squeezed Anabel's hand before striding briskly down the beach.

"What's going on?" I asked.

Scooter cleared his throat. "The chief just got a call from the police dispatcher. Anthony is dead."

CHAPTER 13
PARROT ATTACK

"Anthony's dead?" My eyes widened. "What happened? A car accident? A shark attack? A heart attack?"

Scooter held up his hand. "All I know is that the owner of the Honeysuckle Cottages found him. She called 911, but it was too late."

"Inside his cottage?" When Scooter nodded, I said, "Okay, then it wasn't a shark attack. At least I hope it wasn't a shark attack. If it were, that would mean sharks now have the ability to walk on land and come into our homes. Or worse, they're bipedal, like Bigfoot."

"You're not making any sense," Scooter said gently.

I ran my fingers through my hair. "You're right. I've had sharks on my brain lately. Probably shouldn't have watched that documentary the other night. Let's see, it probably wasn't a heart attack. Anthony was only in his thirties."

"There's no point in conjecture," Scooter said.

"He's right," Anabel said. "Tiny will get to the bottom of it."

I put my hand on her arm. "What a horrible end to your party."

She gave a wry smile. "It wouldn't be the first time that something like this interrupted a party, or a romantic dinner, or even a quiet night in watching a movie."

"It can't be easy being married to a police officer," I said.

"It comes with the territory." Anabel smiled. "Tiny might say that being married to an artist isn't easy either. When I'm in the flow and totally focused on a painting, I forget about everything else. There have been a few times when Tiny and I were supposed to meet somewhere, and I didn't show up. Totally spaced that we had plans. Sometimes, I even forget to eat and sleep."

"I could never forget to eat," I said.

Penny interjected. "Speaking of eating, why don't I start cleaning up the food containers. I think the party is probably over now."

"Ben and I can give you a hand," Ned offered.

"I'll help too," Anabel said.

"No, this is your special day," Penny said. "You should relax, not clean up."

"Well, if you're sure. I'll take the dogs for a walk then." Frick and Frack started yipping at the mention of a walk. When

Mrs. Moto meowed and rubbed against Anabel's legs, she said to the cat, "Do you want to come too?"

As Anabel and her three furry friends strolled down the beach and the others went to clean up, I turned to Scooter. "Do you think it could have been foul play? Could Anthony's death be related to Fletcher's murder?"

He sighed. "I thought we had decided that we weren't looking into that anymore."

"Wait, just hear me out. Remember how Herbert and Anthony came to a sudden agreement that Herbert would retire and sell the business to Anthony? Well, you have to admit that was awfully suspicious. Why would Herbert ever have agreed to that unless he was coerced somehow?"

"Herbert said that he was looking forward to retirement," Scooter said. "In fact, I saw him at the marina a couple of days ago. He was with Penny, arranging to have his boat trucked from Cleveland to Coconut Cove."

"Maybe he wasn't as happy about retiring as you thought." I chewed on my lip, then said, "What if he decided that he wanted to change their agreement permanently?"

Scooter arched an eyebrow. "Permanently? You think Herbert killed Anthony?"

"It's a possibility, isn't it? Herbert hated Anthony. And once you've already killed someone, what's one more death?"

"You think he killed Fletcher and Anthony?" Scooter shook his head. "I don't know."

"Well, who else would it be?"

Scooter paced back and forth for a few moments, then turned to me. "Where's that notebook of yours?"

I grinned. "So the investigation is back on?"

"Maybe." He ruffled my hair, then held out his hand. "Did you bring your notebook?"

"Of course. It's in my backpack, along with my other essentials like the first aid kit and a bag of M&M'S" While he flipped through the pages, I said, "They're headed back this way."

"Who?" Scooter asked absently.

"The chief and Sylvia. I don't know where Madison is."

"What about Dominic?"

"Dominic isn't here," I said.

"Huh?" Scooter furrowed his brow.

"He's not on Destiny Key. Unless you saw him when you guys were at Warlock's Manor?"

Scooter shook his head. "No, what I meant was that maybe Dominic killed Anthony."

"I'm not so sure about that." I quickly filled Scooter in on my conversation with Sylvia. "He's some sort of rich distant cousin."

"So, he's not a loan shark?"

I shrugged. "I'm not sure if he loaned

Fletcher money or just gave it to him."

"But the watch and the car keys? How do you explain those?" Scooter scratched his head. "Who was it again who told us Dominic was a loan shark?"

"It'll be in the notebook, but—" I stopped mid-sentence when Sylvia and the chief came up to us. I passed the notebook to Scooter discretely, then gave Sylvia a hug. "I'm so sorry to hear about your nephew."

"Thank you," she said, her face streaked with tears. "Anthony was helping me make the memorial service arrangements for Fletcher, and now I have to . . ." Sylvia collapsed into my arms. In between sobs, she said, "Now I'll have to help my brother and sister-in-law with the arrangements for their son."

"Why don't we get you back to the boat?" Scooter suggested.

Sylvia nodded gratefully, tucking her hand through his arm. "Will you tell Madison where I've gone? She wanted some time to herself."

"Of course." I glanced over to where the others were cleaning up. "We shouldn't be too long."

After they left, Chief Dalton sighed. "Poor woman, losing two family members in a week."

"What was the cause of death?" I asked.

"It was an accident."

I cocked my head to one side. "What kind of accident?"

"I don't think you'd find it very interesting," he said dryly.

"So not a shark attack, then."

The chief rolled his eyes. "No, not sharks."

"Oh, come on, tell me. You already told Sylvia and Madison, didn't you?"

He exhaled sharply. "Fine. I'll tell you, but only because otherwise you'll pester me to death. He was electrocuted."

"Electrocuted? How? Did he stick a knife in an outlet?"

"The man was in his thirties, not a kid," he scoffed. "Of course, he didn't stick a knife in an outlet."

"Well, then how did it happen?"

"A faulty charger."

I took a deep breath. "That's awful."

"It happens more often than you'd think, especially with cheap knock-off chargers," the chief said. "It's a shame they didn't find him sooner. Maybe he could have been saved."

"Scooter said that the owner of the bed-and-breakfast found Anthony. Is that right?"

"Yes, when she went in to clean the cottage." The chief looked at me. "Your friends might need your help finding another place to stay tonight."

"That's a good point. I don't think that they'd want to stay at the place where Anthony died. Why don't I see if I can make them reservations at the Golden Astrolabe Hotel?"

"I think that would be for the best. Can

you let them know that I'll check in with them tomorrow? Just a few formalities, that's all." The chief frowned. "It will be especially hard on Mr. Tolliver's fiancée."

"Madison and Anthony weren't engaged yet," I said.

"Hmm, I must have misunderstood." He looked at Ned and Ben, who were folding up tables. "I better go and help them out."

As the chief walked away, I called out, "Hey, what kind of charger was it?"

"A phone charger," the chief said over his shoulder.

All I could think of was that being electrocuted by a phone charger seemed like an awfully ironic way to die for the soon-to-be CEO of a telecommunications company.

* * *

On our sail back to Coconut Cove, both Sylvia and Madison were understandably subdued. Sylvia spent most of the trip back stroking Mrs. Moto while Madison stared vacantly into space. That is when Madison wasn't retching over the side of the boat. The poor girl—not only was she afraid of water, she also suffered from terrible seasickness.

"Do you want some ginger tea?" Anabel offered. "That might help settle your stomach."

"Okay," Madison said, then sank back against a cushion.

While Anabel went down below to boil some water, I asked one of the other ladies to take over the helm. I sat next to Madison and asked her if there was anything else we could do to help.

"No, thanks," she said. "I'm starting to feel better."

The greenish hue of her face made me doubt that she was really on the mend, but I didn't say anything. "It won't be much longer. Can you hang on for another half hour or so?"

Madison nodded, then gave Anabel a weary smile when she handed her a mug. As Madison blew on the tea to cool it down, Sylvia let out a deep breath.

"What's wrong?" Madison asked the older woman. "Besides the obvious."

"I was just noticing your lovely manicure," Sylvia said.

Madison held out her hand, inspecting her teal and navy striped nails. "I had them done at a little nail salon in town. The Nail Nook, I think it's called."

"You have such beautiful, long fingers," Sylvia said. "Imagine how lovely the engagement ring would have looked on your hand."

Anabel and I exchanged glances, and I heard a woman behind me gasp. Was now really the time to remind Madison that Anthony had been about to propose to her?

Sylvia looked around at the women in

the cockpit and explained, "Madison was hanging up one of Anthony's suit jackets when she found a velvet box. Well, of course, curiosity got the better of her. I mean, who among us wouldn't be tempted to peek inside? Anyway, it was an engagement ring. Anthony had been planning on proposing." Sylvia turned to Madison. "What did it look like, dear?"

"It was an engagement ring," Madison said before sipping on her tea.

"Well, I know that silly. I assume it was a diamond?" Madison nodded brusquely, signaling that she wanted the conversation to end, but Sylvia continued undeterred. "What kind of cut? A classic solitaire? One with side stones? An emerald cut? What kind of setting? Gold? Platinum?"

"It was a nice ring. Can we just leave it at that?" Madison set the mug down and clutched her stomach. "I think I'm going to be sick again."

After that, Sylvia fell silent. Madison dozed off, only waking when we arrived at the marina. Once I had secured the boat and said goodbye to the rest of the guests, I drove Sylvia and Madison to the Golden Astrolabe Hotel. "We can arrange for you to get your car tomorrow," I told them. "I don't think either of you should be driving right now."

As Madison thanked me, I noticed that her color looked better now that she was back on land. During the short drive to the hotel, Sylvia asked me if I wanted to come view some properties with her later in the week.

"Are you still planning on moving to Coconut Cove?" I asked.

"I'm certainly not going back to Cleveland. It's time for a fresh start." Sylvia looked at Madison. "What about you, dear? What are you going to do?"

"I have no idea," Madison quietly said. "Anthony was my whole life."

As I pulled into the hotel's circular driveway, the doorman opened the passenger door and helped Sylvia out of the car. Before he could do the same for Madison, she pushed past him, striding quickly into the lobby.

"She must be feeling ill again," Sylvia said as I walked around the other side of the car.

"I was surprised that she decided to go out on the boat given how seasick she gets," I said.

Sylvia furrowed her brow. "I was too. But when I was getting ready this morning, she came by my cottage. When I told her where I was going, she insisted on joining. I hope Anabel didn't mind that she crashed the party."

"Not at all," I said. "I'm just sorry that it ended so tragically for the both of you."

"Maybe if Madison hadn't come, this wouldn't have happened. She could have saved Anthony from being electrocuted." Sylvia dabbed at her eyes with a tissue. "Sorry, I'm being unfair. It wasn't Madison's fault."

"It wasn't anyone's fault," I said automatically, not really believing my own words. "Don't forget that Chief Dalton is going to stop by tomorrow to ask you a few questions. Did you want me to be there?"

"No, that's okay. He said it would just be a few formalities." She looked inside her purse. "Did I leave my phone charger aboard your boat? You can't miss it, it's green."

"I'm not sure. I can check for you when I get back. Do you need it right away?"

"No, I can borrow a spare one from Anthony." Sylvia put a hand over her mouth. "I can't believe I said that. He's gone."

"Do you want me to stay with you for a while?" I offered.

She straightened her shoulders, then gave me a quick hug. "Thanks, but I'll be fine."

As she walked into the lobby, I decided that Sylvia wouldn't be the only person Chief Dalton would be speaking to tomorrow. I had a few questions for him as well. For example, if you wanted to electrocute someone with a phone charger, how would you go about it?

* * *

"Mollie, you need to get yourself down to the police station. Pronto," Charmaine Buttercup barked at me the next morning. I squinted at my phone. What time was it?

Rubbing my eyes, I sat up in bed and pressed the phone back to my ear. "What's going on?"

"The chief looks like he's going to explode," she said. "You'll never guess who just barged into his office with a stack of wedding magazines."

"Sylvia." I sighed. Wedding planning seemed to be how Sylvia coped with her grief. And Anthony's death would have her reeling.

"But wait, that's not the best part. She brought a parrot with her. A trained parrot."

"It's seven in the morning," I said. "Where did she get a trained parrot at this hour?"

"Heaven only knows."

I furrowed my brow. "What exactly is the parrot trained to do? Is it an emotional support animal?"

"No, it's for weddings. When the bride and groom are ready to exchange rings, the bird swoops in, wedding bands clutched in its beak. After it drops them in the minister's hand, it calls out, 'Pretty bride, pretty bride,' 'I do, I do,' and 'Nice kitty-cat, nice kitty-cat.'"

"What do cats have to do with exchanging rings?" I asked.

"I didn't ask. Maybe the bird's trainer also has a cat—" Charmaine suddenly yelped.

"What's wrong?"

"That creature just tried to land on my head. Get down here now!" she said before ending the call.

When I got to the station, I had to bite back a smile. Charmaine and the parrot were having a stand-off. She was holding her ground on one side of her desk, her arms folded across her chest and her hair sticking up in all directions. The parrot was perched on a coat stand, squawking, "Pretty lady, pretty lady."

When the bird swooped at her, Charmaine ducked not a moment too soon, just missing her. After it circled back to the coat stand, Charmaine stood and jabbed a finger in the parrot's direction. "Ha ha, you missed. Better luck next time."

I pointed toward the chief's office, and Charmaine nodded before engaging in another round with her nemesis. After taking a deep breath, I knocked on the door.

"Enter," Chief Dalton said brusquely.

Sylvia beamed at me when I walked in, patting the chair next to her. "We were just talking about you."

"Me?" I squeaked, worried that she had plans for me and the parrot.

"What do you think about wearing an eye patch?"

"An eye patch? Um, why?"

"Well, since you and the bridesmaids are going to be dressed as pirate wenches, I thought an eye patch would be a cute touch." She held up her hand. "Now, I know what you're thinking. Eye patches aren't very feminine, but it's going to be made of pink lace to match your petticoat."

"Ah, this explains the parrot." I turned to the chief. "So you're going with a pirate themed wedding now?"

He scowled. "Can you please explain to your friend that I have no intention of wearing any outfit that includes a peg leg and a sword?"

"This sounds more like something Ben would do if he ever got married," I said.

Sylvia's eyes lit up. "Ben? Ben Morretti? That's the young man who suggested the idea."

"Ben is a bit obsessed with pirates," I said.

"I'm going to kill him," the chief muttered.

I put my hand on Sylvia's arm. "Chief Dalton is a pretty busy man. Tell you what, why don't you and I go have breakfast, then we can brainstorm some other ideas for the wedding?"

"Breakfast sounds good. I've been craving a spinach salad." After she got to her feet and stowed the wedding magazines back in her bag, she turned to the chief. "Didn't you want to talk to me about Anthony?"

The chief looked torn. On one hand, he needed to follow-up with her regarding Anthony's death. On the other, he was probably terrified that Sylvia would take the opportunity to turn the conversation back to the wedding.

His professionalism won out. "Yes, I have a few questions. A few formalities really."

Sylvia settled back in her chair and looked at him expectantly. "Go ahead."

The chief pulled a file folder toward him and opened it. "This is probably a long shot, but do you know when and where Mr. Wright purchased his cell phone charger?"

She shook her head. "I'm not sure."

"I seem to remember some sort of discussion on the cruise about some new phone chargers the company had been sent to test out," I said. "Could it have been one of those?"

"I have no idea," she said. "Fletcher didn't discuss business with me."

The chief made a note, then looked back at Sylvia. "Was Mr. Wright in the habit of listening to music on his phone."

"I guess." Sylvia furrowed her brow. "I think he was more into audiobooks."

Chief Dalton nodded. "He would wear headphones when he listened to them?"

"Most of the time," Sylvia said. "I don't think Madison liked his choice of books, so he didn't play them on the speakers very often. She is into historical romance and he always pooh-poohed her taste in fiction."

"What kind of books did he listen to?" I asked.

Chief Dalton frowned. "Mrs. McGhie," he cautioned.

I leaned back in my chair and made a motion of zipping my lips closed.

"He liked thrillers," Sylvia said.

"And what kind of headphones would he use?" the chief asked.

Sylvia shrugged. "The kind you stick in your ears."

"So earbuds, not headphones," I said.

The chief glared at me, then looked back at Sylvia. "Can you describe what your nephew's earbuds looked like?"

"I believe they were white." Sylvia fiddled with her necklace. "Why are you asking so many questions about Anthony's ear buds? Was that how he was electrocuted? Through his earbuds?"

"We won't know the official cause of death until we get the coroner's report back," the chief said.

"But you have an unofficial idea, don't you?" I asked.

The chief spread his hands in front of him. "I can't really say."

Sylvia pursed her lips. "But it was an accident, right?"

"I need to speak with Mr. Wright's fiancée," the chief said, not answering her question. "Is she still at the hotel?"

"Madison wasn't his fiancée. She wasn't actually part of the family yet," Sylvia said quietly. Then she fixed her gaze on the chief. "What color was the phone charger that Anthony was using?"

The chief hesitated for a moment, then said, "Green."

Sylvia rubbed her temples, then looked at me. "Is it okay if we skip breakfast? I think I need to lie down for a while."

"Of course," I said.

"Do you have any more questions?" she asked the chief.

"I think that will do it for now."

As he escorted Sylvia to the door of his office, she turned to him and said, "The two of you made it clear that you didn't want a fancy wedding. This pirate theme is the perfect alternative. Casual, fun, and a bit quirky. What do you think about having Anabel walk the plank instead of marching down the aisle? Do you think they'd let us build a mock pirate ship inside the church?"

Chief Dalton's jaw dropped. "Walk the plank?" he spluttered.

"I'll leave you to look into that, okay?"

She patted his arm, then gave me a wave before leaving his office.

The chief was speechless for a few moments, then he poked his head into the hallway and yelled after her, "Don't forget your parrot."

CHAPTER 14
UNDERWATER BASKET WEAVING

"Anthony's death wasn't an accident, was it?" I asked Chief Dalton.

"That would depend on what your definition of an accident is."

Shaking my head at his cryptic answer, I did a quick search on my phone. "According to this, 'an accident is an unfortunate incident that happens unexpectedly and unintentionally.' So my question is, was Anthony's death intentional?"

The chief grabbed a highlighter from his pencil holder. "I know you like pens. If I give this to you, will you go away?"

"Pink is not my favorite color."

"Fine. Blue then?"

"Yep, I like blue." When he thrust the pen into my hand, I added, "So to recap our conversation—"

The chief pointed at his door. "I thought we had an agreement. You get a pen and I get peace and quiet."

Ignoring his interruption, I continued, "As I was saying, Anthony was electrocuted. Last night you said it was his phone charger, but today, you asked Sylvia about Anthony's ear buds. How exactly does electrocution work?" I grabbed a blank piece of paper from the printer on top of the file cabinet next to the chief's desk. "You don't mind, do you?"

He rolled his eyes. "Of course not. Please, help yourself."

After scrawling down 'electrocution' on

the top of the page using my new highlighter, I drew a rough sketch of an electrical outlet, phone charger, cell phone, and earbuds underneath. "Let's see, power comes in from the outlet, through the charger, into the cell phone, and pops out through the earbuds."

"Did you just describe power as 'popping out'?"

"Hey, it's not like I went to college to study electrical engineering."

Chief Dalton bit back a smile. "No, somehow I can't picture you with an engineering degree. What did you major in?"

"It's not important." I thrust the paper onto his desk and pointed at my sketch. "Focus on this."

"Underwater basket weaving. That was it, wasn't it?"

I shook my head. "How about if we make a deal? You give me your undivided attention for the next ten minutes and then I'll tell you what I majored in."

"You're not exactly reliable when it comes to deals." He pointed at the highlighter in my hand. "But I know from experience that you're not going to leave my office until you've had your say."

I pointed at my sketch. "Now, if there was a power surge that came through the outlet, then Anthony's death could have been an unfortunate accident. I assume that they're checking the wiring at the bed-and-breakfast, but I bet they won't find any issues with it. We didn't have a lightning storm yesterday, and I'd guess that there weren't any issues on the power company's end."

The chief nodded his head ever so slightly. "Go on."

Indicating the picture I had drawn of the phone charger, I said, "This could be the problem. If it was one of those cheap counterfeit chargers, it might not have been able to prevent electric shock."

"That could be the cause." The chief held up his hand when I leaned forward. "I'm not saying it is. Just speculating, that's all. But if it was the cause, then it was still an unfortunate accident."

I grabbed a yellow highlighter from the pencil holder, then drew a circle around the phone charger for emphasis. "Unless someone deliberately gave it to Anthony to use, because they knew it could be hazardous."

Chief Dalton looked skeptical. "That's not a very smart way to murder someone. Give them a charger and hope that it kills them. While counterfeit chargers can cause electric shock, it's still pretty rare."

"But what if the killer upped the odds by doing something to the charger? I don't know, messed with the wiring somehow?" I tapped the highlighter on the table. "Now, let's see, who knows enough about phone chargers to do something like that?"

When the chief didn't respond, I said, "Do you want me to give you a hint? His name starts with an 'H' like, say, Herbert."

"Why would Herbert Miller have murdered him? From what I understand, the two men came to an amicable agreement about the company."

"Amicable, yeah right," I scoffed. "Herbert decided to alter the terms of their agreement, permanently. It would have taken some planning on his part, though. He had to swap out the chargers and . . ." My voice trailed off as I pondered the scenario. Finally, I sighed. "Actually, there still is a big element of chance. How could Herbert have been sure that Anthony would use his phone while it was charging? How could he have been sure the electrical shock would have been strong enough to kill him?"

Chief Dalton cocked his head to one

side and smirked. "That underwater basket weaving degree of yours sure isn't helping here."

"Your sarcasm isn't helping either," I retorted. Then my eyes widened. "Where exactly was Anthony when he died?"

"In his cottage at the bed-and-breakfast," the chief said.

"Where exactly in the cottage?" I made a quick sketch on the piece of paper, then jabbed my finger at it. "Was he in here?"

The chief raised an eyebrow. "What is that? A frog?"

"No, it's a bathtub. Anthony loved taking long, hot baths in the mornings. Was he listening to his phone while he was in the tub? Was his phone plugged in at the time? Even a first grader knows that electricity and water are a deadly combination."

Chief Dalton shrugged. "No comment."

I scooped up my new highlighter,

folded up the piece of paper and stuck them in my purse. "That's fine. I have other ways of getting to the bottom of this." I started to walk down the hallway to the reception area, but doubled back to stick my head in the chief's office. "Did you want me to tell Sylvia that it's all systems go for a pirate wedding?"

* * *

After Charmaine's early morning wake-up call and having to deal with Chief Dalton's evasiveness, I needed a hefty dose of chocolate. Naturally, I headed to the library.

"Any news on the job interview?" I asked Hudson as I examined the chocolate selection. It looked like there had been a recent run on the candy bars, so I had to settle for a dark chocolate pomegranate one. It wouldn't have been my first choice, but beggars can't be choosers.

Hudson waited until a mom and her

two pre-school aged kids walked into the children's reading room, then leaned over the counter. "I had it on Friday. No news back yet, but I think it went okay."

"Were you nervous?" I asked.

"So nervous, but I did some breathing exercises and meditation before the interview. That helped a lot."

"I've never meditated. You're not supposed to think about anything, right? My mind gets distracted easily. I doubt that it would cooperate."

"I was the same way at first. But you just have to practice. There's a great app you can try." Hudson pulled it up on his phone and showed it to me. "It has different types of guided meditations, including some for beginners."

"That looks like the app Scooter has on his phone," I said. "Sometimes, I wonder if my husband has been replaced by an alien. If you had mentioned meditation to him a year ago, he would have scoffed. Now he seems to have gone all New Age on me. Next thing you know he'll be burning scented candles and wearing crystals around his neck."

"Meditation is pretty mainstream these days. Even some high-powered business types on Wall Street meditate before they close an important deal. It's not just for hippies and celebrities." Hudson cocked his head to one side. "To be honest, I would have thought you'd be open to this sort of thing. It seems like it's right up your alley."

I held up my hand. "Oh, I'm open to it. It just surprised me to find out that Scooter is into it. But it seems to have worked wonders when it comes to his ability to deal with, um, let's just say, more gruesome things."

"Gruesome things? Like murder?" Hudson asked wryly. "By the way, what's going on with the investigation? My aunt hasn't mentioned anything about it lately."

"Which murder are you referring to?"

Hudson's body tensed. "There's more than one? When did this latest one happen?"

"Yesterday during Anabel's party."

"One of the guests was killed … That's horrible. Please tell me you're kidding."

"No, it's nothing like that. I mean someone was killed, and it is horrible, but it wasn't one of the women at the party."

"Then who died?" Hudson asked, his shoulders relaxing.

"Do you remember Sylvia, the wedding planner? The one who got in a fight with her husband here at the library?" Hudson nodded. "Well, she was at Anabel's party. Chief Dalton was on the island as well. He got a call that her nephew, Anthony, had been killed and he informed her."

"Oh, that poor lady. First she lost her husband and now her nephew." Hudson chewed on his lip. "I'm really surprised that Aunt Nancy didn't get on the phone right away to tell me about it. Two murders in, what, less than a week? That's the kind of thing she's all over."

"It was actually a little more than a week, but who's counting?"

Hudson smiled. "Other than the entire town of Coconut Cove? You do realize that people keep track of this sort of thing. Especially my aunt."

"Nancy doesn't know that it was murder. That's why she didn't call you. Anthony was electrocuted while he was taking a bath. Everyone just assumes it was an accident." I pointed at Hudson's phone. "He was listening to an audiobook at the time."

Hudson grimaced. "Yikes. That sounds like a horrific way to go."

"It makes the top ten list, for sure," I said.

"You've become quite the expert in death, haven't you?"

I furrowed my brow. "You make it

sound like I'm the Grim Reaper."

"No, you just have an unlucky tendency to stumble across dead bodies," he said.

"Well, I didn't find Anthony. So, thankfully, that won't get added to my body count." I pursed my lips. "I still can't believe people keep track of that sort of thing."

"It is a small town," Hudson said. "We find the strangest ways to amuse ourselves."

"Is the librarian role you interviewed for in a small town too?" I asked.

"Uh-huh. It sounds like it has some similarities to Coconut Cove. I think that will make it an easier transition." He crossed his fingers. "Assuming I get the job."

I smiled. "My gut tells me you're going to get it."

Dr. McCoy jumped onto the counter and rubbed his body against Hudson's face. "Where have you been, buddy?"

Hudson asked the cat.

I tucked my dark chocolate pomegranate bar in my purse, somewhat amazed that I hadn't eaten any of it yet. Who says I don't have willpower? Okay, it might have had more to do with the fact that I was going to have to pluck the pomegranate pieces out before the chocolate would be edible, and that was going to take some time.

"I should get going," I said. "There are some people I want to track down about this latest murder."

Hudson picked up a pen that Dr. McCoy had knocked on the floor, then asked, "So if everyone else thinks it was an accident, why do you think it was murder?"

"Too many things don't add up." I scratched Dr. McCoy's head, then did a double take when I saw Dominic walk through the entrance. "There's someone I never expected to see in a library."

As the muscular man walked past the display of new releases, he knocked some of the books off the table. Dr. McCoy leaped off the counter and padded over to inspect the mess. Dominic grinned when he saw the cat, crouching down to stroke him. "Pretty kitty, pretty kitty," he cooed.

Hudson walked over to help pick up the books. "Dr. McCoy seems to like you," he said to Dominic.

"Nice kitty," Dominic said as he scooped the cat into his arms. He stood, cuddling Dr. McCoy against his chest while Hudson rearranged the new release display.

"Can I help you with anything?" Hudson asked.

Dominic gently deposited the cat on the table, then said, "Cookbook."

"Sure, what kind of cookbook?"

"Rutabaga."

"Ah, I have just the thing for you." Hudson grinned as he grabbed a book from the table. "Trixie Tremblay's newest release."

Dominic pointed at the book. "Read."

"Are you from Coconut Cove?" When Dominic shook his head, Hudson said, "Unfortunately, I can't check it out to you, but you're more than welcome to read it here."

"Okay." Dominic opened the book and began to leaf through it.

"You might be more comfortable at one of the tables," Hudson suggested. "Dr. McCoy, why don't you show him the way?"

Dr. McCoy meowed, then raced over to a table by the window. Dominic turned to follow, then caught my eye. "Lady Luck."

Hudson looked at me quizzically. "It's a long story," I told him before greeting Dominic.

Dominic held up the cookbook, then pointed at me. "You, read."

"You want me to look at the book with

you?" Dominic nodded, and I followed him over to the table that Dr. McCoy was perched on. Dominic pulled out a chair for me, then sat next to me. As he flipped through the pages, I asked him what he was still doing in Coconut Cove.

"Take care of Sylvia," he said.

"That's sweet of you," I said. "She told me that you're a distant cousin. Where was it that you're from? She mentioned Bratslavia."

"Brat . . . bratwurst?" Dominic shook his head. "No. Bratwurst, bad. Rutabaga, good."

"Well, I would beg to differ," I said. "Have you seen Sylvia since Anthony was killed?"

Dominic furrowed his brow. "Anthony dead?"

"Yes, he died yesterday. Didn't you know?"

Dr. McCoy rolled over onto his back. Dominic rubbed the cat's tummy, then looked at me. "Sylvia sad?"

"Devastated. Madison too."

"Pretty kitty," Dominic cooed before removing a chain from around his neck. "I cheer up."

"You're going to cheer Sylvia and Madison up?"

"Magic." He pulled a small metal ring from his jeans pocket. Then he proceeded to hold the chain up and show me that it was clasped. Next, he held the chain in one hand and the ring in his other. Passing the chain through the ring a few times, he said, "No fall."

He waited patiently for a few moments when Dr. McCoy started batting at the chain. I pulled the cat into my lap. "Go ahead."

Dominic squinted, as though channeling his magical powers, then flicked the ring. He grinned, showing me that the ring was now attached to the chain. "Ta da!"

"Very impressive," I said. "I didn't

know you were a magician."

"No, no magician." He pulled out his phone and showed me a picture. "This, magician."

"Hey, that's Ragno, the Master of Illusions, isn't it? When did you take this?"

"Cruise ship."

"Oh my gosh, you went to the magic show the night Fletcher was killed. I forgot that you told me about that when we were at Trixie Tremblay's seminar."

"Yes. I see magic. I see Ragno. Ragno, good." He grinned as he swiped through his photos. "See, spiders."

I shuddered. "That's why I didn't stay for his act. I can't stand spiders. What did you think of his trick with the snakes?"

"Snakes?"

"Yes, Sylvia told me that Ragno does an impressive illusion with boa constrictors."

Dominic shook his head. "No snakes."

"Oh, you don't like snakes? I'm not a big fan either."

"No, no snakes." Dominic put the chain back around his neck and tucked the ring into his pocket. He pulled the cookbook toward him, "Rutabagas."

"Yeah, I'm not a big fan of rutabagas either. Tell you what, I'll let you look at the recipes on your own." As I grabbed my purse, I asked, "Where are you staying, by the way?"

Dominic looked up at me. "Gold. Gold compass."

"Hmm … I think you mean the Golden Astrolabe." When Dominic didn't respond, no doubt entranced by the glossy picture of Trixie Tremblay peeling a rutabaga, I shrugged. That was about as much useful information as I was going to get out of the man from Bratslavia. Time to track down my other suspects.

* * *

As I walked to the car, my phone rang. "It's your wonderful husband. Please pick up," the Bob Newhart soundalike said.

"Hey, Scooter," I said. "How was the dentist?"

"Fine. He put the new crown on. Pretty painless. What happened at the police station?"

"Sylvia showed up with a parrot."

"A parrot?"

"For the Dalton's pirate-themed wedding."

Scooter chuckled. "Pirates, huh? I never figured Chief Dalton as a swashbuckling kind of guy."

"Trust me, it wasn't his idea."

"That was the big emergency? Wedding planning?"

"Well, the parrot was trying to make a nest in Charmaine's hair, and the chief was desperate to get rid of Sylvia."

"So desperate that he asked you to come to the station? Wow, that is desperate."

"I'm pretty sure it was Charmaine's idea, but it worked out well. I got a chance to talk to the chief about Anthony's murder." After I told Scooter about my diagram and filled him in on the finer points of electrocution, I said, "Herbert had motive to kill both Fletcher and Anthony. I just can't work out how he managed to switch Anthony's phone charger."

"Sounds like we need to question him," Scooter said. "I have an appointment now, but we could try to track him down later today."

"What appointment? You already went to the dentist."

"Oh, um, this is something else."

"Are you keeping secrets from me?" I joked.

Scooter sighed. "It isn't really a secret, it's more that I'm not sure what you'll think if I tell you. It's kind of embarrassing."

"Your standard of embarrassment is different from mine," I said. "Is it as bad as the time when I tried to do a truck and trailer maneuver on the roller derby rink, ended up going head over heels and split the back of my pants? That was not the time to be wearing polka dot underwear."

He laughed. "No, nothing like that."

"Okay, then, tell me," I said, opening the car door and slipping onto the seat.

"I'm seeing a hypnotist. He's been helping me with my squeamishness."

"It's strange—"

Scooter interjected, "What, that I'm seeing a hypnotist?"

"No, that's not strange. Well, it's strange for you. Or at least unexpected."

"Then what's strange?"

"It seems like everyone has been talking about hypnotists these days. Hudson suggested I try it to help with my chocolate addiction. Sylvia is into it too. She recommended a guy named

Hank, who lives near Coconut Cove. Maybe the universe is trying to tell me something."

"Hank? Hypnotist Hank? That's who I've been seeing. In fact, I'm on my way there right now." Scooter paused for a moment, then said, "Want to meet me there? You can check it out for yourself."

After Scooter gave me the address, I drove to the outskirts of town. Hank's office was located in a small strip mall next to Pete's Gator Farm. Pete's was a popular tourist attraction in the area. I didn't get it. Why would anyone voluntarily pay good money to get up close and personal with alligators? People even paid extra to get a picture of themselves holding a baby gator. Personally, it seemed crazy to me, but not nearly as crazy as holding a large, hairy spider. Maybe Hank had strategically located his office for just that reason—helping people cope with being face-to-face with scary reptiles through hypnosis.

When I pulled into the parking lot, I saw Scooter chatting outside with Sylvia. She had dark circles under her eyes that even the best concealer in the world couldn't disguise. After I gave her a hug, I told her I was surprised to see her out and about. "I thought you weren't feeling well."

"I'm hoping to get an emergency appointment with Hank," Sylvia said, clutching at her necklace. "The stress is getting to me."

"Understandable," Scooter said. "Losing your husband and your nephew in a week would be too much for anyone to deal with."

"How does hypnosis help with stress?" I asked.

"I've been falling back into bad habits as a way of dealing with the stress. A hypnotist plants suggestions when you're in a trance. The suggestions help you control your behavior better."

"I eat chocolate in certain conditions," Scooter said. "Hank's techniques are helping me cope when those situations arise."

"How does it work?" I asked.

"He helps me visualize having a more positive reaction when confronted with disturbing situations," Scooter said. "The suggestions that he plants are things like, 'When I see a dead body, I feel calm and collected,' and 'When someone is bleeding, I administer first aid without fainting.' He also taught me a ritual to do, which helps ground me in stressful moments."

"The one where you do that breathing thing, tug your earlobes, and press your nose?" I asked.

"That's the one," Scooter said. "It really helps."

Sylvia pressed her hands together so tightly that I thought she was going to lose feeling in her fingers. "I have a ritual like that myself, but it isn't working these days."

The door to the office opened and a tall man wearing a green cape poked his head out. "I thought I heard someone out here." When he saw Sylvia, he pulled her into an embrace. "Oh, sweetheart, I heard about what happened."

"Is there any chance you could see me, Hank? I've been . . ." her voice trailed off as tears streamed down her face.

Hank put an arm around the distraught woman's shoulders, then gave Scooter a questioning look. "Do you mind waiting?"

"No, that's fine," Scooter said. "Sylvia needs your help more than I do right now. Mollie and I can go get some coffee and come back later."

"So this is the famous Mollie." Hank drew his cape around himself, then bowed with a flourish. When he drew himself back up, he snapped his fingers and a bouquet of paper flowers suddenly appeared in his hand. As he presented them to me, he said, "It's a pleasure to finally meet you."

"Likewise," I said, pretending to smell the flowers. "Sylvia told me that she used to work with you back in Cleveland as a magician's assistant."

"I was lucky that she graced me with her presence on stage. She was a marvel. Such a stunning woman." He winked at Sylvia. "The audience couldn't take their eyes off you."

I cocked my head to one side. "A pretty woman is good for misdirection, huh? That way people don't notice how you pull off your tricks."

Hank put his hands on his hips and said with mock indignation. "Misdirection? Never. I'm a magician, not a con artist."

Sylvia tugged at his arm. "Did I tell you I saw Ragno on the cruise ship?"

"Oh, that would have been a treat," Hank said. "Did he conjure up boa constrictors?"

"Of course. Making snakes appear and disappear is his trademark illusion," she said.

"What about the volunteers from the audience? Did any of them faint?" Hank turned to Scooter and me. "Did you see Ragno's act as well? The last time I saw it, one of the ladies collapsed on stage."

"Honestly, if I had been there and someone dragged me up on stage, I would have fainted too," I confessed.

"We can sign you up for a series of sessions," Hank suggested. "After you've finished, you'll be able to hold a dozen snakes in your arms without batting an eye."

Scooter laughed. "You might want to start with something easier, like Mollie's chocolate addiction."

I furrowed my brow. "I'm not really sure if that would be easier."

"Imagine if someone offered you two choices," Scooter held out his right hand, then his left. "Give up chocolate or hold a snake. Which would you pick?"

"I'd find someone with better choices."

Hank chuckled, then looked at his watch. "I should be finished with Sylvia around noon. Will that work for you?"

"Sure," Scooter said.

I turned to Sylvia. "Did you and Madison want to get together later today? We could go out to dinner. Try to take your mind off things."

She shook her head. "We have a plane to catch this evening."

"Where are you going?" I asked.

"Back to Cleveland. I need to organize Fletcher's memorial service, and I also want to be there for Anthony's parents. Losing a husband is one thing, but to lose your son, that's unimaginable."

"Did the chief say that it was okay to leave town?" I asked.

Sylvia looked puzzled. "Why would he

care if we left?"

"Because the investigation is still underway," I said.

"You heard Chief Dalton. It's a routine investigation. If he has any follow-up questions, he can call me." She shrugged. "Or he can wait until we're back."

"So you are coming back to Coconut Cove?" I asked.

"Yes, the real estate agent is showing me some more properties on Saturday. You should join me. I'd love to get your opinion."

"We have the fundraiser at the yacht club that evening and a million other things to do during the day, so I'm not sure," I said. "I'll let you know."

After Hank ushered Sylvia into his office, Scooter asked if I was ready to go get some coffee.

"Sure, want to take your car or mine?" I replied.

"We'll take—" Scooter's phone rang,

and he glanced at the screen. "It's Herbert."

"Answer it," I urged. "And make an excuse for us to get together with him. We need to find out more about Anthony's murder."

I leaned against my car while Scooter chatted with Herbert. There was a lot of discussion about telecommunications-related things, so I tuned their conversation out, trying to figure out how Hank did the trick with the paper flowers instead.

Scooter nudged me. "Uh, can you hang on a minute," he said to Herbert. Then he turned to me and said, "Herbert wants me to become his partner."

"Partner? Partner in what?" I asked.

"His company," Scooter said. "He's decided not to retire after all."

CHAPTER 15
ALLIGATOR PIÑATAS

"What do you mean Herbert wants you to become a partner?" I asked after Scooter ended the call. "What happened to his big retirement plan?"

"Apparently, Anthony's death changed things," Scooter said. "The paperwork hadn't been finalized so Herbert still owned the company when Anthony died."

"Sounds awfully convenient," I said. "How did Herbert sound? Upbeat?"

"He seems pretty excited about the

direction he's planning on taking the company in. There's a multi-million dollar contract which he wants to bid on. If the company gets it, it would be huge. That's why he wants to bring me on board, initially to help with the bid, then to oversee implementation if it's successful."

"Excited, huh? That doesn't sound like a man who just days ago was trying to convince everyone that he was looking forward to retirement." I paced back and forth in front of Hank's office, thinking through these latest developments. "I had told you that I thought Anthony had somehow coerced Herbert into turning the company over to him. Now that he's dead, Herbert doesn't have to. He retains complete control over the business. Sounds like a good motive for murder, don't you think?"

Scooter removed his tortoiseshell glasses and rubbed his eyes. "You must have heard me on the phone. I agreed to meet with him for lunch to talk about his offer. Not exactly a bright idea."

"Why do you think that? It's a great idea. It will be the perfect opportunity for us to question Herbert."

"But if he's a murderer . . ." Scooter's voice trailed off, and he quickly did his calming ritual. After exhaling sharply, he said, "Don't you think it would be dangerous to be face-to-face with Herbert?"

"Where did he want you to meet him?" I asked.

"At Alligator Chuck's BBQ Joint."

"A restaurant. Perfect. It's a public place, and it's always crowded. If Herbert thought you were on to him, he wouldn't be inviting you to meet him there. He'd meet you someplace out of the way, a dark, desolate place where no one would see if he—"

Scooter held up his hand. "I get the picture. So, you're coming with me?"

I looped my arm through his.

"Absolutely. You're not going to invest our money into the company without my sign-off."

"Oh, I have no plans on investing," Scooter said quickly. "You don't need to worry about that. Especially given what I know about it's finances."

"Is this because of that document someone put under our cabin door on the cruise?" I asked. "You never did explain exactly what that was about. All you'd said was that it was proof their investment opportunity was a scam."

"Tell you what, let me go in and leave a note for Hank telling him that I have to reschedule, then I'll explain it to you on the way. We'll come back and pick up your car later."

By the time we got to Alligator Chuck's, my head was pounding. Scooter had reeled off all sorts of numbers and financial terms. I couldn't make heads or tails of it, but I trusted Scooter. If he said that it was evidence of Fletcher's company committing fraud, then it was.

As we sat in the car waiting for Herbert to arrive, I asked Scooter what he had done with the document that night.

His face turned red. "I'm kind of embarrassed to admit this, but I destroyed it. I know that you would never have done something like that. It could have been used as evidence later. But I think I was in shock at having discovered what Fletcher was really up to. I wasn't thinking."

I put my hand on his. "It's okay. Hopefully, you didn't eat it."

He laughed. "I still can't believe Dominic did that. But, no, I tore it into tiny pieces and threw it in the recycling bin."

"Obviously, it wasn't meant to be put under our door. Who do you think it was intended for?"

"I assume Fletcher. But I'm not sure

who left it for him. It could have been Herbert."

"Since it had to do with the company's finances," I said. "Makes sense considering Herbert is the CFO."

"It also could have been Anthony," Scooter said. "He has an MBA and knows all about corporate finance. Don't forget, he was, for all intents and purposes, managing the so-called investment opportunity."

"But why would either Herbert or Anthony have left that document for Fletcher? Especially something so incriminating. Isn't that the type of thing you don't want in writing?"

Scooter drummed his fingers on the steering wheel. "Unless you were trying to blackmail someone. It might have been Herbert's way of saying to Fletcher, 'I know what you're trying to pull.'"

A knock on the passenger side window startled me. When I saw it was

Herbert, I rolled down the window and smiled brightly. "We'll be right in."

"Oh, are you joining us, Mollie?" Herbert asked.

Scooter leaned across me. "Mollie is the CFO in our marriage. I don't make any financial decisions without her input."

"That's fine with me," Herbert said. "I'll go see if they can change the reservation to a table for three."

Once Herbert walked into the restaurant, I burst out laughing. "Chief financial officer? Me? I couldn't even remember the password to our online account."

"Don't worry about that," Scooter said. "If you really want to know more about finances, I can teach you."

"You've got a deal," I said, shaking his hand. "Now, let's go trick a killer into confessing."

* * *

Scooter and I slid into the booth on the opposite side from Herbert. As the waiter handed menus to us, Herbert looked around the restaurant. "I can see why they call this place Alligator Chuck's. I don't think I've ever seen so many alligators in one place before."

"Thankfully, they're not alive." I pointed at a dark green piñata hanging over our heads. "That's the only kind of alligator I like. One you can fill with candy."

Scooter twisted in his seat and gestured at a large wooden statue by the hostess station. "A local chainsaw artist carved that. The detail is remarkable. You'd almost think it was real."

"Penny mentioned alligators at the marina," Herbert said. "Do you ever worry about them attacking your cat?"

"It's a huge worry," I said, feeling my heart start to race at the thought of losing my beloved calico. "Mrs. Moto loves swimming, but we've told her that absolutely under no circumstances is she to dive into the water at the marina."

"She's a smart cat," Scooter said. "I think she's figured out that it's not safe to go for a dip there. I haven't heard any reports of the marina alligators being dangerous. If there was, I'm sure they'd remove them."

Herbert pointed at a lifelike alligator stuffed and mounted on the wall. "I suppose that's what happens to the dangerous ones."

"It's a shame when it comes to that," Scooter said. "If you're really interested in seeing a lot of alligators in one place, you should go to the Everglades or to Pete's Gator Farm."

"Pete's is on my list of things to do," Herbert said. "I saw one of their brochures at the hotel."

I leaned forward. "But you're not going to have much time for leisure activities like that now if you're not retiring."

"You're probably right," Herbert said as he looked through the menu. "Have you had the alligator bites before?"

"I have," Scooter said. "They're pretty good, especially with the dipping sauce. Want to split some as an appetizer?"

"Will it be enough for three?" Herbert asked.

Scooter smiled. "Mollie refuses to eat them. Don't worry, it will be plenty big enough for the two of us."

After placing our order, I turned the conversation back to Herbert's change of heart. "You seemed pretty enthusiastic about retirement. What made you decide to go back to work?"

Herbert placed a napkin on his lap. "While Anthony and I had agreed that I would sell the company to him, the paperwork hadn't been signed prior to his death. Since I still own the company, that took retirement off the table."

"So when Fletcher died, you got complete control of the company?

Sylvia didn't inherit his shares?" Scooter asked.

"Correct." Herbert hesitated for a moment, then looked at Scooter. "Normally, I wouldn't share this kind of information, but since I'd like you to come on board, it's important that you know how the current partnership agreement is structured. We can use it as a starting point for our own agreement. According to provisions that we made, upon Fletcher's death, his shares reverted to me."

"Sorry, I'm kind of slow when it comes to this type of thing," I said. "What do you mean by his shares reverting to you?"

"Basically, Fletcher and I had a fifty-fifty split in terms of ownership of the company," Herbert said. "When Fletcher died, all of his shares were transferred to me. I own one hundred percent of the company now."

"And what would have happened if

one of you had left the company to pursue something else?" Scooter asked.

"In that case, the shares would have been split differently. The person who remained would get fifty-one percent and the person who was leaving would get forty-nine percent."

"That means the remaining partner would call all the shots?" I asked.

"That's right. He would have the controlling interest," Herbert said.

I cocked my head to one side. "But why the original fifty-fifty split? Fletcher was the CEO. Doesn't that mean that he had the bigger role? Why didn't he own more of the company in the first place?"

"No, not at all. When we set things up, we each took on a role that best suited our skillsets. I have a finance degree. It made sense for me to take on the CFO role." Herbert gave a self-deprecating laugh. "I'm kind of a nerd if you haven't noticed. Fletcher was better with people than I was. He was good at making presentations and closing deals."

"You mean he was good at schmoozing people," I said, as the waiter set our appetizers on the table.

Herbert shrugged. "It's part of the job. That's one of the reasons why I want to bring Scooter on board. He has good people skills. I know what my strengths are. I'm better in the background, crunching the numbers."

Scooter chewed thoughtfully on one of the alligator bites, then said, "Being in charge of the finances is a serious responsibility. The books have to stand up to the scrutiny of auditors. Have you ever had any problems before? Things not matching up or audit findings that required additional investigation?"

Herbert slowly wiped his mouth with his napkin. "What exactly are you asking?"

"If I do go ahead with this partnership, I need to make sure that everything is legit," Scooter said. "Fletcher had a reputation for not exactly doing things by the book."

Herbert sighed. "It's true that sometimes Fletcher put the company, and me, in a difficult position. But that's another reason why I'm hoping you'll join, Scooter. You're a straight shooter. You don't play fast and loose with the rules."

After taking a bite of my fried cheese, I said, "I'm curious. What would have happened if you had retired when Fletcher was still alive?"

Herbert furrowed his brow. "But I didn't."

"Just humor me. I like to think through hypothetical scenarios," I said, dabbing at a bit of greasy cheese which had fallen on my lap. "Pretend that you had retired. Would you have retained your shares? That fifty-one percent forty-nine percent split you described?"

"Under normal circumstances, yes."

"Normal circumstances. What does

that mean?" I asked.

Herbert dunked an alligator bite into some dipping sauce. "You know, when things are normal."

Scooter gave me a sideways look, then turned back to Herbert. "I think what Mollie is getting at is if there were any provisions in your partnership agreement which would cause your shares to revert to Fletcher. Perhaps a morality clause or something to do with financial irregularities? That kind of thing."

Herbert looked at Scooter sharply. "Are you implying that I've done something immoral?

"Gosh, no," Scooter said. "You know what lawyers are like. They're always insisting on including clauses like that in contracts."

"Oh, lawyers." Herbert rolled his eyes. "They can be such a pain, can't they? Sure, we had all the standard clauses in our agreement."

I leaned forward, fascinated as Scooter continued to drill into the intricacies of legal documents. "Okay, hypothetically speaking, if one of those clauses applied, then would you have had to relinquish your shares to Fletcher?"

"Correct," Herbert said.

"Okay, let's just play this through. Say you were out of the picture and Fletcher owned all the shares in the company. Once he died, what would have happened? Who would have gained control of the company?"

Herbert shrugged. "I'm not sure. It probably would have depended upon his will. The company might have gone directly to Sylvia, or potentially bypassed her, and gone directly to their two daughters."

"Not to Anthony?" Scooter asked.

"I really don't know." Herbert furrowed his brow. "I'm not sure this line of hypothetical questioning is fruitful. What we need to discuss is a partnership agreement between the two of us. How someone structures their will is a personal matter."

While the waiter set our main dishes down, I considered the best way to take the conversation forward. Scooter appeared to have exhausted the line of questioning around the partnership agreement. It's not like I could come right out and ask Herbert to tell us how he killed Fletcher and Anthony. Getting someone to confess to murder wasn't that straightforward.

Before I could figure out a strategy, Scooter jumped back in. "What are your top short-term priorities for the company, Herbert?"

Herbert scowled. "Fire Madison. That's job number one."

"Really? Isn't she a good secretary?" Scooter asked, trying to mask the surprise on his face.

"That woman spends more time

deciding what lipstick to wear than she does answering the phones," Herbert said. "Don't even get me started on her filing system."

"I suppose you had to keep her on, because of Anthony," Scooter said.

"That's one reason," Herbert muttered as he cut into his steak.

"Oh, are there other reasons?" I asked casually.

"You mean like the fact that she's a back-stabbing little . . ." Herbert clamped his mouth shut and shoved his plate back. "Did you know that little strumpet and her no-good boyfriend tried to tell everyone that the person who murdered Fletcher was me?"

I cocked my head to one side. "So, you think it was murder? When I saw you at the community center with Anthony, you told me that Fletcher's death was an accident."

"To be honest, I don't really care if someone killed Fletcher. Good riddance, however it happened."

"Some people might say that it's in your best interests that they're calling it an accidental death," I said. "After all, you don't have an alibi for when he was killed."

Herbert took a deep breath. "Actually, I do have an alibi. I just didn't want to get the young lady into trouble."

Scooter and I exchanged glances, then I asked, "You mean you were with someone when Fletcher died?"

"Yes. Cindy works on the cruise ship. If her manager found out that we were together, she would have been fired." Herbert put his head in his hands. "I feel like a fool. When she offered to go to my room with me, I thought that she really liked me."

"So the two of you were in your cabin?" I prompted.

"Turns out she was after money," Herbert said bitterly. "That's like all women, isn't it? They're always after something."

Scooter cleared his throat. "Not all women."

Herbert's face flushed, then he looked down at the table. "No, you're right," he said quietly. "Not all women. You're one of the lucky ones, having Mollie by your side. I was lucky too. My wife was an amazing woman."

"She was sick for a long time, wasn't she?" I asked gently.

"That was the hard part. She lingered for so many months." Herbert took a deep breath, then got to his feet. "Is it okay if we do this another time? I can email you the draft agreement. Take a look at it. Have your lawyers check it out, and then we can talk on the phone while I'm in Cleveland."

"You're going to Cleveland too?" I asked.

As Herbert threw some cash on the table, he said, "What do you mean?"

"Sylvia and Madison are flying back

home tonight as well."

"Great. Two people I really don't want to see. I hope they're not on my return flight."

"So you're planning on coming back to Coconut Cove?" I asked.

"I'm thinking of relocating here," Herbert said. "If Scooter can work from here, I can too. There's no reason why the business has to be in Ohio, right? If I live in Florida, I'll be able to sail more frequently. Plus, not shoveling snow would be a bonus too."

After Herbert left, Scooter turned to me. "Well, I didn't see that coming."

"Yeah, our number one suspect has an alibi," I said. "But we still need to check it out."

"You're going to ask Velma if she can help?" Scooter said.

"Uh-huh. Hopefully, she knows Cindy and can get her to confirm what Herbert said. No reason to go through official channels at this point. We don't want to jeopardize Cindy's job."

Scooter picked at his hamburger. "Now, we just have to figure out who the murderer is."

"It's not going to be easy," I said.

"Good thing my best girl is so smart." Scooter grinned at me. "You'll figure it out in no time."

CHAPTER 16
ABRACADABRA!

Turns out, I'm not that smart. Our investigation came to a standstill. It seemed like everyone and their brother had jetted off to Cleveland. Okay, maybe that was an exaggeration, but Herbert, Sylvia, and Madison had all left Coconut Cove. Even Dominic seemed to have flown the coop. Without any of the people who had a connection to Fletcher and Anthony around, it was impossible to make any progress.

The only thing we managed to

accomplish was to confirm Herbert's alibi for when Fletcher had been killed. Unfortunately, the others had alibis as well. Sylvia, Madison, and Dominic had all been at the magic show.

Scooter and I did go see Chief Dalton, trying to get an update on what was going on with the investigation into Anthony's death. Except he stonewalled us, throwing out his usual response of "No comment." Frankly, he seemed relieved that Sylvia had left town. No more talk of parrots, gangplanks, and pirate outfits was a good thing in his books.

By the time the weekend rolled around, both of us were dispirited. Usually when we were feeling down, it had something to do with *Marjorie Jane* —a boat project gone wrong or an unexpected expense. That kind of thing. Only this time, we were in a funk all because we hadn't been able to bring the killer to justice.

Bringing a killer to justice. Yeah, I know that sounds corny. Though there are bad people out there. Some really bad people and some of them escape justice. They're out there roaming around, enjoying life, while the friends and families of their victims struggle to get back to some semblance of normal. Sure, sometimes the victims aren't the nicest people on the planet. Take Fletcher, for example. But murder isn't the solution.

I took a bit of pride in the fact that what Chief Dalton liked to label as my "unwanted nosiness" had actually helped bring killers to justice in the past. Unfortunately, this time, whoever had killed Fletcher and Anthony was out there free as a bird, laughing at how stupid the rest of us were.

Scooter interrupted my thoughts, wrapping his arms around my waist and kissing my cheek. "Are you ready to go, my little super sleuth?"

I frowned. "I'm no super sleuth. Maybe you should go back to one of your other pet names for me."

"Just give it time," he said. "You'll figure it out when you least expect it."

I smoothed down my skirt, then slipped on a pair of cute flats. It was a refreshing change of pace to get dressed up after days of working on boat projects. Unfortunately, there were still lingering traces of grease on my hands from working on the diesel engine.

"Ready," I said, grabbing a cardigan. "Although to be honest, I'd rather stay home cuddled up in bed watching old movies. Can't we just make a donation instead of going to the fundraiser?"

Scooter smiled. "Oh, I think you'll change your mind once I tell you who's going to be there tonight."

"Well, go on, tell me. The suspense is killing me."

"Sylvia, Madison, and Herbert."

"Wow, all three of them." I furrowed my brow. "I can see why Herbert is going. He's an avid sailor. But why Sylvia and Madison?"

"According to my source, Sylvia wants to check out the yacht club as a potential wedding venue. Madison is accompanying her."

"You're kidding. For the Daltons' wedding?"

"I assume so," Scooter said. "They're coming tonight, right?"

I grinned and rubbed my hands together. "Yes, it should be fun, watching the chief try to avoid Sylvia."

Scooter motioned toward the door. "Come on, we're going to be late."

"Hang on a minute, I can't find my phone."

"Did Mrs. Moto make it disappear again?" Scooter crouched down and pulled up a small door set into the floorboards. We didn't know how she did it. Though we were convinced that, despite her lack of opposable thumbs, Mrs. Moto had figured out how to open the door on her own and knock our stuff into the bilge. I wondered if this was some sort of payback for the fact that she hadn't been as involved in this investigation as she had been in past ones. Cats have their special ways of letting you know that they don't like being left out.

Scooter reached his hand into the bilge, then presented my phone to me triumphantly, "Abracadabra!"

After wiping it off, I popped it in my purse. "Abracadabra," I mused while I petted Mrs. Moto. "That's what magicians say. Magic, magic, magic. What is it about magic that's bugging me?"

"You mean besides our cat performing disappearing tricks with our possessions?"

"No, that's not it." I shook my head. "Never mind, let's get going."

* * *

When we got to the yacht club, Ned and Nancy were seated at a table by the entrance. After Scooter paid Ned for our tickets, Nancy stamped our hands.

"Ouch," I said. "I don't think you needed to do that so hard."

Nancy peered at me over her reading glasses. "We want to make sure the ink doesn't come off, don't we, dear?"

"I'm not sure why you're stamping people, anyway," I said. "Don't you know everyone who's attending the fundraiser? It's not like people are sneaking in. Especially with you sitting out here. No one would dare to try to get past you."

Nancy beamed, proud of the fact that people were terrified of her. If she and Ned really did sell the marina, she should consider a career change and become a bouncer.

"Do you want to buy some raffle

tickets too?" Ned asked. "The grand prize is a cruise to the Bahamas."

"On the same ship that we took?" Scooter asked. "I can't say that I'd really want to do that trip again."

Ned looked sheepish. "You're not the first person to say that. But when the cruise line offered us the tickets, well, how could we say no?"

"Not many people want to go aboard a boat that someone was murdered on," I said.

"Fletcher wasn't murdered," Nancy said. "It was an accident."

"Or so they want you to believe," I muttered.

"So, what about those raffle tickets?" Ned said. "Second prize is a fifty-dollar gift certificate to Melvin's Marine Emporium."

"Count us in," Scooter said. "This will be the first time I've ever hoped to win the second prize instead of the grand prize."

"You better hurry if you don't want to miss the magic show," Nancy said.

I furrowed my brow. "Magic show?"

"A local magician is performing. Then, later in the evening, Ben's band will be playing."

"The magician's name isn't Hypnotist Hank by any chance?"

"Yes, that's the one." Nancy looked pointedly behind us. "There are other people waiting. Are you going to stand here all evening?"

As we walked into the main room, Scooter nudged me. "There's Sylvia and Madison."

"We need to find a way to have a quiet word with them," I said. "I think I figured out something important about the case."

Scooter's eyes widened. "How did you do that?"

"A magician never reveals her secrets," I said, waving my hands mysteriously in front of me. Then I turned and pointed at a hallway. "The boardroom is back there, isn't it?"

"Uh-huh. What did you have in mind?"

"We need to find a way to get Sylvia in there by herself. I'll have a little chat with her while you're standing outside with Madison, eavesdropping. I want her to hear what Sylvia says. If I'm right, then the case will get blown wide open."

Scooter ran his fingers through his hair. "How are we supposed to manage that?"

"I'll tell Sylvia that I want to talk about the Daltons' wedding. Make sure that you and Madison are standing outside the door to the boardroom in, say, ten minutes. I'll leave the door ajar."

"Getting Sylvia to go with you sounds simple, but what am I supposed to say to Madison?"

"Flirt with her." I grinned. "You're a handsome guy. She'll be putty in your hands."

Scooter's jaw dropped. "You want me

to flirt with another woman?"

"Do you want to nab the murderer? Then, trust me on this."

Scooter was right. It was easy to convince Sylvia to come with me. When we walked into the oak paneled room, she made a beeline for the far corner.

"I think those chairs are broken," I said, crossing my fingers behind my back. "Apparently, the last time they had a meeting in here, several people ended up on the floor."

"Did anyone get hurt?" Sylvia asked, looking dubiously at the leather wingback chairs.

"Uh, yeah. Broken tailbones all around." I motioned to two chairs at the end of the conference table closest to the door. "It would be safer if we sat here."

After Sylvia took her seat, she asked, "What was it you wanted to discuss? The wedding cake?"

I always wanted to talk about cake.

Except if we went down that path, I was likely to get distracted from keeping an eye on the time. Scooter and Madison would be here any minute. "You mentioned the bridesmaids wearing eye patches."

"Yes, pink lace ones."

"Well, I'm the matron of honor. Shouldn't my eye patch be different?"

She pursed her lips. "Well, I can see where you're coming from. I assume you're a bit older than the other girls?"

I stifled a laugh. There weren't actually any other girls lined up. When Anabel had first started talking about her wedding, she asked me to be her matron of honor. "I want to keep things small," she said. "Just you and Tiny's best man."

"I suppose I will be the oldest," I said. "Is there anything you can do to make me look younger?"

"With an eye patch? Sure. Let me pull some photos up on my phone."

While she scoured her go-to wedding sites for eye patch ideas for older ladies, I kept an eye on my phone, watching the time. I heard a slight rustling from the hallway, then I said loudly, "It was nice to meet Hypnotist Hank the other day. He mentioned Ragno's trick with the boa constrictors. I didn't get to see the act. Could you tell me about it?"

Sylvia furrowed her brow. "I thought you wanted to talk about eye patches?"

"Well, the chief mentioned something about having a magic theme for the wedding. It might help to hear more about Ragno's act."

"Magic, hmm . . . we could do some interesting things with that." Sylvia leaned back in her chair. "Well, let's see. After his trick with the tarantulas, Ragno—"

"Do you mind speaking up? I'm a bit hard of hearing," I said.

"That happens to all of us as we get older, dear. I can give you a lead on some great hearing aids. They make all the difference."

"Okay, maybe later," I said. "But what about Ragno?"

Sylvia leaned forward and said loudly, "Ragno takes a boa constrictor and puts it in a large velvet sack. First, he shows the audience that the sack is empty. Then he invites some members of the audience up on stage. He passes the sack around, asking each of them to confirm that there is only one snake inside. Next, he says a magic spell and there's some smoke, then abracadabra. When he opens the sack back up, there are multiple snakes inside."

"Just to be crystal clear, you saw Ragno perform that trick on the cruise ship?"

"Of course, we were sitting right next to the stage. I saw it as clearly as I see you sitting across from me."

"And Madison saw the snakes too?"

Sylvia pursed her lips. "I'm going to let

you in on a little secret. Madison didn't stay for the magic act."

The door burst open, startling Sylvia. She spun around in her chair and gasped when she saw Madison standing there. "What are you doing here?"

Madison strode into the room, Scooter following closely on her heels. She leaned down and jabbed a finger at the older woman. "You're lying. There weren't any boa constrictors that night."

"Of course, there were."

Sylvia attempted to push her chair back, but Madison grabbed hold of the armrests. She took a moment to flick her long hair back, then said darkly, "No, there weren't. If you had actually been at the magic show, you would have known that."

I waved my hand in front of Madison's face. "Excuse me, I have a question."

Madison took a step back, then looked at me. "What's that?"

"Are you saying that Sylvia wasn't at the magic show?"

"No, she left, saying that she was going to the ladies' room. But she never came back."

"Okay, it's true. I wasn't there. I was feeling ill," Sylvia said. "I went to my cabin to lie down."

"Hah, that's what you want them to believe happened, but we both know that isn't true either," Madison said. "You were too busy killing your husband to have a chance to go back to your cabin."

Scooter pulled me back and whispered. "If Sylvia killed Fletcher, what was Madison's cigarette butt doing at the crime scene?"

Sylvia's hearing aids must have been super powerful, because she got to her feet and took a step toward Scooter. "You found a cigarette butt?"

"Um, yes."

"What did it look like?" she asked.

"It was pink," Scooter said slowly.

Sylvia waved her hands in the air dramatically. "Pink cigarettes. I know someone who smokes pink cigarettes. And that person is Madison. Remember? I told you how I ordered them from Paris for her."

Madison snatched Sylvia's purse off the floor, then shook the contents onto the table. She pulled a foil pack out of the pile, then popped a piece of gum out of it. Holding it up, she turned to Sylvia. "Want to tell them what this is?"

Sylvia folded her arms across her chest and stared at Madison without saying a word.

Scooter looked at me sideways. I said quietly, "It's a special kind of gum."

Madison seemed too young to be wearing hearing aids, but who knows. In any case, she spun around, clearly having heard what I said. "Yes, it is special gum. Nicotine gum. Sylvia is a smoker."

"Ex-smoker," Sylvia said.

Scooter arched an eyebrow. "Oh, is that why you were at Hypnotist Hank's? To quit smoking?"

"Go on, tell them," Madison urged. "Tell them how you've tried to quit smoking for years. You've tried everything—gum, hypnosis, even patches."

"The patches didn't work. They gave me a rash," Sylvia said.

Madison rolled her eyes. "Nothing worked. When you're not next to me inhaling my secondhand smoke to get a nicotine fix, you're always bumming cigarettes from me. Sometimes, you don't even bother to ask first, you just steal them."

"So Sylvia took one of your cigarettes," Scooter said.

Madison nodded. "That's right. She knew about the secret smoking spot I had on ship. I don't know if she lured Fletcher up there, killed him, then had a cigarette or if she had a smoke, then killed him. Either way, she was stupid and left the cigarette butt at the scene of the crime. I would have never done that."

"Done what?" I asked.

"You mean would I have killed Fletcher? Of course not. And I always pick up my cigarette butts. I wasn't born in a barn."

I pursed my lips. "But I overheard you on the cruise talking with Fletcher. He made you promise to take care of Herbert or else. You didn't seem very happy about it."

"Where was this?" Madison asked.

"Outside the ladies' room. You guys were on your way to dinner."

Madison shook her head. "Oh, that was nothing. Fletcher had wanted me to try to convince Herbert to retire so that he could take over the business. Besides, as I already pointed out, I couldn't have killed Fletcher. I was at the magic show. Sylvia wasn't. She's your murderer."

Sylvia put a hand to her chest. "Me? Kill my husband? You're out of your mind."

"You hated him," Madison said. "And when he told you he was going to divorce you, you lost it. You went up on that deck and pushed him overboard."

"Mollie, Scooter, the two of you know me," Sylvia said. "You know that I believe in the sanctity of marriage. I'm a wedding planner, for goodness sake."

"How do the vows go, Sylvia?" Madison said dryly. "Until death do we part, that's how. There was no way you were going to let Fletcher divorce you. You couldn't bear to be humiliated like that. You had put up with his affairs, always turned a blind eye to the other women, but divorce, no, not you. Murder, though? No problem."

Scooter raised his hand, as if to ask a question.

"What?" Madison barked.

"Why would Sylvia kill her own nephew?" he asked. "He was her flesh and blood."

"Because Anthony knew what she had done. He had finally decided he couldn't bear to keep lying for her and had decided to turn her into the police."

"What?" Sylvia spluttered. "That is absolutely not true."

"Of course, it is. He told me. Don't you remember that conversation we all had? The one where you made us swear to cover for you? The one where you tried to get us to pin everything on Herbert? I was supposed to pretend you were at the magic show with me." Madison gave a bitter laugh. "That was fine for you. But Anthony needed an alibi too."

"So, that's why he tried to pay off Velma," I said.

"Exactly. But that didn't exactly go as planned," she spat out. "As usual, Anthony blew it. He didn't pay that girl enough. He let us down. And not for the first time. I think that's when he realized that he couldn't keep trying to cover for his aunt."

"You can't pin Anthony's murder on me. Like Scooter said, he was my own flesh and blood. I would have never killed him." Sylvia fiddled with her necklace for a moment, then added, "Besides, I was on Destiny Key when he died. How could I have killed him from there?"

"Madison was there too," I said. "You both had a very convenient alibi."

"Don't let the old lady act fool you," Madison said. "You know that it was her charger that killed Anthony. It was green, wasn't it?"

I held up my hands. "Hang on a minute, I have a question about the charger. Was it one of the ones the company was testing?"

"That's right. Anthony gave each of us a charger to try out. We all had a different color. Mine was pink, Anthony's was blue, and Sylvia's was green. She switched out her charger with Anthony's."

"Wouldn't Anthony have noticed the switch?" Scooter asked.

"He was color blind." Madison shrugged. "Sylvia was his aunt. She knew that."

Sylvia made a low guttural noise, then she grabbed a marble statue from the sideboard and flung it at Madison. When it missed the younger women, Sylvia screamed, "You stole the charger from my room. You switched them. You're the reason why my nephew is dead."

The older woman paused for a moment, her shoulders slumping. After taking a deep breath, she glared at Madison. "You get seasick on boats. I should have known something was up when you invited yourself to Anabel's party on Destiny Key."

"What in the world is going on in

here?" a deep voice said behind me.

I turned and saw Chief Dalton looking at the broken statue on the floor.

Sylvia rushed over to the chief and put her hand on his arm. "You have to arrest Madison. She killed my husband and my nephew."

Madison straightened her shoulders and said coolly, "No, Sylvia killed them."

I stepped forward. "Actually, they both did it. Sylvia killed her husband and Madison killed Anthony."

CHAPTER 17
HERE COMES THE BRIDE

After my pronouncement, both women were speechless for a moment. Then they lunged at each other, fighting like cats and dogs. Hair was yanked, nails were used as weapons, and shrill screams punctuated the air. Somehow, Chief Dalton and Scooter managed to pull them apart. A couple of off-duty police officers, who happened to be at the fundraiser, heard the ruckus and rushed in to assist. Chief Dalton told them to escort the two ladies to the police station and hold them for questioning. Then he turned to me and shook his head.

"Now do you believe me?" I asked him.

"All I know is that you accused two women of murder," he said.

"If that's the case, why did you have them hauled down to the station?" I asked.

Chief Dalton pointed at the broken statue on the floor, then showed me the scratch marks Madison had left on his cheek. "They were disturbing the peace."

"They both just confessed to murder," Scooter said. "I was here and heard the whole thing."

I held up my hand. While I appreciated my husband's enthusiasm, he wasn't entirely correct. "Actually, neither of them confessed yet. But we know that they did it."

The chief sat down in one of the chairs

and sighed. He pointed at the seats across from him. "Let's get this over with. What do you think happened?"

After Scooter and I sat down, I leaned forward. "Fletcher was a horrible husband to Sylvia. He cheated on her, gambled their money away, and then he threatened to divorce her."

"We don't know that he was going to divorce her," Scooter said. "Madison is the one who said that."

"True," I said. "But it fits. Remember, we heard Fletcher say to his killer, 'You're never going to get what you want.' Sylvia probably confronted him about the divorce, saying that she wanted to stay married. He told her that wasn't going to happen, she wasn't going to get what she wanted."

Chief Dalton frowned. "So, this bit about divorce is just hearsay."

"I have faith in you," I told the chief. "You'll get her to admit to it."

"Tell him about the pink cigarette butt

we found," Scooter said.

"Sylvia is a closet smoker," I said. "She stole a cigarette from Madison, smoked it at the crime scene, and left the butt behind."

"How do you know it was Sylvia that smoked it?" the chief asked. "Couldn't it have been Madison?"

I smacked the table with my hand. "Oh, my gosh. We still have the butt. It's back on our boat. You can test it for Sylvia's DNA."

The chief narrowed his eyes. "You kept evidence of a crime?"

"Seriously?" I scowled. "No one believed that it was murder. Not the captain of the cruise ship, not the FBI, and not even you. Who would I have given it to?"

"Is that the only evidence you have?" the chief asked.

"There's also the matter of Sylvia's alibi," I said. "She said that she was at the magic show when Fletcher was killed, but she wasn't. Sylvia has seen Ragno's act before. She assumed that he was going to do his illusion with the boa constrictors, but that night he didn't for some reason."

Scooter cocked his head to one side. "Is that how you figured it out? You mentioned something earlier about magic."

"When I saw Dominic at the library, he showed me a magic trick. When I complimented him about being a magician, he said that he wasn't one. Then he showed me a picture of Ragno. He had gone to see the magic show. When I asked him about the snakes, he said, 'No, no snakes.' At the time, I thought he was saying that he didn't like snakes, but later I realized that he meant Ragno didn't perform his trick with the boa constrictors."

Scooter leaned back in his chair, pondering this. "But when we saw Sylvia at Hypnotist Hank's, she said that

Ragno had done the snake trick."

"Exactly. When Nancy mentioned that Hank was performing tonight, it all clicked."

"And then you set them up." Scooter grinned. "But how did you know that Madison would contradict Sylvia? Why didn't she stick with the alibi they had all agreed to?"

"I'd be interested in knowing that, too," Chief Dalton said.

"Because she tried to set Sylvia up for Anthony's murder. Making sure everyone knew that Sylvia had also killed her husband would make it more plausible." I looked directly at the chief. "You knew there was something fishy about the phone charger."

The chief held my gaze for a moment, then checked his phone. "Excuse me, I need to take this."

Scooter and I exchanged glances while the chief listened to the other person on the line. After a couple of minutes, he ended the call, saying. "Interesting. I'll be there momentarily."

"Was that about Sylvia and Madison?" I asked.

"Tell me more about the phone charger," he said.

"If I do, will you tell me what's going on with them?" The chief nodded his head slightly, so I filled him in. "Madison used to compete in beauty pageants. When we were at Chez Poisson, Anthony told us that her talent was twirling batons with all those flashing lights on them. Apparently, she was a whiz with electronics and wired the batons herself. It would have been a simple matter for her to steal Sylvia's charger and rewire it so that the electrical circuit would overload."

Scooter furrowed his brow. "But how did she get Anthony to use the charger?"

"That part I don't know." I smiled at Chief Dalton. "But I'm sure that you'll be able to get her to tell you."

"Hypothetically, how would you have gone about it?" the chief asked.

"Anthony liked to take baths in the morning while listening to an audiobook. I would have made sure Anthony's phone battery was drained or close to it. He might have complained about it, so I would have suggested that he plug in his phone while listening to his book, even offering to get his charger for him. The same charger that I had rewired." I tapped my finger on the table. "Remember our discussion about earbuds?"

Chief Dalton scowled, probably hating that I had reminded him that he hadn't known the difference between headphones and earbuds. "Yes."

"I'm going to guess that Anthony had a pair of those fancy cordless ones. If he had used those, he could have plugged his phone in safely somewhere and listened to his book in the tub without worrying about being electrocuted. I'll bet you anything that Madison hid his earbuds, then just happened to have a pair of wired ones, which she offered him." I arched an eyebrow. "Something you'll want to look into when you question her."

Scooter scratched his head. "Sorry, but there's something I don't get. Why would Madison have killed Anthony? They were going to get engaged. Remember how we had thought he was going to pop the question that night at Chez Poisson?"

"Good question, Mr. McGhie," the chief said.

"It is a good question," I said before turning to Chief Dalton. "The answer is going to require a little legwork on your part. When we were getting ready to sail to Destiny Key, Penelope recognized Madison. She said that she had seen her at the jewelry store and . . ."

When I paused for dramatic effect, the

chief rolled his eyes. "And what?"

"Madison was upset. I think what happened was that Anthony had returned the engagement ring to the jewelry store. Somehow, she found out and that was the last straw. She had been waiting for him to propose and when he didn't, well, it wasn't a very happily ever after to their fairy tale."

The chief got to his feet. "Okay, I think I've heard enough."

"Where are you going?" I asked.

"To the station."

I stood and walked toward him. "Wait a minute, we had a deal. You were supposed to tell us what's going on with Sylvia and Madison."

The chief suppressed a smile, then said. "They both confessed in the squad car."

"Well, I'm glad we could help," I said as he started to walk out the room.

The chief paused, then turned back around. "By the way, Anabel and I made a decision about the wedding. The first weekend after Thanksgiving, save the date. She'll fill you in on the details later."

* * *

When Scooter and I walked out of the boardroom, Herbert pulled us aside. "What's going on? I saw Sylvia and Madison being taken away by the police."

"They confessed to murder," I said.

"Both of them?" Herbert asked.

Scooter nodded. "Fletcher was going to divorce Sylvia. She killed him before he could go through with it. And when Madison realized that Anthony was never going to propose, she decided to end their relationship on a more permanent basis. Mollie figured the whole thing out."

"To be fair, they confessed in the squad car, not directly to us," I said.

Herbert put his head in his hands and

groaned. "They say confession is good for the soul," he muttered.

"Is there anything you want to confess?" I asked.

He stared at me vacantly, then said quietly, "I cheated on my wife when she was on her deathbed."

I put my hand on his arm. "Did she know?"

Herbert shook his arm free. "Of course not. How could I tell her that I had slept with Madison? She would have told me what a fool I was to be seduced by a pretty, young woman."

Scooter's jaw dropped. "Madison?"

"Yes, it was when I was a judge at a beauty pageant that the company sponsored. Madison was desperate to win, so desperate that she slept with me. Like an idiot, I had thought she really liked me."

"Did Fletcher know?" I asked.

Herbert laughed, the kind of laugh that sends shivers down your spine. "He saw her come out of my hotel room. Why else do you think I covered for him when he embezzled money from the company? He threatened to tell my wife unless I cooked the books."

I fixed my gaze on Herbert. "Ah, so that was what Fletcher was holding over Madison's head. He threatened to reveal her affair with you to Anthony unless Madison convinced you to retire."

"The fact that you cooked the books would have given him leverage over you later too," Scooter said.

"He reminded me of it every chance he got," Herbert said bitterly. "Do you know that Fletcher actually sent that half-witted cousin of his to threaten me?"

"What's the deal with Dominic, anyway?" I asked. "You said that you saw Dominic threaten Fletcher."

"That's right," Scooter said. "You told me that Dominic wanted to collect what Fletcher owed him. Is Dominic really a loan shark?"

Herbert shrugged. "All I know is that Dominic did time, but I don't know why. My conversations with him have been limited. He only talks about spy and gangster movies.   Maybe he likes pretending that he's some sort of tough guy. Who knows? His English is really limited, so it's hard to know what really goes on in his head."

"Sylvia told me that Dominic won the lottery," I said.

"That would explain all the cash he was always flashing around. Fletcher even wrote Dominic checks from time to time, but he never cashed them," Herbert said. "Listen, since I'm confessing everything anyway, you might as well know that I made that whole thing up about Fletcher and Dominic fighting. Scooter was asking a lot of questions about Fletcher's death, so I threw that out there in case anything came back on me."

"Well, they all did try to accuse you of murder," I pointed out.

"They all wanted me out of the company one way or another," Herbert said. "When the murder charge didn't stick—"

"That was mostly down to the captain of the cruise ship," I interjected. "It was more convenient for him if it was an accidental death."

"Right," Scooter said. "Then when Anthony's alibi was blown, they all decided to stick with the accidental death story. They were worried that a murder charge would come back to bite them. That's when they decided to really put the pressure on you to sell the company to Anthony and retire, didn't they?"

"It was worse than that. They weren't even going to pay me for the company. They wanted me to sign everything over to Anthony without any compensation. They said if I didn't do what they wanted, they would expose the fact that I had falsified the company's finances." Herbert clenched his fists. "Records I had falsified to cover up the fact that Fletcher had embezzled from the company in the first place. They were blackmailing me. Can you believe their nerve?"

"The timing must have seemed opportune to them," Scooter said. "Fletcher was dead. Assuming Anthony hadn't been involved with the falsified financial records, then he could turn you over to the authorities with little risk to himself."

I furrowed my brow. "Did you by any chance send a note to Dominic about it while we were on the cruise ship?"

"Yes, I told him that there was no way that I would be a victim of extortion." Herbert ran his fingers through his hair. "Of course, Anthony called my bluff later."

"That happened at the community

center, right? You guys were suspiciously all buddy-buddy. You never did want to retire and sell the company. Anthony forced you." I cocked my head to one side. "Did Anthony know about you and Madison?"

"I doubt it," Herbert said. "Why would he have thought about getting married to her if he knew that she did?"

"When we were at Chez Poisson, Anthony pretty much accused Madison of having an affair with Fletcher," Scooter said. "What do you think that was about?"

Herbert looked at Scooter. "Oh, I see what you're getting at. Fletcher had a reputation as a womanizer. Maybe Anthony saw his uncle hitting on his girlfriend. That might have given him second thoughts about proposing."

"We think Anthony returned the engagement ring," I said. "Maybe the thought of Madison and Fletcher together factored into that decision."

Herbert leaned against the wall. "Fletcher wasn't a bad guy in the beginning. But when he started gambling and losing lots of money, he changed. It was an addiction and something we shared. I tried to help him; I really did."

"That's all we can do," I said gently. "Try to help."

Herbert was quiet for a few moments, then he looked at Scooter. "Are you still interested in becoming a partner?"

"No, I'm sorry," Scooter said. "I want to enjoy my life, go sailing, and not get caught up in the rat race again."

"Yeah, you might be right," Herbert said. "Maybe I should retire after all."

* * *

A few weeks later, the Daltons had their dream wedding. No edible gold-leaf and caviar canapes. No handmade Italian lace wedding veil. And, most importantly, no pink lace eye patches, parrots, or gangplanks. Instead, they had a simple celebration of their love on the beach. The chief wore a white button-down shirt and khaki shorts. Anabel had flowers in her hair and wore a flowing white dress with pastel fairies and unicorns embroidered on it. Both of them were barefoot. Their Yorkies, Frick and Frack, walked Anabel down the aisle, yipping with excitement.

After the "I dos" were said, rings were exchanged, and the groom kissed the bride, everyone cheered. The cheers turned to laughter when Anabel tossed her bouquet.

"Hey, look at that," I said to Scooter. "Ben caught the bouquet. That means he's going to be the next to get married."

"Guess you better hurry up and introduce him to that girl on the *Orangutan*," Scooter said. "She might be the one."

While we were standing in line at the

buffet—desserts provided by the Sugar Shack and barbecue from Alligator Chuck's—Melvin came up to us.

"You didn't need to do that," he said to Scooter. When Scooter started to protest, Melvin held up his hand. "But I appreciate it. My whole family appreciates it. Thank you."

"What did you do?" I asked after Melvin left.

"Remember how we won the grand prize at the fundraiser?" Scooter asked.

I wrinkled my brow. "I really have no desire to go on another cruise to the Bahamas. At least not on a big cruise ship. A sailboat, yes."

"Well, I talked the cruise line into giving me the cash equivalent. I gave it to Melvin. He's been trying to raise money to help Velma's sister pay for her son's medical bills. I thought we could contribute."

"Oh, that's the perfect use for that money," I said. "On a related note, did you know that Velma is going to stick around Coconut Cove? She got a waitress job at the Sailor's Corner Cafe."

Scooter and I snuggled up on a beach blanket, stuffing ourselves with ribs, baked beans, coleslaw, and corn on the cob. We ate so much that we were barely able to get back on our feet to watch the newlyweds cut the cake.

While Scooter went to get us a couple of slices of cake—yes, we still managed to find room in our tummies for cake— Nancy and Hudson walked over to me.

"Did you hear Hudson is moving to North Dakota?" Nancy asked. "He was offered a job as a head librarian. I don't know how he managed to keep the fact that he was interviewing a secret from me."

Hudson kissed her cheek. "I don't know how I got that past you either, Aunt Nancy."

"Congratulations," I said. "We're all

going to miss you."

"Come visit anytime. Bring Mrs. Moto., Dr. McCoy would love to see her." He nudged Nancy. "If you and Uncle Ned sell the marina, you'll have plenty of time to visit too."

Nancy smiled. "Only during the summer, dear. It gets cold in North Dakota during the winter."

After everyone finished their cake, Ben's band started playing. "Come on, let's work off some of these calories we've eaten," Scooter said, sweeping me into his arms. As we swayed to the music, he said, "Seeing the chief and Anabel get remarried makes me want to propose to you all over again."

"Maybe we could renew our vows instead?" I stood on my tiptoes and gave him a quick kiss on his cheek. "On board *Marjorie Jane* while we're anchored near a tropical island with Mrs. Moto by our side. How does that sound?"

"That sounds perfect," he murmured into my ear. "We should set sail tomorrow."

"After Christmas, I promise."

Scooter cupped my face in his hands and kissed me. "I'm going to hold you to that, Mrs. McGhie. Or should I say Cap'n?"

AUTHOR'S NOTE

Thank you so much for reading my book! If you enjoyed it, I'd be grateful if you would consider leaving a short review on the site where you purchased it. Reviews help other readers find my books and encourage me to keep writing.

My experiences buying my first sailboat with my husband in New Zealand (followed by our second sailboat in the States), learning how to sail, and living aboard our boats inspired me to write the Mollie McGhie Sailing Mysteries. You might say that there's a little bit of Mollie in me.

It was bittersweet writing *Overboard on the Ocean*. This will be the last full-length novel in the Mollie McGhie series. (Don't worry, if you need one last

Mollie fix, there's a Christmas novella planned. We couldn't let Mollie leave for the Bahamas without one more murder to solve, could we?) I've grown to love Mollie, Scooter, Mrs. Moto and all the other regular characters who inhabit Coconut Cove. It's hard to say goodbye to them. But who knows? Mollie and the gang may appear again one of these days in a spin-off series.

I want to thank Duwan Dunn, Greg Sifford, and Scott Jacobson for reading an earlier draft and providing their insightful and thoughtful feedback. Their support and encouragement means so much to me. They're the best! Many thanks as well to my editor, Alecia at Under Wraps Publishing, for being so easy to work with and for her great suggestions.

If you'd like updates on new releases, my current projects, sales and promotions, and other fun stuff, please sign up for my newsletter at ellenjacobsonauthor.com/newsletter.

ABOUT THE AUTHOR

Ellen Jacobson is a chocolate obsessed cat lover who writes cozy mysteries and romantic comedies. After working in Scotland and New Zealand for several years, she returned to the States, lived aboard a sailboat, traveled around in a tiny camper, and is now settled in a small town in northern Oregon with her husband and an imaginary cat named Simon.

Find out more at ellenjacobsonauthor.com

ALSO BY ELLEN JACOBSON

Mollie McGhie Cozy Sailing Mysteries

Robbery at the Roller Derby
Murder at the Marina
Bodies in the Boatyard
Poisoned by the Pier
Buried by the Beach
Dead in the Dinghy
Shooting by the Sea
Overboard on the Ocean
Murder aboard the Mistletoe

Smitten with Travel Romantic Comedies

Smitten with Ravioli
Smitten with Croissants
Smitten with Strudel
Smitten with Candy Canes

North Dakota Library Mysteries

Planning for Murder

Made in the USA
Monee, IL
05 December 2023

48221345R00288